ACT OF EVIL

ACT OF EVIL

Ron Chudley

Ron Chudley

Dear John,
Here is the latest epic.
Hope you enjoy.
Love Ron

TouchWood
Editions

TouchWood Editions
www.touchwoodeditions.com

Library and Archives Canada Cataloguing in Publication
Chudley, Ron, 1937–
Act of evil / Ron Chudley.
(Hal Bannatyne mystery series ; 1)

Print format:
ISBN 978-1-926741-06-2 (bound).—ISBN 978-1-926741-14-7 (pbk.)
Electronic monograph in PDF format: 978-1-926741-70-3
Electronic monograph in HTML format: 978-1-926741-71-0 (epub)

I. Title. II. Series: Chudley, Ron, 1937–. Hal Bannatyne mystery series ; 1.

PS8555.H83A73 2010   C813'.54   C2010-902100-2

Editor: Frances Thorsen
Copy Editor: Rhonda Bailey
Cover image: Harald Tjøstheim, istockphoto.com

BRITISH COLUMBIA ARTS COUNCIL
Supported by the Province of British Columbia

Canada Council   Conseil des Arts
for the Arts   du Canada

We gratefully acknowledge the financial support for our publishing activities
from the Government of Canada through the Canada Book Fund, Canada
Council for the Arts, and the province of British Columbia through the
British Columbia Arts Council and the Book Publishing Tax Credit.

Mixed Sources
Cert no. SW-COC-001271
© 1996 FSC
FSC

The interior pages of this book have been printed on 100% post-consumer
recycled paper, processed chlorine free, and printed with vegetable-based inks.

1 2 3 4 5 13 12 11 10

PRINTED IN CANADA

For Joan Bryan . . . first believer.

ONE

With the camera rolling, Hal Bannatyne tripped on one of the fake cobblestones and fell flat on his back.

While still on the ground, twisted about so that he happened to be facing the crowd of spectators in the nearby roped-off area, he found himself looking directly up at . . .

Mattie?

He hadn't thought of his old flame in years, wouldn't have believed that he retained a clear image of her face. Yet he knew beyond question that it was she.

Then the assistant director and the makeup girl and a couple of extras all descended at once, helped him up and brushed him down, laughing in spite of their concern. Jack Naesby, the director, came out from behind the camera, hands on hips. "Great stunt, Mister Chaplin. But we should probably stick to the script, don't you think?"

Hal was a loose and very secure actor, not at all bothered by providing a little unplanned comedy relief.

"I'm fine, Jack. Thanks for the concern, buddy."

"Okay. Let's go again, please. *Take two.* Positions, people. Let's put this baby to bed."

Hal prepared to move to his mark. But first he swiveled to regard the line of spectators, the place where he'd seen Mattie.

She was no longer there.

IT HAD BEEN a long day. Victoria, British Columbia, is a picturesque little city, a fact well known in the movie business. A number of the downtown streets can dress up prettily in period attire and plunge into earlier eras as easily as an actor dons a fancy costume. This lane leading off Humboldt Street in the downtown core had stood in perfectly for a quiet Victorian-era street, as required by the script. They had been filming here for a week. Today was not just the last at the location, it was the end of the shoot. When the current scene—the first take of which Hal had just wrecked—was in the can, filming would be complete.

Although this shot was not, in continuity, the last in the movie, it was crucial; the climax of a moving scene where Hal's character bids a final farewell to his lover. Juliet Jeffries, his co-star, was an intense and accomplished performer. They'd worked well together, their screen relationship all the more electric for the fact that they'd not become personally involved. Half a dozen takes were in the can before the director declared himself satisfied. "Right, thanks very much, everyone. That's a wrap."

The traditional burst of applause was genuinely enthusiastic. Jack Naesby, though a stickler and inclined to over-direction, was respected and had a good rapport with cast and crew, so it had been a happy company. Just *how* happy would no doubt become evident tonight at the wrap party.

Because of the scarcity of downtown space, there was room for only the minimum of production trailers. Jack shared his with Darcy Shadbolt, an elderly actor playing a support role, who was an old compadre. Such a setup wouldn't have been acceptable to a star in Hollywood, probably, but Hal didn't care; having built most of his reputation in the quasi-democratic world of theater, he was unimpressed by the hierarchy games of the movies. On entering the trailer, he found Darcy, who'd already changed into street clothes, quaffing a beer. "Congrats, old man," Darcy chirped: despite fifty years in Canada, he still sounded as BBC Brit as when he'd crossed the pond. "That last scene was a corker—as, I might say, has been your entire performance in this pale epic."

Hal smiled. "Thanks, Darc."

"I mean it, dear heart—though I thought for a mo' we were to be robbed of your shining talents for that final shot: how's your bum?"

Hal hadn't thought of his battered rear since the incident. It might be stiff tomorrow, but felt okay now. What did surprise him, however, was the vividness with which the *other thing* came back: after the fall—that unmistakable glimpse of his old sweetheart.

It had been Mattie: he knew that as surely as he knew his own name.

Having reassured Darcy on the state of his gluteus, he was offered and accepted a beer. While he changed, they chatted about trivialities, but Hal's real thoughts were elsewhere.

How long had it been since they'd broken up? Incredible as it seemed, twenty-five years! A full quarter century: just thinking about that made him feel decrepit. The life of a performer provided any virile, not-too-ugly guy with ample opportunities for romance, and Hal had scarcely been inactive. No nuptials or kids, to be sure, but several quite serious relationships, and a steady array of pleasant companions in-between. Affectionate impermanence: that was the state best suited to an actor—or so he'd come to believe. So the real surprise today lay not just in seeing Mattie—nor even the unnerving immediacy of the recognition—but an emotion that had slipped unexpectedly from a place he hadn't even known existed: something that felt oddly like regret.

Bullshit!

He told himself that firmly, as he left the trailer and walked the half-dozen blocks to his hotel. Surely, the strength of his reaction to Mattie had been due to nothing more significant than surprise. By the time he reached his destination, he'd more or less convinced himself. Yet, throughout the trip, he couldn't prevent his eyes flickering across passing faces. He didn't see her again.

He arrived at his room and ran a bath, meaning to have a rest and a decent supper before the bash to be held in the production suite at the same hotel. At least getting away would be reasonably easy. Cast parties didn't do much for him any more, the result largely of a decreased interest in getting hammered; life had begun to seem too short to be wasted in a stupor, plus he'd really come to loathe hangovers. His position in the company meant that he couldn't exactly *not* show. But he intended to slip away as early as possible.

Ouch! Getting into the tub produced a twinge of his recently battered posterior. Hot water would soon ease that. He lay back, intending to do nothing but soak and veg out—

Mattie . . .

They'd met at the University of Victoria, both members of what was then a fledgling theater department. He'd grown up in the city, she was from a small town up-island. Hal was in his second year when Mattie arrived. They gravitated to each other within a week, their coming together swift, hot, and inevitable. During the first academic year Mattie had lived in the dorms. But in the summer she stayed in town to get a job, at which time they dispensed with pretenses and took an apartment. For the next two years they were scarcely apart, both anticipating a bright and happy future together.

Except it hadn't worked out that way. Prior to graduation, on the advice of his acting prof, Hal had auditioned for the National Theatre School. To his surprise, he was accepted, which meant three years in Montreal, on the other side of the country. Up to then, he hadn't even been sure that he wanted to make acting his career. But being accepted for the National gave him exciting prospects and a real boost. During the first year apart, he and Mattie wrote and phoned constantly. When he came back in the summer, it appeared for a while that nothing had changed. But it had: *he* had, if Mattie was to be believed. More to the point, she'd decided she wanted no part of a full-time stage career, while he'd become committed to nothing less. Older heads would have called it quits right then. But they were still "in love," with much emotional capital invested. Hal returned to Montreal, vowing that somehow they'd find a way. His immediate idea was that she move east and join him. If she didn't want to act, there were plenty of other things she could do, and at least they'd be together. But it turned out she wouldn't do that either; though she wouldn't come right out and admit it, apparently her family and life on the West Coast were more indispensable than her relationship with Hal. So unless he gave up acting and slunk back to BC, to teach or something equally tedious, there was no way they *could* be together. Coming to this conclusion was probably inevitable; his mistake had been breaking it to Mattie by way of a long-distance phone call . . .

His tub was getting chilly. He got out and dried off, and while he was dressing the telephone rang.

"Hi, sugar. How's your backside?" The musical voice of Juliet Jeffries managed to sound classy, even in ribaldry.

"Fine. Nothing broken. You want to go eat somewhere?" They'd taken to sharing meals in the evenings, sometimes running lines afterward, if they had a scene next day. Now there were no more lines to run or scenes to play. After tomorrow, they mightn't see each other for years, such was the rhythm of the work. This had been a good partnership, so a quiet farewell supper before the closing riot was a pleasant prospect.

"Our last chance in a while, I guess. Come by when you're ready."

He said he'd be there in half an hour and prepared to dress. He'd been up since 6:00 AM, and his chin already sprouted a mat of black stubble. In honor of the last night, he decided to shave again. The features that confronted him in the mirror were broad, square and even, a face classically handsome. Fortunately, he was a good enough actor not to have suffered the label of "pretty boy." His hair was thick with barely a trace of gray. In his late forties, he could still pass for a decade younger. When he entered a room, the heads of most women—plus a fair contingent of men—inevitably turned. Hal took all this for granted; the mug in the mirror was pretty much routine to him, except that this evening something was different.

Staring at himself, he was reminded once more of that glimpse he'd had of Mattie. Did the immediacy of recognition mean that *she* hadn't changed? At twenty, she'd been really beautiful. People had thought they looked like a couple of movie stars together: quite an ego trip. Today she'd seemed unchanged, though she had to be in her mid-forties. In the shock of the moment, he must have imposed an ancient memory upon present reality. His imagination placed that memory beside his own reflection—and something odd occurred: there, gazing back at him, was not himself but his father.

Jesus! What the hell's this about? But it was fairly obvious. When he'd first met Mattie, his dad would have been about the age Hal was now. The mirror guy was old enough to be parent to the girl who'd once been his lover, so his mind had made the embarrassing—if appropriate—switch. But *she* was no longer that girl. Despite appearances, Mattie must have aged as much as he. And so . . .

So this whole train of thought was nonsense. If he didn't know better, he'd think he was having some weird mid-life crisis. He'd had a few problems in his career—due largely to his actor's curiosity, which had led him into trouble on more than one occasion—but emotional insecurity wasn't his style. Hal chuckled ruefully. He finished dressing, and headed out for a last supper with his co-star.

Juliet Jeffries' suite was just down the hall. Actors, when touring or on location, spend a lot of time in each others' company—if not beds—such is the nature of the business. Performers are not necessarily more promiscuous than other folk, their lifestyle just provides a lot more opportunities. Also, fantasy-romance, onstage or for the camera, needs genuine immersion; being believably in love requires the evocation of emotions which—at least at the time—can be hard to differentiate from the real thing. That Hal's and Juliet's spirited performance had *not* translated into an off-screen affair had taken a certain discipline, and as soon as she opened her door, he found himself regretting it.

Juliet was ten years his junior, a willowy thirty-seven; with auburn hair, large brown eyes, and a mouth that crimped sweetly at the corners, offsetting a strong chin. During filming, he'd seen her only in the dark, high-necked gowns of the late Victorian period, or the work-sweats of the theater gypsy. Tonight there had been a transformation. She wore a mauve, clingy dress that did wonders for her very good figure, while her hair had been lifted into a bronze halo, framing a face ready for a *Vogue* photo-shoot.

"Wow!" Hal said, mimicking a cavernous jaw-drop. "Lady, you look awesome."

Her grin broke the *Vogue* image, but made her look even more desirable. "Thanks, Mister B. You look pretty damn hot yourself."

It was a warm evening, and as they headed out in the direction of the waterfront at a leisurely stroll, the release from work pressure began to sink in. Juliet was new to the Island. Hal had been away so long he felt like a stranger. In the month they'd been in town, the schedule had left little time for recreation, but this evening they could actually feel part of the tourist throng around the neat harbor. Hal realized just how much had changed. Oh, the stately old Empress Hotel was much the same, likewise the neo-Gothic pile of the legislature and the flock of pleasure craft bobbing by the quay. But there was also a heap of new construction: office towers, huge hotels, and an array of fancy condos, like turreted sentinels guarding the farther reaches of the bay. On the water, apart from the usual seaplanes buzzing in and out, a flock of tiny, comical ferries darted to and fro. The scene was busy, ridiculously charming. In the twenty-plus years of Hal's absence, his old town had quite grown up.

They found a Greek restaurant a block from the waterfront and had a leisurely meal. Juliet was due to fly back East next day, to start rehearsals for *A Midsummer Night's Dream*, in the role of Titania. Hal thought this was a terrific piece of casting, and he told her so in no uncertain terms.

"Thanks, Hal, you're sweet." Along with her glamorous accoutrements, his co-star was showing a side of her personality he'd seldom seen, light and fancy free; a reaction to finishing the job, no doubt, and borne along pleasantly by a couple of glasses of Chardonnay. "I'm not exactly nervous. But this *is* the first time I've done Shakespeare in ages."

"What was the last thing?"

"Ophelia, but that was years ago."

"And got some rave reviews, I seem to recall."

Her eyebrows lifted. "Do you, indeed?"

"Well, didn't you?"

Juliet smiled. "I guess I did at that."

"There you go then. You're going to be fabulous and you know it."

"Thanks." She reached across and took his hand. "You'd make a terrific Oberon, Hal. I only wish you were going to be in the company."

Her grip was strong, as forthright as her acting and as compelling. So was the look that accompanied it. Hal returned the pressure and felt a pleasant glow suffuse his whole body. "Me too!" he said sincerely. "Though I must admit I haven't attacked the Bard in an eon either."

"From what I heard of your King Henry at Stratford, 'attacked' is the right word." She giggled, but didn't let go his hand. "Anyway, I just wanted to tell you how much I've loved acting with you."

"Me too."

"And to say how much I appreciated not getting—entangled— while we were working. I always find that a distraction."

"My pleasure. Except . . ."

"What?"

"I guess I have to say—tonight—I *do* rather wish I hadn't been such a bloody gent."

Neither eyes nor hand released him, and the crinkle-corners of her mouth twitched provocatively. "Well, sweetie, now the work is done, isn't it? . . . and I'm not leaving until tomorrow."

They got a cab back to the hotel, arriving shortly before eight. The wrap party would be just getting going. They would put in an appearance and then cut out as early as reasonably possible. Juliet headed for her suite to freshen up, having arranged to meet him at the party. Hal, who'd been expecting a call from his agent, went to the front desk to check for messages.

At the rear of the lobby, opposite the bell captain's counter, was an alcove where visitors could wait to meet hotel guests. As he approached the desk, Hal happened to glance in that direction. There—sitting quietly and looking straight at him—was Mattie.

TWO

"Hello, Hal," Mattie said. Hal was so surprised to see her that, considering they hadn't spoken in twenty-five years, the first words out of his mouth were so banal as to verge on the ridiculous: "How did you find me?"

She gave an odd little shrug. "Oh . . . I followed you back here earlier . . . from that place you were filming." Then, finally, as he still said nothing. "And I appear to have given you a rather bad shock!"

After he'd approached, Mattie had remained seated, looking almost as if she'd been hiding in the quiet little corner. Her expression, which had never been better than uncertain, now moved into embarrassment as she rose. "And this was obviously a really bad idea. Sorry!"

With a brisk twist of her body, she veered around him, starting to walk away.

Coming to his senses, but unable to bring himself to make physical contact, Hal executed a none too graceful dance, stepping in front and forcing her to stop. "I *saw* you today," he blurted.

She stared, trying to push him aside with her eyes. Close up, he could see that years had indeed done their work—but *what* work: her features had matured into lines of real beauty. What his co-star, Juliet, had achieved with makeup and cunning, Mattie had been vouchsafed by the simple passage of time. Imagining that face onstage, or lighting up a screen, the phrase drifted into his mind, *God, what a waste.*

Then he felt guilty, made what sounded to himself like an adolescent titter, and said, "I've been thinking about you ever since."

She drew in a breath, as if to make some rejoinder, then slowly let it out again. Almost inaudibly, she said, "Me too!"

Something like coherence returned to his brain. "How come you were there—at the shoot, I mean?"

She shrugged. "Coincidence, really. Oh, I knew you'd been making a film here. Read about it in *Times Colonist* a while back. It made me start thinking about you but—well—that was all, I guess. Then today I came to Victoria to do some shopping and noticed a crowd on Humboldt Street. I went to see what was going on and . . . there you were."

Hal laughed. "Yeah, flat on my back. Well, it's great to see you. Do you hear me? *Great!*"

If nothing else, his intensity produced a pale smile. "If you say so."

"I *do* say so!" He grew flustered then—*like a ridiculous kid*, his mind babbled—and was overtaken by indecision as to whether to shake her hand, or kiss her, or what the hell to do. He was saved by the sight of the hotel coffee shop over her shoulder, and by some perverse miracle recalling her long-ago drink preference. "You *do* have time for a cup of tea?"

She shrugged, but drifted along with him in the direction of the coffee shop. The place was almost empty. They took a table near the door, Mattie sitting tentatively, as if she might at any moment bolt. A waitress appeared, walking with an end-of-shift slump. "We're closing in ten minutes," she said.

"That's okay, just coffee for me." Then, to Mattie. "Is it still Earl Grey—with milk?"

She looked surprised, then nodded. After the waitress left, they sat stiffly, avoiding each other's eyes. Finally Mattie muttered, "I'm afraid this is just silly."

That did it. Exasperation jolted his tongue loose. "It's not silly at all. A surprise, okay—but, as I said, absolutely great. After I saw you earlier, I *did* start thinking of you a lot—and wondering how I could find you." (That last was a bit of a stretch, but what the hell: sooner or later, he was sure, he would have.) "But you say you followed me back here? Why? I mean, why not just stick around and say hello?"

"I don't know . . . shy, I guess. All those people fussing about. You seemed like such a grand star. I wanted to leave but I couldn't quite do that either. Then all the way back here—this will sound *really* childish—I was trying to sum up courage to accost you. But before I could, you disappeared into the hotel and it was too late."

"You could have left a message at the desk."

"I know. But by that time the whole thing had got to seem so absurd I just left. I'd been planning to have dinner in town anyway, so I went off and did that. But all the time it kept bugging me what a chance I'd missed. I mean . . . I don't think I realized how much it'd mean to—you know, just say hello after all this time—till I saw you again. And I'd blown it. So I came back here and asked at the desk, but they wouldn't tell me anything. I was just trying to decide what to do next when . . . well, here we are."

At that point the tea and coffee arrived. Hal scribbled his room number on the check and they were left alone. He'd already come to the conclusion that, before they could really talk, one thing had to be got out of the way. A short while ago, he wouldn't have thought that he cared—or even remembered—much about this. But, yes, it had been there, skulking in a back alley of his mind, ever since his first glimpse of her. So he drew a deep breath and said, "Mattie—before anything else, I must say one thing: I want you to know I'm very sorry."

She looked startled. "Why?"

"For how things ended with us."

She thought about that for a moment. "It couldn't have been any different. We both know that."

"I mean—the *way* they ended: me dumping you on the phone and not making any more contact. It was a shitty thing to do."

She gave him a long look, and he noticed the attractiveness of maturity had been abetted by something else. What, exactly? It seemed like an undercurrent of sadness. But the impression was fleeting, and it faded as Mattie firmly shook her head. "That's a sweet apology, Hal. But really, it's not necessary. What happened was inevitable. We both needed the kind of lives we understood more than . . . well, more than we needed each other. Anyway, that was all a very long time ago."

"Yes."

She nodded, closing the subject, then sipped her tea. "You remembered Earl Grey. Impressive."

"Blind luck, I think."

"Well, it shows you hadn't *entirely* forgotten me . . ." She shook her head in annoyance. "No—I'm sorry, that's just stupid small talk."

He laughed, starting to unwind. "Of course it is. Mattie—we haven't seen each other in twenty-five years: how else can we start catching up? And I'll say it again: I'm *really* happy to see you."

"And me, you."

"And you're not going to dash off again?"

"I guess I can stay a little while."

They looked at each other, neither knowing what to say next, but at least comfortable. Eventually, it was Mattie who spoke. "The years have been good to you, Hal."

He chuckled. "That sounds like a line from a play."

"Well, it's true."

"Thanks—you too, I might say."

"Mmm . . . Are you married?"

"No, I never did that. Almost, a couple of times—but I managed to escape." Which was *really* juvenile, and not the way he wanted to appear to her at all. He continued hurriedly, "How about you?"

Before she could reply, there was a blur of movement and Hal looked up to see Juliet Jeffries approaching. "Oh, there you are, darling," she said. "You *are* a dark horse. Who is this amazing looking creature?"

Mattie flushed. Hal introduced the women and saw his old friend draw into herself under Juliet's frank scrutiny. Then, matter-of-factly, the actress switched her beacon to him. "Listen, darling, I'm sorry to interrupt your tête-à-tête, but I've got to get up at one hell of an hour tomorrow. If we're going to duck out of the party in time for some romps of our own, we'd better hustle."

Mattie rose. "I must be off too."

She began to walk away fast. Hal knew that this time only physical intervention would do. She was across the foyer when he caught up and placed a hand on her shoulder. The bones felt disturbingly fragile. He let go, but she stopped anyway. "Goodbye, Hal."

"Mattie—we've hardly had the chance to—"

She cut him off by kissing him on the mouth. It was a dry peck, such as might be delivered by an aunt, but her lips were so tense they quivered. She turned and strode away.

This time he didn't try to follow.

The wrap party was everything that might have been expected; thankfully short on ceremony and producers' speeches, and long on gifts, food, booze, and sentiment, so everyone had a noisy good time. True to their plan, Hal and Juliet drifted off early and unnoticed.

On the way up in the elevator, she kissed him. This was nothing like the movie embraces they'd exchanged as Victorian lovers. Juliet's approach to sex was strictly modern and as dedicated as everything else she did. Any movie that included the scene, richly begun by the time they reached her room, would certainly have been X-rated.

After that, it all went according to a script which—though never performed together—they both knew very well. Hal always took special delight in lovemaking with a new partner. Juliet was not just novel, she was expert, enthusiastic and more uninhibited than most men. Despite the hot and heavy start in the elevator, they didn't continue that way. In private, they slowed right down, removing each other's garments gently, doing much caressing and delicious exploration; bringing patience and imagination to an endeavor as old as history but—since both were actors versed in the art of keeping a performance fresh—as new as if it were their very first time.

Altogether the best kind of ending to a day.

Only when Hal returned to his own suite did he remember he'd never checked for messages. There'd been some question about a voice-over job in Vancouver after the end of filming, and he'd been expecting to hear. He phoned down—there were no messages. He was cynically unsurprised; if things followed the usual pattern, he'd be back in Toronto by the time the idiots here made up their minds. He was about to hang up when the desk clerk said, "Oh, Mister Bannatyne—I almost forgot—there *is* one thing for you. An envelope was handed in just a while ago."

"Envelope."

"Yes, sir—shall I have it sent up?"

Who in hell would be leaving an envelope at this time of night? But then he had an intuition—or maybe just a hope. "Hold it there," he said, "I'll be right down."

The desk clerk had the envelope waiting. It looked used, stuff having been crossed out and replaced by his name. Inside was an old department store invoice—scribbled on the back, two words.

SORRY—MATTIE!

Plus a phone number.

THREE

The night beyond the house was as dark as the wrong side of the grave. Had Fitz not lived on this land all his life, known every square foot like he knew the warts and wrinkles of his own aging carcass, he wouldn't have had a fool's chance of doing what was necessary.

There was no sign of them yet, but they'd be coming, he was convinced of that now. When people like that were frustrated, when they'd used every means of persuasion or coercion and still hadn't got what they desired, they didn't just give up.

The same rogues, he now knew, had been behind the big development near Nanaimo, the Island's second largest city. In that case, a large parcel of land which had been extracted from the province's sacred Agricultural Land Reserve—pretty surely by political chicanery—had been slated for an expensive new subdivision. The land was on a promontory overlooking the water, making it ideal for an exclusive gated community, the problem for the developers being that the owner of a key piece of access land had refused to sell. That individual thus became the darling of conservationists and those against the ever increasing urbanization of Vancouver Island—a lone knight against the forces of the developers and crooked politics. But one night the knight's castle had mysteriously burned, with himself and his family inside. Although the fire was undoubtedly arson, no one was apprehended, and a while later the crucial land was sold and the development quietly went ahead. That's the way things were done in this part of the world: everything civilized and quiet—with the big operators winning out in the end.

Fitz was the one in their way now.

Sitting on the porch of the big old house, looking out toward his invisible domain, he absently stroked the stock of the shotgun resting across his knees. It was a side-by-side twelve gauge, as ancient as himself, and probably hadn't been fired in half a century. Coming upon it in the attic had been blind luck, and right now he could use every bit of that he could get.

He reached over and took a swig of rye. Strange to think that the root cause of this debacle was the stock market boom of the 1920s: that and his dad's laziness and ill-judgment. Stranger still to remember that once the family had owned half the land around here, much of the south end of Maple Bay. Fitz's grandfather, William, had bought the property back in the 1880s, cleared it, farmed it, loved it well. But he'd worked too hard and died too young and his son hadn't loved it at all. Seeking a life of ease, George Trail had sold off most of the farm, retaining only a small parcel overlooking the bay, which included the house over which his son now stood guard.

The irony of this piece of history was threefold. First, the stocks purchased by the sale of the land became valueless within a year, wiped out by crash of '29; second, George got his sought-after leisure all right, but only because he couldn't find the work he then desperately needed—he'd been saved from actual starvation by produce from the piece of land he *had* retained; third, that remnant not only came to be loved by his own son, Fitz, but, because of its strategic location, became the cause of the present problem.

Also, it had be admitted, the fault was as much Fitz's own. He hadn't taken the early overtures seriously. Of course, he hadn't known they were from a development company, and the offers weren't high enough to alert his suspicion. Only later, when he discovered that a lot of properties nearby had suddenly changed hands, did he realize something was going on. Finally, when he received notice of a public hearing for a big hotel and marina complex slated for Maple Bay, it all came clear. He went to that meeting—discovering that his own property was slap in the middle of the proposed development site. Worse, the meeting itself seemed like a whitewash: most of the people present being merchants who were solidly *for* the proposed development.

Fitz was appalled. He hated what it would do to the quiet community, and was outraged to find his own precious land included. He voiced his opposition in no uncertain terms. This was politely noted, but was obviously going to be ignored. Only later, when contacted by a protest group offering support, did he learn what had happened to the holdout to the plans of the same company in Nanaimo.

Not long after that the real pressure on him began.

First it was financial; they'd simply offered a lot of money, in fact, a small fortune. He wasn't even tempted. What they were doing was wrong, they were rogues who'd tried to trick him with those earlier attempts to buy his land. He spurned all offers. Then the legal threats began, to see if the old man could be intimidated. But that was a crock. The land was his, free and clear, all taxes paid; it hardly needed a lawyer to tell him that no one could force him to sell.

So then came actual harassment. Nothing obvious at first, just incidents that could be put down to kids: stuff stolen, trash dumped, tires slashed, graffiti sprayed everywhere. The police were sympathetic, but what could they do? And they certainly weren't impressed by accusations against developers.

But he knew.

Worst of all, not even his own family believed there was any real threat. They thought he was just a paranoid old fool. He was almost beginning to believe that himself when the phone calls started.

Cunningly, the calls always came when he was alone. At first there would just be silence, then a click. On later occasions, breathing. Finally a deep voice said the words, *Get out!* Then, *Leave!* Finally,

Save yourself! This sequence was repeated several times. Significantly, the word *sell* was never used.

But he knew.

However, after the calls started the vandalism stopped. So, with no witness, he had no proof that the harassment was even still happening. He hadn't even told anyone about the calls anyway; the way things had been going, who'd have believed him?

Then he received a quite different communication. A cheerful woman, identifying herself openly as from the development company, had made what she called "a final offer," giving him the deadline of a week to decide. He'd told her what to do with her offer.

The next day he got another anonymous call. "*Six days left—or you die!*"

Each day thereafter the same thing—a countdown. But he hadn't responded. He hadn't caved. He hadn't done a thing—except hunt out the shotgun. Then today—the final call.

"*Okay, buddy—tonight's the night.*"

Was it really? Or was it just a bluff like everything else? Waiting alone in the dark, nursing his gun, Fitz wondered about that for the hundredth time. Well, if the threat was real, whoever showed was going to get a big surprise. Thinking of that as he took another swig of rye, Fitz chuckled and mis-swallowed, the liquor burning even as it half choked him. He coughed till his eyes streamed. By the time he'd got himself under control, he felt exhausted, too weak to get out of his chair—let alone use his precious gun. *Oh, God*, he thought, *what a mouse-fucking catastrophe it is to be old.*

But, damn it! DAMN IT! He was *not* going to let himself—and the remnant of his clan—get walked over. He might well be a pathetic old fart, (a "geri"—as he'd heard his granddaughter elegantly put it) But this could also be an advantage: no one would be anticipating an armed response from a geri.

The night was very still. From the blackness beyond the drive came a ghostly hoot-hoot, then an answering call. Since he was a boy, there'd always been at least one owl pair nesting in his woods, a detail that the incinerated eco-knight would no doubt have appreciated. From the road beyond, he could hear the murmur of passing traffic. Sooner or later, one of these vehicles would stop. Through the ensuing silence, *they* would come creeping . . .

Okay, buddy—tonight's the night.

The hand that steadied the gun had begun to ache badly. How long had he been out here? No idea, but already he was feeling exhausted. He probably shouldn't have brought along the bottle. But, hell, a man had to have something to keep up his spirits. Still, he'd better not drink too much more. Otherwise, when the time came, he might not be able to get out of his chair, let alone all the rest.

He pushed the rye away, settled the gun more comfortably—and found himself wishing that Will could be there to keep him company. Immediately he regretted the thought. Not only was Will long-dead, if he *had* been there the poor lad wouldn't have been much help. He hadn't had much feeling for the land as it was, and the idea of defending it with firearms would have sent his mild accountant's brain into shock. Too bad. Fitz took another swig of rye, remembering too late that he'd meant not to. Ah, well . . .

He settled back and began to consider resting the gun on the ground. He thought about it carefully, trying to balance the comfort of not having to nurse the heavy weapon against the difficulty of retrieving it quickly in the dark. This was a simple matter of logistics—benefit derived versus problem created—but somehow it got more complicated. He'd closed his eyes, and in his mind he could visualize the gun—which, as he examined it more closely, he found to be even older than he'd realized. Also, its barrels appeared not properly aligned, a crack had opened between them, and one had an ominous twist to the side. *My God*, he thought, *if I fire this thing, it's going to explode in my face.* He tried to put the gun aside—but found that he couldn't. It was too heavy—no, his hands were stuck to it—no, he seemed to be paralyzed, incapable of movement of any kind . . . and then he saw something else: at the edge of vision, just beyond the porch, something moved. Out of the dark a figure appeared, creeping on all fours. He couldn't make out its face but, he could see it was carrying a gas can. He tried to yell, but couldn't, since he was a frozen statue. The figure poured gasoline over the steps, over the porch, finally over the old man himself. He could feel the evaporating chill, was drowned in the sweet, pungent smell. There was the flash of a lighter, the spurt of a tiny flame, that kissed his gas-drenched world and exploded. He screamed . . .

And he was in his chair, clutching the gun and lurching forward—awakened by something very real, something bright and *coming*. He'd dozed off—and now he could see lights amongst the trees. A vehicle had entered his drive and was approaching fast.

God—this is it! They're here! And not even trying to hide.

Which could only mean they didn't care. Instead of stealth, they were going to swoop in, torch the house, and get out before they could be identified. He'd never thought of that. Probably the same thing had happened to that poor bastard in Nanaimo.

The car came around the last curve of the drive, headlights raking the lawn and bathing the front of the porch. The glare was so blinding that all he could make out was its source. Still, he succeeded in lurching to his feet. His body felt like it was made of crumpled tin. All he could manage was an arthritic hobble, but that was okay, it would serve. He might be a sad old wreck, but he was *here*—and, by God, he was going to give the bastards the shock of their lives.

The car stopped. Fitz came down the porch steps, closing in from behind. The driver's door opened. A figure emerged, straightened, started to turn.

The gun went off, the roar like a celebration.

"Get off my land," Fitz man croaked. "The next one won't be a warning."

The intruder gave a gasp. After an involuntary step back he froze, silhouetted against the car lights.

Damn! The old man thought, *He's calling my bluff. Scaring won't do it. Ah, well . . .*

Slowly he brought the gun level, his finger reaching for the second trigger.

The figure still was immobile. There was a slow intake of breath. Then a voice said, "Dad—Dad, for God's sake—it's me! Mattie!"

FOUR

The phone rang at 6:00 AM. Mattie hadn't been even close to sleep, so it didn't matter. Her first thought was that it must be the police, but that wasn't logical: despite the horror of what had almost happened, no one could possibly know. Even if it *was* the law, surely they wouldn't call at this time in the morning.

"Hello?"

"Hey, Ma—how are you doing?"

Her daughter's voice filled Mattie with relief. "Oh, it's *you*, darling. What a nice surprise. I'm so glad."

"You don't sound so happy," Jennifer said. "Is everything okay?"

Mattie tried to pull herself together. "Everything's fine. You just woke me, is all."

"Whoops. Of course—sorry, I forgot. What time *is* it there?" Her voice had a new flavor, almost a trace of a French accent.

"It doesn't matter, dear. It's lovely to hear your voice any time. How's Toulouse?"

"Great. I'm so busy, time just seems to fly. Only a week and we start vacation."

Mattie was surprised, then realized she shouldn't be. The French academic year would likely not be that different from Canada's. Jennifer, who'd graduated from Simon Fraser University only two years before, was teaching English in France. Bright and meticulous like her father had been, she was probably already a better teacher than her mother, which made Mattie both proud and slightly ashamed. "Of course," she said. "It's almost summer break, isn't it. Have you anything planned?"

"I might do a bit of traveling—with a friend. We thought we'd explore southern Italy. Maybe even get as far as Greece."

Mattie might once have hoped Jennifer would come home for the holiday, but under the circumstances, she was relieved. "Sounds lovely. Who's the friend? Someone from your school?"

"No, just a guy." Jennifer chuckled, "I sort of picked him up, if you want to know. But he's really cool."

"I'm sure he is, dear." Mattie squelched the urge to ask more personal questions. "How are you going to travel?"

"By car—Hans has a Peugeot."

"Hans? Is he Dutch?"

"That's what I wondered when we met. But he's just a regular French boy. I think the name comes from one of his grandparents. Speaking of which, how's Grandpa?"

The talk had diverted Mattie from the grim happenings that had left her still sleepless when the phone rang. She longed to blurt it all out, but of course that was out of the question. *If you want to know, when I got home last night, your grandfather was waiting with a shotgun. It was only the sheerest luck that he didn't kill me.* No! The truth wouldn't do at all, Jennifer, who adored her grandpa, would be horrified, and what would be the point? They would get through this. They had to. Until then, if one family member could remain untouched, that at least was something. "Your grandpa's—fine. If it weren't so early, I know he'd love to talk to you."

"Okay, well give him a big kiss from me."

"I will, dear."

"And Ma . . . ?"

"Yes, dear."

"I love Toulouse, and teaching kids, and—well—just being out in the world on my own. But I really miss you guys. I hope that doesn't sound too mushy?'

"Darling, we miss you too. So mush away. I'll take all I can get."

"Right on, Ma. And speaking of *getting* . . ."

"Yes?"

Jennifer chuckled. "Well—are *you* getting—?"

"*Jennifer!* For heaven's sake."

"Just kidding! But what I *really* mean . . . Look, I'm fine; seeing Europe and having a really cool time. And I guess Grandpa's okay too, what with the house and his precious land . . . By the way, is he still fretting about those takeover people?"

Recalling the latest incident, Mattie felt a chill. "Yes—off and on."

"Well, it's something to occupy him, I guess. But, Ma, it's you I've been worried about."

"Me?"

"Well—just having school, and Brian being—you know, like gone—and living in the middle of nowhere . . . it must be kinda lonely."

"Sweetie, this is *not* the middle of nowhere. You're suddenly this world traveler, so I understand how it might *seem* that way. But the Cowichan Valley is the most beautiful place in the world; I wouldn't live anywhere else. As for being lonely—I just wish I had *time*. Dear, it's sweet of you to worry, but I'm not pining away, believe me."

Jennifer laughed. "Okay, Mum, I get it!

They continued to talk of lighter matters for a while. Then Jennifer said that her phone card was running out, so they said goodbye and broke the connection.

It was now bright day with the robins in full blast. Mattie lay back, feeling the residue of Jennifer's phone presence like a sweet balm. This would fade all too soon, so she was determined to enjoy it as long as possible. However, there was no longer any question of trying to sleep. She got out of bed, donned her raggedy old robe, and headed for the kitchen.

Exiting the master bedroom—which she'd now occupied alone for twelve years—Mattie moved past Jennifer's room. Next came the closed door of the room that had been Brian's; for once the dull ache, always just below the threshold of attention, did not intensify. This morning, her full concentration was on the room at the far end of the hall—Fitz's room.

The house was over a century old, built as a colonial statement in a then-young province. Huge and solid, a West Coast echo of Arts and Crafts design, it was made of timbers the like of which, even in this wooded world, had not been seen in decades. The floor boards gave not the smallest creak, which was good, since she didn't want to wake her father-in-law; the last thing she could handle now was a confrontation.

Reaching his open door, she saw that she needn't have worried. Fitz was lying fully clothed on the bed: eyes closed, head thrown back, mouth agape, as if about to give birth to a giant snore, which never came. Though the old man's chest slowly rose and fell, he was as silent as the dead.

Stupid, stupid! a voice muttered in her head. *I wish you WERE damn dead . . .* Which, of course, she didn't mean and had to cancel, even as a peevish thought: there had been too much death associated with this family already. What she had to do was regard the nocturnal near-disaster as a warning and bless the blind luck that had allowed her to survive it.

Last night, after she'd recovered, calmed the drunk old coot and got him to bed, she'd taken the shotgun—which she'd not known existed till she was staring down its barrel—and hidden the dreadful thing. This morning, before her father-in-law woke, she was determined to make the vanishing permanent.

She put on the kettle and sat at the kitchen table while waiting for it to boil. She felt sleep-deprived and old. Morning sunshine, already warm, glowed through the window. The room faced east, overlooking the broad spread of Maple Bay. It was a magnificent outlook, unimpeded, since only a narrow garden strip, bounded by a sixty-foot-high cliff, separated the house from a vast panorama of islands and sea and sky. This was a significant reason—if not the main one—why the location was so coveted; old Fitz was right about *that*, at least.

The kettle boiled and she made tea. She sipped on it gratefully, settling back at the table, and had just begun to feel slightly more relaxed when the *other thing*, pushed into the background by the trauma of her return, stumbled back into consciousness: the incident with Hal Bannatyne.

Oh, dear God, she thought, feeling embarrassment and annoyance, plus a sneaking subsonic of pleasure, *I must be out of my mind. What on Earth was I thinking?*

It had all started so innocently. When she'd first come upon him in Victoria the moment had been startling—and at first comical, to see him fall flat on his elegantly tailored tuchus. Mattie was surprised, dismayed, and amused equally. But what happened next was disturbing and set the note for everything that followed: still sprawled on the ground, Hal glanced in her direction . . . *and their eyes locked.*

Thinking of it, Mattie embarrassed herself all over again by re-experiencing the strange buzz that had occurred: they'd known each other—not just recognized, *known*—and something had been reactivated. As a result, she'd initiated a fiasco of a meeting, which in turn had ended in her flight. But then, still not done with self-immolation, she'd scrawled an apology—*plus her phone number*—and crept back, while Hal presumably was making out with his exotic actress, and left her pathetic note at the hotel desk.

Of course, he'd never get it.

Please God, he'd leave town today and never come back.

But, oh—to see him just once more . . .

"Christ, I'm even crazier than Fitz!" Mattie blurted to the empty kitchen. She slammed down her cup and stalked out to the mud room, where she fumbled into her old garden boots. Dressed in these and her robe, neither of which could quite disguise the elegance of her still-slim form, she strode out into the side yard.

Across a shallow courtyard was a small outbuilding, mostly used as a woodshed. Last night she'd hurriedly stashed the shotgun in the shed behind a pile of logs. She fished it out, feeling a fresh jolt of nausea at the memory of what had almost happened, and—though her hands shook—determinedly broke it open. There they were, one spent cartridge, and the other—which, if fired, would likely have ended her life. "God damn you, old man," she muttered, shaking both cartridges onto the ground, Her impulse was to throw down the gun and take an axe to it. Instead, she snapped it shut and fetched a spade. Behind the shed was a shaded place, with a thick mat of needles from the overhanging firs, where not even weeds grew. She raked aside the needles, dug a trench, dropped in the gun, covered and stomped down the earth, and finished by raking back the needle cover, noting with relief that there was no trace of her efforts. *Rust in peace, you nasty thing!* she thought, grimacing at the sour pun.

She returned to the house—to discover she was not alone. Con Ryan was sitting on the stoop.

"Hi, Miz Trail," Con said, "You're gardening early."

Mattie glanced guiltily at her spade. But Con's artless expression told her he knew nothing of what she'd been doing. Though he'd startled her, his presence was no surprise: today being Saturday, he was here to go fishing with her father-in-law. She discarded the spade and pulled the top of her robe tighter. "I doubt if Fitz is up to fishing today," she said as she headed inside. "He really tied one on last night."

Uninvited, Con followed. He treated the house like home, also unsurprising, since he was almost family: Brian's best friend since childhood, and now the frequent companion of her dead son's grandfather. Mattie was warmed—if mystified—by the boy's attachment to the old man. Brian, by contrast, especially in later years, had been almost aloof from his grandpa, perhaps as a reaction to the pressure— real or imagined—he'd felt being made the substitute for his own dead dad. Now, son and grandson were gone, and all Fitz had in the male department was Con. The young man lived nearby with his mother, but still seemed to inhabit their house more than his own.

For a while after her son's death, Mattie had found Con's presence almost unbearable, because of the awful absence it bleakly implied. Since childhood the two had been inseparable; through kindergarten and grade school and Cow' High; playing and sailing and fishing together; all the stuff that kids do—until that day . . .

She knew that, in his own way, Con missed Brian as much as any of them did, which was why he kept coming around. So, though it was sometimes hard, she could not deny him. She was also familiar enough with the perversity of the human heart to know that without him, things might well have been worse.

Certainly that was the case for her father-in-law. Mattie knew that Fitz blamed himself for what had happened: as if teaching the boy to sail made him responsible for the weather. Con, by just continuing to visit, had somehow made him feel better; in fact, without him, Fitz likely would not have survived.

To become a paranoid old fool, running around with a shotgun.

But she wouldn't think anymore about that. "I'm just making breakfast," Mattie said, as Con followed her into the kitchen. "You want scrambled eggs?"

"Thanks, Miz Trail, cool. Afterwards maybe I'll see if I can wake up the old guy."

"Good luck," Mattie said, trying not to sound too grim. She got out eggs and started to make breakfast. "How's your mum?"

"Oh, pretty good. A bit better, right now, I think."

This was a sort of code. Unlike Mattie's father-in-law—who though capable of getting drunk, was not one—Mabel Ryan was an old-established alcoholic. She came from a wealthy family and, despite having been abandoned by her husband, was able to maintain both a substantial house and a quietly insidious addiction. "A bit better," in her son's words, meant that either she was just out of rehab, or had not yet reached the stage where she required re-admittance. It was a sad business, but seemingly intractable. "I'm glad to hear that," Mattie answered sincerely. Beyond that, there was little to be said.

Con sat as his usual place at the table, and by long habit, picked up the binoculars from the sill and scanned the long reach of Maple Bay. Since the house was only yards from the sheer drop-off to the beach, the view was uninterrupted. Mattie found herself thinking, *I wonder if he's like me: I wonder if he thinks if he just keeps looking long enough, maybe one day Brian will come sailing home?*

Immediately she added that to the list of this morning's canceled thoughts. Con was as aware as any of them of the reality: the bones of his buddy were out in the bay, forever lost, somewhere in the deep. Brian Trail was never coming home.

Mattie wanted to tell Con to put down the binoculars, but she didn't. As she worked at the stove, she began to take quiet yoga breaths, to clear her mind of all negative thoughts—of Con and poor Brian and her sad old coot of a father-in-law—but found herself instead thinking of Hal Bannatyne.

And trying not to wish that the phone would ring.

FIVE

The phone rang at an ungodly hour. Hal, who'd been solidly asleep, came up out of a dream-jumble to find his cell in his hand, before he was even sure that he was in the waking world: actors have a particular dependence on the information phones bring, which becomes ingrained very early.

"Hello?"

"'Morning, Hal, laddie—sounds like it was a good wrap party."

"Damn, Danny—do you know what time it is?"

Danny Feltmann, Hal's agent, laughed without hint of apology. "Sure I do, three hours earlier than it is here in TO—which is lucky for you."

"*Do* tell why."

"Gives me a chance to catch you before you leave. You were flying home today, right?"

"Not actually."

"But you're done shooting?"

"Yeah! But I wasn't planning on coming back quite yet."

"Why on Earth would you want to stick around that God-forsaken place?"

"It's personal."

"Really? Hey, you haven't been playing real-life detective again?"

"What's that supposed to mean?"

"Well, the last time you had personal reasons you didn't want to tell me about was when you got involved with the death of that actor in LA."

"I wasn't *involved*, idiot. I just happened to find out some stuff that I had to follow up on."

"Nearly got your ass killed, as I recall. You're supposed to *play* cops, not *be* them."

"That was just a one-off, as you well know."

Danny laughed. "Okay, already! Just make sure it stays that way."

"Anyway, I've got family here. I'd been hoping to—"

"Yeah, yeah!" Danny cut him off. "Listen . . ." The bantering tone left his voice as he became all business. "The idiot agency just got in touch. Freakin' *finally*! They met our outrageous demands—and they've decided they want you to start the gig in Vancouver on Tuesday, So—you talented fellow—you don't have to leave the lotus-land of your freakin' fathers quite yet."

Danny had a smartass streak and a skin as thick as a rhino—both of which somehow combined to make him a really good agent. Hal got all the necessary details, and after the usual ritual of pleasantries and insults, the call ended.

By this time he was not only thoroughly awake but starving. Having been on an early-rising film schedule for a month, his body clock wasn't about to let him become a slugabed. He rose, showered and shaved, then went down to pick up breakfast in the hotel coffee shop, sitting at the same table as he'd briefly occupied last night with Mattie.

The scrap of paper with her number was tucked away in his wallet. Before starting the job in Vancouver, he had three free days. Inevitably, he found himself considering the idea of phoning her: to do . . . what? Arrange a visit? Have yet another go-nowhere conversation about lives that now meant nothing to each other, that had fractured irrevocably twenty-five years ago? The idea was ridiculous . . . and yet he couldn't help thinking about it.

Last night, he realized, he hadn't learned a single thing about her.

A few meager details of his own life had come out—he cringed at the recollection of the "escaping marriage" crap—but before Mattie could open up, sexy whirlwind Juliet had blown in and his old friend had evaporated. Remembering that moment, Hal was annoyed to find himself embarrassed. So, what the hell did she expect after twenty-five years, that he'd become a goddamn monk? But that wasn't fair; knowing Mattie, she'd probably just figured that he had more exciting things than herself to bother with, and . . . No, in fact, he had no idea *what* she thought; why she'd come, or why she'd gone . . . or subsequently left her phone number.

Or why he was thinking about this at all.

By the time he'd finished breakfast he'd decided on a plan of action. The hell with Victoria. What he'd do was head for Vancouver and spend the three days until his gig started being a tourist. Right! He finished breakfast and headed across the hotel foyer, intending to check out. The clerk at the desk was on the phone. As Hal approached, he looked startled. "Oh, just a minute—you're in luck," he said into the phone. "Here he is *now*."

As the instrument was held out to him, Hal looked enquiringly at the clerk, but what he thought was, *Mattie!*

The desk clerk said, "It's some guy, Mister Bannatyne—says he's your brother."

HAL FELT BOTH surprise and relief. He did indeed have a brother, apparently now living right here on the Island, but had almost given up expecting to hear from him.

Several years younger than Hal, Trent Bannatyne had also shown an early interest in the theater. But that was as far as it went, his real talent being for numbers and money. He'd graduated with a degree in economics and moved to Toronto at about the same time Hal finished theater school. For a while they'd seen each other often enough. But then, Hal's itinerant lifestyle and Trent's increasing involvement with the world of high finance, had resulted in fewer and fewer opportunities to get in touch, gaps finally building into years. Their father having died of a stroke, their mother had moved to live with her sister in Florida. Both kept in contact with her, Hal going down to visit quite regularly, Trent mostly by phone calls. Nonetheless, by passing back and forth as much information as possible, Marcie Bannatyne had managed—as parents will—to maintain some semblance of family. Then, about a year ago, she'd given Hal surprising news. Trent, for reasons his mother couldn't explain, had given up his high-flying business career and moved back to Vancouver Island. The last time Hal and his mother had talked, just after he started the film, she'd even given him a new phone number for Trent, hoping as always that her boys would get together. Hal had tried the number several times, to no avail, and had just about given up hope of contacting his long-lost sibling.

"Hello. Trent?"

"Hi, bro! How ya doin'?"

Trent's voice was brisk, warm, and self assured.

"I'm fine," Hal replied. "I've been trying to get in touch with you."

"Really?"

"Yes, but the number Mum gave me didn't seem to work."

Trent chuckled drily. "Oh, that . . . I had it changed. Sorry, man!"

"Never mind, you found *me*. But how did you know where I was?"

"Whatja think? From our mudder, brudder!"

Hal's eyebrows raised. That kind of verbiage didn't sound like the old Trent, and gave him a slightly odd feeling. "So where are *you*? Here in Victoria?"

"Not exactly. But on the Island. Unlike certain globetrotting 'movie stars,' *I* came home."

"Amazing! Mum told me you were back but didn't seem to know why. I figured—what with the internet and all—you could probably just as easily work from here as anywhere."

Trent chuckled. "Good thinking, but no! I gave up all that big business shit. I'm into the arts now."

"The arts? Which one?"

"Acting, actually."

"*Really*!"

"Well, right now it's just an idea. But don't sound so surprised. I know you're the big star in the family. But, who knows, maybe I'll give you a run for your money. Anyway, we can talk about that later—when you come up."

"Up?"

"To *see* me. You do want to see me, bro?"

"Of course, you idiot. Where are you exactly?"

His brother told him. When the call ended, instead of checking out, he found out from the desk clerk where he could rent a car.

SIX

The route out of town, Hal discovered, was as much changed in twenty years as everything else in Victoria. Instead of the pokey little road he remembered, there was a new highway—not huge by big city standards, but four fast-moving lanes with decent overpasses—swooping north almost as far as the mountains. Climbing the Malahat Range, which fenced off the city from the rest of Vancouver Island, was still a tortuous exercise. But the resulting view of islands and sea, the Fuji-like cone of Mount Baker on the US mainland, and the emerald slopes that garlanded the road itself, was breathtaking. With surprise he recollected that once he'd taken all this beauty entirely for granted. *This is paradise*, he thought, as he swung his little rental car over the summit. *A real pretty place for an actor to starve to death*.

He kept going on the Island Highway, down from the mountains, skirting the villages of Mill Bay and Cobble Hill. These places had really grown, but the feeling of country tranquility was much the same. He came to a crossroads and, following his brother's directions, turned west toward Shawnigan Lake. He reached Shawnigan Village, turned left, and followed the winding road south, to the rear of a succession of lakeside properties. The modest summer cottages of the old days had been converted into year-round residences, the gaps between now packed with expensive real estate that filled every bay, cove, and headland of what had once been a quiet stretch of water. Hal drove on for a couple of kilometres, looking for the address he'd been given. Then he saw it: two large dogwood trees flanking high gates of oiled cedar, beneath an exquisitely crafted timber arch that sported the legend LAKE HAVEN carved in bas-relief across its apex. Beyond, the drive curved down toward the water, bisecting a steep bank covered by moss, sword ferns, and the deep green of wild erythronium. At the bottom was the solid mass of a house. From the rear, this was mostly windowless, cut stone and heavy wood, topped by an intricately gabled roof of dark slate. Through gaps in the trees, the lake could be seen, plus an elabo-rate series of decks, which began at one end of the house, sweeping around and joining it by descending levels to the shining docks and waters beyond.

Hal sucked in an admiring breath. What he was looking at must have cost a fortune; obviously, when Trent had said he'd quit finance to become an artist, he must have been kidding. Hal started through the gates, now more intrigued than ever to see his brother.

The drive ended in a courtyard, cut back into the side of the hill, with space for several cars. Already parked was a Mercedes convert-ible, and Hal swung in beside it. As he got out, a figure appeared from around the front of the house, stopped, hands on hips, staring.

It was only five years since Hal had seen his brother, but he was shocked by how much he had aged. His first thought was, *Christ, the guy looks older than me*. But this was Trent all right. Instead of the sober business suit of old, he was dressed in shorts and a wild Hawaiian shirt, which went well with his shock of prematurely white hair and deep tan. His cheekbones stood out and his eyes were bor-dered by a network of deep wrinkles—but the grin that grew on his face was of unmistakable delight.

A second after the smile, came motion. Trent Bannatyne charged forward, sandaled feet slapping on the courtyard stones. "Bro!" Trent grinned. "Bro, you old bastard, hello, hello! So here we are again—back together in old BC."

A SHORT WHILE later, after they'd exchanged a barrage of greetings and general sibling camaraderie, Trent led the way into the house.

Only then did the full splendor of the lakeside dwelling become evident. The place was a modern symphony in stone and plaster and polished wood. Every room had many windows, affording a series of unobstructed lake views. Beyond, the decks he'd glimpsed could now be seen in detail, the nearest overtopped by a succession of beamed arches which extended the feeling of the house, making the transition from designed interior to rugged outdoors artfully seamless. In his capacity as performer and sometime celebrity, Hal had been entertained in a number of quite grand houses. This outshone most.

Trent led the way into a living room filled with elegant furniture and a lot of expensive-looking art, through sliding doors onto the nearest deck. There was a glass-topped table and chairs beneath a huge umbrella. Trent indicated a seat with a grin. "Take a load off. You like my little place?"

Hal laughed. "Trent, it's fabulous! What did you do? Make a killing in the stock market?"

His brother shrugged. "Actually, that's not too far from the truth. Back in '08 I was heavily into oil futures, you remember how the black shit was going through the roof: one hundred and fifty bucks a barrel? Then, right about the time when the housing market started to go sour with all those toxic loans, I had this premonition. I *saw* the crash coming. I mean, hell, *now* it doesn't seem like you needed to be a genius to work out what was going to happen, but *then* most people had their heads in the sand. Anyhoo—I had this hunch and followed it. Unloaded my futures at top dollar and invested the lot in safe-as-dullsville shit like Great West Life and came back home to the Island, and—well—here you see me. Now I just sit around and love my woman and think about what I want to do next."

"Which, you said, may be acting?"

Trent shrugged. "That—or something else. Right now, honestly, I haven't decided."

Hal chuckled. "Well, it looks like you can afford to take your time. Good for you."

There were sails and powerboats towing water skiers out on the sparkling lake. The hills beyond and the cloudless sky shimmered with a late-morning haze. The sounds of seabirds and dogs and distant marine engines and occasional far-off laughter blended in a summer chorus so idyllic that Hal felt entranced.

Under a separate awning to one side of the deck was a wet bar, from which Trent produced a bottle of cold Chardonnay, opening it as they talked. And what talk it was. Trent might have left the world of finance, but he seemed to take considerable pleasure in reminiscing about the life he'd led. His stories of business deals, stock market coups, and intriguing corporate ventures made his older brother's showbiz career actually seem almost pale. Yet Trent never seemed to boast. His voice was quiet and modest. And perhaps most surprising was a final revelation: Though they hadn't had much personal contact, Trent had followed his brother's career quite closely, helped by information from their mother. He remarked on a number of Hal's film roles, mentioned reviews that he'd read of stage shows, and dredged up a more thorough account of Hal's career than the actor might have been able to manage himself.

This took them into the early afternoon. They retired to the sumptuous kitchen, and Trent, without a pause in the conversation, fixed lunch. As they were finishing, Trent said. "By the way, bro, I've been meaning to ask: how much longer will you be in this part of the world?"

"Filming's finished here on the Island. Now I'm off to Vancouver to do some work on an animated feature. But I don't start for a couple of days. So we could hang out, if you like."

Unexpectedly, Trent looked glum. "Ah—now, there's the thing."

"You're busy?"

"Not busy—committed. I've lately become interested in—er—things spiritual. Not *religion*, you dig—Eastern philosophy and mysticism—and I've arranged to go to this conference in New Delhi. It starts day after tomorrow, and I'm afraid I'm flying out tonight. In fact . . ." He looked at his watch and rose. "It's been a wonderful catch-up, but I'm afraid I'm going to have to start getting ready to leave."

Hal got up quickly. "Gee, I'm sorry, Trent—you should have said . . ."

Trent raised his hand in dismissal, then dropped it onto Hal's shoulder. "Don't be a nerd. I wouldn't have missed this for the world. It's been so great, I only wish it could go on all night. But when I get back from India I'll fly out to TO—maybe as early as the fall—and we can jaw for a week. Now that we've done this today, I'm embarrassed we didn't do it ages ago. Mum'll be tickled as hell to hear about it, eh?"

"No kidding!"

Trent's eyes twinkled. "And when you talk to her, don't forget to tell her what you think of my place."

Hal looked around appreciatively. "You bet. And when you get back from New Delhi, why don't you give me a call." He scribbled on a scrap of paper and handed it to his brother. "Here's my cell number: it'll get me anywhere, anytime."

"Thanks, bro." Trent pocketed the paper, then moved toward the house, the meaning clear. Mildly surprised at this somewhat abrupt end to their meeting, Hal followed. They were just entering when there was the sound of footsteps behind them.

"Hey, darling!" a voice said.

Trent stopped, and they both turned. Moving along the deck from the direction of the side of the house was a woman. She was in her early forties, fit and athletic, as tanned as Trent, with a pleasant, open face and a shock of brown hair pulled into a loose braid. She was wearing a shirt, shorts, and sandals—and a really big grin. She marched up to the pair, planted a kiss on Trent's cheek then turned to Hal. "I know who *you* are. You're Trent's famous actor brother, Hal. Trent, you didn't tell me he was coming to visit today." She laughed.

"And, by the look of your face, I'll just bet you didn't even tell him about *me*. So I guess I'll just have to introduce myself. Hi, Hal, I'm Stephanie—your brother's fiancée."

Hal remembered Trent saying something early on about "my woman," and realized no mention had been made of her since. Embarrassed, he introduced himself, finishing with what he hoped would be a believable fib. "Actually, Trent told me a whole lot. Congratulations. I'm just so glad we had a chance to meet before he has to leave."

"Leave?" Stephanie raised her eyebrows in what appeared to be surprise. "Leave for where?"

"You know—India: he told me about flying out tonight. Are you going too?"

Stephanie shook her head. "No!" Abruptly she moved past them into the house. "I've got to go in now. Nice to meet you, Hal."

She was gone. Trent sucked in a breath, then gave an embarrassed chuckle. "Sorry about that, bro. Truth to tell, Steph *wants* to go to Delhi. But she's . . . not spiritually ready, And she's kinda mad that I won't take her. Bit of a sore point, I'm afraid. But she'll get over it. Hey, I know—when I come out to TO in the fall, I'll bring her along. That'll make her happy. And you guys can really get to know each other then." By that time they were through the house and entering the back courtyard. When they reached Hal's car, Trent paused and stood regarding his older brother, crinkled eyes shining. "Hal," he said, "it's been special! What was the matter with us, eh? Seeing each other so little through the years! Now I just can't wait to do it again. 'Bye for now, you beautiful bastard. You know I love you."

Hal grinned, "Yeah, Trent, me too."

As he was getting into his car, there was a sudden flurry of movement as Stephanie appeared from the house. She passed her fiancé and moved in, reaching Hal before he closed the door. "Sorry, I was rude, Hal," she said breathlessly. "Rushing off like that. It was lovely to meet you at last. I hope it'll be longer next time."

She leaned down and pecked him lightly on the cheek, at the same time squeezing his hand. Then, with a nervous smile, she was gone.

Hal closed the door and started the car. The brothers exchanged final goodbyes, then Hal started up the steep drive. Only when he was out of sight of the house, did he stop to examine the thing which, under cover of her farewell, Stephanie had pressed into his palm. It was a scrap of paper. Unfolding it, he read:

Fran's Restaurant—Duncan—anytime after 4:00 PM. There's something I really need to tell you.

SEVEN

The Trail house sat in an open area in the center of the heavily wooded property. The eastern perimeter of this clearing was a cliff, with the beach directly below. At cliff's edge was a stone wall, solid but low enough not to impede the view. At one end of the wall, to the right of the house, was an opening for a path, which descended the cliff diagonally. Halfway down, this turned into steep steps. They were sturdily built, embraced by the twisted roots of arbutus trees, which thrust and clung, as if fashioned from the very rock that gave them life. These tough evergreens covered the lower cliff face. They provided shade for ferns, Oregon grape, and patches of intruding broom and overhung the thing to which the steps descended—the boathouse.

This was a large wood structure, not as old as the dwelling above but venerable in its own right. It sat snugly at the bottom of the cliff, built on stout pilings so that originally craft had been floated inside at high tide. This was no longer possible, since the beach had silted up, so the sea end had been enclosed. High up in the new wall was a big bay window, providing a commanding view of the ocean. To one side of the boathouse, connecting it to the water, was a sturdy dock. At the rear, where the steps arrived from above, was the building's only entrance. The roof was of shakes, the walls weathered cedar. Nestled in its sheltering cove, the place was private and peaceful, a quiet haven by the rocky strand over which it stood watch.

Two men descended the steps, one slow and careful, the other with the sure agility of youth. The young man reached the boathouse first. He glanced toward a boat that was tied up at the dock, then stopped and waited for his companion. "You wanna beer first, Fitz," he said, "You look like you could use one."

The old man glared. "What's that supposed to mean?"

"Hair-of-the-dog. Fitz, your head's gotta be splittin'. Miz Trail told me what went on last night."

"What did she say?" the old man said carefully.

"That you got pie-eyed."

Fitz sighed resignedly. "She had that right. I guess. Okay, one beer. Then we'll head out." He brushed past his companion, who followed him inside.

The interior of the boathouse revealed that it had long since evolved from its original purpose. It was now a workshop, fishing lodge, and all around old-man's den. The central slot where boats had once been moored was covered with stout boards. A workbench ran down the entire north wall, on which was a profusion of ropes, chains, paint pots, and an extensive collection of woodcarving tools: knives, adzes, awls, rasps, mallets, and chisels. In a cleared space stood a work in progress: a half-finished rendition of a fish, carved skilfully in cedar, which seemed to leap from the pile of chips and shavings that surrounded it. Scattered about the shop were many more carvings, mostly animals or birds, all strikingly executed.

At the ocean end of the building, where the bay window projected, was an old kitchen table, a couple of chairs, and a crumbling couch. Nearby was an ancient fridge, and a mess of books, newspapers, and overflowing ashtrays scattered all about. Beside the window, which commanded a stunning view of the east end of the bay, was a battered rocker. On the window ledge was yet another carving, different from the rest: a delicate rendition of a sailboat, windswept, broaching hard, with the suggestion of a solitary figure at the tiller.

Fitz headed straight for the fridge, and extracting a couple of cans of beer, one of which he thrust in the young man's direction. Both cans popped and hissed almost in unison. The old man headed for the couch, his companion following and perching on the end. They drank and Fitz sighed profoundly. He had white hair and beard, both neatly trimmed, sharp, prominent features, and a high forehead. His skin, though weathered, showed little of the discoloration of age. His eyes were pale and piercing. After a while he said, "So—how's your new job going, Con?"

Con shrugged and sucked on his beer. "I'd hardly call waiting tables for minimum-and-tips a *job*—more like a fuck-off. But it'll do till I get something better."

"If you want 'better' you should go back to school."

"Oh, man, don't start that again."

"Well you should. You need education to get anywhere these days. Con, you used to be so—"

The boy cut him off with an explosive gesture. "Oh, Jeez! Can it, old man, will ya? I came to do some fishin', not to be preached at. Seems like that's all you ever do these days. When you're not jawin' on about damn developers."

Fitz sighed. "You're right. Sorry, kid. Did Mattie . . . tell you what happened last night?"

"Like I said, that you got plastered."

"Nothing else?"

"No! But she did seem pretty mad."

Fitz shook his head sadly. "She had a right, Con. Seems like I nearly killed her."

Con stared. "No shit! How?"

"Don't ask! Believe me, you don't want to know."

"Yeah?"

"But maybe you should—so you can keep an eye on me."

Con laughed. "*Me*—keep an eye on *you*? Fitz—what happened?"

Fitz took out a cigarette and lit up. He inhaled deeply, letting the smoke out in a cloud from which his companion just perceptibly recoiled. "As you know, I hardly ever touch hard liquor." Fitz said. "Years ago, after Brian's dad was killed, I hit the stuff pretty bad. I got over it. But it wasn't easy. Ever since—even after what happened to Brian—and in spite of everything else that's been going down lately— I've managed to keep it more or less together : . . until last night."

"Christ! What did you do?"

"Give it time, I'm getting there." He took another swig from his beer, coughed, and sighed. "Do you know how long our family has been in these parts, son? Since 1875, four years after BC got lured into damn Confederation. At the start we owned almost all this end of the bay. Even after the First War, we still held a whole hunk on either side of here: that same land my neighbours sold out to those damn developers."

"Yeah, yeah, I know. But what happened? Why'd you sell the land in the first place?"

"My dad did that before I was born. The fool took it into his head to play the market—sold the land then lost all the money in the crash of '29. It's lucky we didn't lose the house as well . . . Anyway, a few days ago, after I started getting those weird phone calls I told you about—"

"You mean that shit's still goin' on?"

"Of course! Those guys don't give up, I told you that. Anyway, this last week it's been a sort of countdown."

"Come again?"

"You know—five days before something bad happens. Then four, then . . . you know, *countdown!*"

"Jesus! Didn't you call the cops?"

Fitz gave a derisive snort. "What good have they ever been? In the other stuff that went down, all they could think of was vandals or kids. I know they think I'm just a crazy old coot. And what proof have I ever had anyway? Those bastards are far too clever for that."

"Yeah—but what's all this got to do with almost killin' Miz Trail?"

"Stop interrupting—I'm getting there. Halfway through this

countdown thing—a few days back—I got to thinking that if this *wasn't* just empty threats this time, if they really planned to *do* something—like maybe burn me out, like that poor bugger in Nanaimo . . . I told you about that, eh?"

"About fifty times. Go on!"

"Well, I reckoned I'd better be prepared. I remembered this old shotgun in the attic. I thought, if things ever get ugly, this could come in real handy. Then yesterday, when Mattie was away in Victoria, the last call came. I figured, that's it, if someone *does* come—to try to scare shit out of me, or maybe worse—*they're* the ones gonna get the surprise."

"Good thinking."

"Yeah, but I made this one big mistake. You see, I figured I'd wait out on the front porch in the dark. But it was cold out there—and I remembered this bottle of rye that's been hanging round for years. Great, I thought, couple of swigs of that'll not only keep out the cold but settle my nerves."

"Fair enough."

"Mistake! Instead of helping, it got me to brooding on all the troubles this family's had: my son killed, Brian lost, now this whole damn problem with the property. After a few drinks, I became certain something bad was going to happen. Then I fell asleep and dreamed it really *was*: a terrifying nightmare where I was being burned to death. Christ! I woke up . . . *and it seemed like it was all coming true*. There were these lights in the drive—coming down fast! I rushed out and when I saw what I thought was an attacker I fired a warning shot, trying to scare him off."

"Jesus, Fitz—you could have killed someone."

"I nearly did—*Mattie*."

"Oh, man!"

"When I realized it was her, I was shocked stone sober, I can tell you. I nearly passed out. I don't remember much after that. Ever since you woke me today I've been feeling like such a stupid fool. Damn, son, I could hardly look the poor girl in the face. She must think I'm senile—and maybe she'd be right."

"No, Fitz!" Con said hotly, "You just got drunk, is all. Anyone can do that. My mum never stops."

"That's different."

"Because she's an alcoholic, you mean?"

"I guess so, sorry. Anyway, I should never have let it come to this." Fitz sighed heavily. "I couldn't say it to anyone but you—but I really think I may be going gaga."

"Fitz, no way!"

"One thing's certain, anyway: I never want to see that damn gun again."

Con shrugged. "That's okay—I think maybe Miz Trail took care of it."

"Really—how?"

"When I arrived this morning, I saw her burying something."

"The gun?"

"I couldn't see exactly. But it sure was *something*."

"In the garden?"

"Behind the shed. I saw her when I went to get my rod . . ." Con grimaced. "Or maybe I shouldn't tell you."

"It doesn't matter. I don't care. If Mattie got rid of the gun, she'll have done a good job. And I'm pleased as hell."

Fitz crushed his empty can and tossed it in the direction of the trash. With a grunt he heaved up from the sofa, stamping his cigarette underfoot. The combination of the beer and the confession seemed to have done him good. His movements were almost sprightly and he looked years younger. At the door, he turned to Con, who was still on the couch, watching him with a bemused look. "Well, come on, don't sit around looking like a funeral, boy. No one's dead. Leastways, not yet. Let's go fishing."

EIGHT

The City of Duncan, a hundred kilometres north of Victoria, had grown up around the E&N Railway. For much of its existence, it had remained a quiet country town. But now, Hal discovered, it had changed considerably. The center of what was once the old village had become a haven for bookstores, coffee shops, and boutiques. The area around City Hall was now a pleasant pedestrian square, with tables and hanging baskets. Nearby, the railway easement had been transformed into a park, featuring an impressive selection of native carvings.

Hal found Fran's Restaurant in a side street across the road from the train station. He could see it from where he parked in the square, and sat regarding the place in indecision. He wasn't at all sure that he'd done the right thing in coming to meet his brother's fiancée. But that message: *If you care about your brother, there's something I really need to tell you.* What the hell was *that* about? When he'd first read it he'd been almost perturbed enough to go back to find out. But though Stephanie's action had been strange, he'd had no feeling of anything actually *wrong*. Still, it was intriguing, and anyway, he'd never been able to resist a mystery. For an actor, curiosity was a necessity, since it prompted one to dig to the roots of characters and their situations. But too much of it in real life could prove hazardous, as he'd found with that business in LA that his agent had teased him about. But this wasn't anything like *that*. This was his brother, for heaven's sake, and he had to find out what was going on.

Fran's Restaurant was a small café with a bright green awning and a couple of trees in tubs outside. The interior was cool and not too dim, a dozen tables with yellow checkered cloths, hanging plants, and framed Audubon prints on the walls. The place was almost empty, four customers in all, none of these being his brother's fiancée.

Hal was surprised. Stephanie had said any time after four, meaning, presumably, she intended to wait from then on. It was now four-thirty and she wasn't here. Had she come and gone? Or was the whole thing just some stupid . . .

"Oh, you came! Good!"

Hal whirled to find his brother's fiancée standing behind him, seeming to have appeared from nowhere. She was carrying a tray—and wearing the neat uniform of a waitress. Without another word, she led Hal to a table, fetched him coffee, moved off to check on the other customers, and finally returned and sat. Her braid was now pinned in a neat circle at the back or her head. Her broad features, in contrast to the somewhat severe uniform, were open and warmly attractive. "It's lucky you came when you did," she said. "We'll start filling up soon, and then I get busy. But thanks so much for coming!"

Hal could only stare. "So . . . this is your restaurant?"

Stephanie looked startled. "Goodness, no. I just work here."

"You're a *waitress*?"

Her voice had a hint of defiance. "Yes—what's wrong with that?"

"Nothing. I'm just wondering what the fiancée of a millionaire is doing waiting tables?"

She chuckled, raised her eyebrows. "So—he told you *that* tale, did he?"

"What tale?"

"The oil futures tale."

"That was a *tale*?"

Stephanie sighed. "Sorry you had to come all the way here to find that out. I'd have phoned, but I didn't know your number."

"I gave it to Trent."

"I didn't know *that* either. Anyway, even if I had, I could hardly have asked him for it,"

"Right. So you're saying—what?—that he *didn't* make a fortune in the market"

"Just the opposite, actually. Listen, Hal, though I haven't known your brother all that long, I love him very much. And I really *am* his fiancée. But as for all the rest . . . I'm afraid the poor guy's flat broke."

"But, that house . . . ?"

"The property has a little cabin in back. That's where Trent lives. When we first met today, that's where I was coming from. I was looking for your brother—expecting to find him working."

"Working?"

"Sweetie—Trent's the *caretaker*!"

Hal gaped. He began to speak, then stopped, as a whole lot of things began to fit together.

Stephanie, her expression at once wry and tender, continued. "In fact, the house *is* owned by a millionaire, but not Trent. It's Terry Bathgate, an old buddy from Toronto days, who moved out here at about the same time and took pity on him."

"Jesus!"

"I believe Trent *did* have a lot of money, but he lost it in the crash."

"But . . . what about that trip he's making to India?"

Stephanie laughed. "That's just another fib! Hal, Trent's not going anywhere."

"But why . . . ?"

"He told you that so he could cut short your visit and you wouldn't find out what's really going down."

"But this is all . . . preposterous."

"Of course it is. When I arrived, I couldn't even give Trent away till I found out what was happening. After you left, know what he told me? It had all started as a joke. Caused by embarrassment, I think, at what had happened to his life. He swears he *meant* to tell the truth eventually, after he'd had some fun for a while. But it got out of hand and he didn't know how to stop. Then he got this idea of pretending to have to fly off, so that by the time he *did* see you, hopefully, he'd be rich again and it wouldn't matter."

"But why would the idiot go to such lengths . . . just to impress *me*?"

Stephanie laughed. "Oh, come *on*, Hal!"

"What?"

"You're Trent's big brother: successful actor, famous Canadian star. That may not be Trent's world, but he admires the hell out of you. And I think there really *is* part of him that might have liked to have done the same thing. So to have to admit he messed up big in his own career is very hard. That's no excuse for what he did. I told him that. But I can certainly understand it."

Hal whistled softly through his teeth. "Wow—I had no idea."

A couple entered the restaurant and Stephanie rose to attend to them, returning after a moment. "Listen," she said, "I hope this nonsense isn't going to make you think your brother is a complete flake. When he's not down, Trent is charming and brilliant and he's really a very loving and caring guy. That's why when we met, which is less than a year ago—and he was *really* messed up then, I can tell you—I took to him at once. Since then we've come a long way. Also, I believe that sooner or later he's going to get back on top again. Whether he does or not, I don't much care: I just love him. But nothing's going to work for him—or us—if he has to go around pretending he's someone he's not. Do you understand what I mean?"

"I think so, yes . . ."

Stephanie leaned across the table earnestly. "Look, it's going to get busy soon. I only suggested you come here because I didn't want to embarrass him. I'm not going to tell him we've talked; not because I'm scared to do that, but because I think that for his own sake he needs to tell you the truth himself."

"I understand."

"I don't know if he purposely waited till Terry Bathgate was away so he could invite you to the house and impress you. He says it was just spur of the moment, and I believe him. In one way, he was tickled to death to have pulled if off. He can be quite an actor when he wants to."

Hal chuckled. "He even said he was thinking of taking it up."

"That's just hot air." Stephanie's eyes, kind but strong, held his own. "Look, I know he hopes he'll get back on top and it won't matter. But if he doesn't, how's he going to explain himself to you? It's an awful burden and there's got to be some way of getting him out from under."

Hal shrugged. "So get him to call me."

"Easier said than done. He knows he's been stupid, but he's very proud. I can probably persuade him, but it'll take time."

"Then I'll get in touch with him."

"No, no! Since you're supposed to think he's in India, he'd realize something was up. And he can't know you heard the truth from me. That'd be too embarrassing, and might also seem like a betrayal."

"So what do we do?"

Stephanie sighed. "Honestly, I don't know. Trent makes me mad as hell sometimes. But I also happen to love him. I need him to find a way out of this mess while somehow keeping what's left of his self-respect. Will you help me do that?"

"Of course."

More people entered the restaurant and Stephanie rose. "I'm here, four till ten, every day but Sunday. If you think of some way to contact Trent again without making him suspicious, phone me here—or come by—and we can talk."

"Are you really sure he wants to come clean?"

"He may not *want* to, but deep down he knows he *must*. Let's just hope we can help him find a way to make it happen." With a rueful little smile, she hurried off.

Hal sat, bemused, realizing after a while that he was hungry. He thought of ordering something, but decided it'd be better to eat elsewhere. He waited until Stephanie glanced his way, gave a farewell wave—which included a phoning mime that was also a gesture of encouragement—and left the restaurant.

As he walked to his car, through the newly gentrified little city of Duncan, he realized that, though still surprised and concerned, the idea of being able to help his brother gave him an unexpectedly strong sense of satisfaction.

NINE

On the trip back to Victoria, it was still light when Hal reached the Malahat Drive. But the highway, shielded from the westering sun by the swell of the mountains, was already in deep shadow. As he climbed higher, he again caught glimpses of Mount Baker to the east, now stained golden by evening light. Approaching the summit, the car came into full sun and he was momentarily blinded. Then he was over the top and beginning the long descent back to the city. As the car rounded a curve, a large sign caught his eye: MALAHAT MOUNTAIN INN—CASUAL DINING. The place looked inviting and his empty stomach made the decision for him. He just had time to get into the turn lane, then hang a left across the highway into the parking lot.

The restaurant turned out to be a find. The interior was classy and subdued, with polished wood floors, modern furniture, and low lighting, To the rear was a covered balcony, with a spectacular view of the inlet separating the main body of the Island from the Saanich Peninsula. Hal's arrival coincided with a table coming free on the balcony. He ordered a drink and examined the menu: it all looked good and he decided to just take whatever was recommended.

While waiting for his food, he took note of the Saturday evening crowd, a fairly even mix of tourists and locals, he guessed, casually dressed but mostly well heeled. They were enjoying themselves quietly, the exception being one mildly boisterous table in a far corner of the balcony. Hal took this all in, but soon his thoughts returned to what had consumed them most of the day: his perplexing brother.

How was he going to get back in touch with Trent? Or, more correctly, how were he and Stephanie going to maneuver the guy into contacting *him*? The whole situation was pathetic and somewhat ridiculous, and it'd have been nice to be able to move on to Vancouver and forget it. But he couldn't. The reunion, bizarre as it had been, nevertheless reminded him how much he cared about his kid brother and engendered unexpected regret at all the years they'd missed out on. Just as, albeit for other reasons entirely, he'd forfeited a whole lifetime with . . .

Mattie!

With surprise Hal realized that the Trent thing had driven that surprising blast from the past right out of his mind. Yet here she was, *here they both were*, once more knocking at the door of his life. And it didn't take a genius to figure he wouldn't be thinking about it if, on some level, it wasn't important.

What was it about this island? He'd only come here to work, to make a simple little movie, for Christ's sake. Now all hell seemed to be letting loose. As if to emphasize this thought, the loud party erupted into a particularly strident chorus of laughter. Someone rose and, after a remark that caused more mirth, threaded his way toward the interior. His trajectory caused him to pass nearby, and as he did so, Hal's casual glance became more studied.

The man was unusually short, hardly more than five feet, but wiry and strong-looking, with proportionately broad shoulders, like a well-dressed acrobat. His face was narrow, sinewy, with a big mouth but thin lips, and eyes of a blue so pale as to be almost colorless.

White eyes. The term floated into Hal's mind, not merely as a description but from some remote memory corner. He *knew* that face . . . and, as he realized that, the small man stopped and stared at him. The white eyes blinked, rolled up, then snapped back into focus. The thin-lipped mouth broke into a grin that was almost wolfish.

"Goddamn *Hal Bannatyne!*" he breathed, Not a question but a brisk statement.

That did it. Hal recognized the little guy. His name was—wait for it, of course—*Vince Smithson*—an old buddy from Vic High. "Vince?" he blurted.

"You *know* it, man!"

"For crying out loud!"

"For crying out louder!"

"Wow!"

"WOW!"

Thereafter at a loss for words, Hal finally said lamely, "You're looking good."

Vince grinned. "And you, buddy! Big shot actor now, eh?"

"I've had some success, I guess."

"Always the modest bastard. I've seen your stuff, man. You're not only famous. You're good."

Coming from such an old acquaintance, this made Hal feel inordinately pleased. The meeting wasn't all that remarkable, since the city was small and he'd once known a lot of people there, but it certainly was a surprise, especially after such an odd day.

"Thanks," Hal said. "So . . . what have you been up to?"

Vince gave that grin again that Hal so well remembered. "More than you might imagine, my friend."

"I can believe it."

"So . . . what are *you* doing?"

"Well, I've been in Victoria making a—"

"No, I mean, *right now!*'

"Oh! Nothing much. Just stopped in for a bite before heading back to town."

"So head for my place instead! It's only five minutes away."

AND THEN HE was going to a party. It happened so fast, with such irresistible momentum, that Hal was carried along in spite of himself. He remembered Vince from school as being an extraordinary salesman, a kid who could make anyone do almost anything. Hal, at six feet three, and Vince, more than a foot shorter, had been like a sort of Mutt and Jeff team. Not that Vince needed Hal as a protector. He was far too valuable to intimidate, being an expert procurer: cigarettes, booze, condoms, even drugs—in those days that meant marijuana—for the right price, Vince could get hold of anything. Strangely, his school friendship with Hal had stemmed largely from the fact that he was one of the rare ones who wanted nothing; while Hal admired the guts and imagination of his diminutive buddy.

Three decades later, Vince's powers of persuasion were undiminished. "I've got a little place up on the mountain," he had said, waving vaguely toward the west. "Near the Aerie Resort, but with ten times the view as those losers. Saturday nights I often throw a bit of a bash. Damn! Tonight you can be the guest of honor."

Ancient habits die hard, and Hal didn't argue. He didn't have any plans, and a party might take his mind off other matters.

Vince had a sleek Jaguar, into which he packed his dinner guests from the restaurant. With Hal following in his rental car, they headed back toward the Malahat summit, leaving the highway at the Spectacle Lake turnoff. Climbing again, they soon reached Vince's "little place." This was a futuristic construction of concrete, floating beams, and glass, sprouting like a living thing from the mountainside, with a view encompassing the entire south end of the Island. Getting out of his car, Hal could see Victoria, spread like a carpet of lights in the distance, and beyond, outlined by the last glow of sunset, the crags of the Olympic Mountains in the State of Washington.

But he was given little time to ogle scenery. The Jag's occupants emerged, and Vince grabbed his arm, hustling him inside. Already there were a lot of people present, chatting and drinking, with a couple of waiters hovering about. Evidently, the party had started without the host.

The interior of the house was spectacular; glass walls on the sides that faced the view, marble slabs covered with tapestries and bright wool hangings where the building nosed into the mountain. For the second time that day, Hal had happened into a dwelling that was the expression of great wealth. But this made the house by the lake seem almost modest, and—unlike his unhappy brother—Vince Smithson was undoubtedly the owner.

As evidence of this fact, after fetching them drinks, his host took Hal by the arm and dragged him from room to room, making introductions at machine gun speed, but with flawless recall, to his guests. Befitting the surroundings, there was much wealth here: expensively dressed young men with glittering girl friends; older fellows with trophy wives; bankers, CEOs, smart women executives; politicians, local personalities, and a few individuals who looked a little dangerous. Everyone was on a first name basis with their host—little Vince who'd once been the fixer in high school—and Hal could see why: his old friend was dynamic, the magical mover of the old days now in full flower. *God*, Hal thought, *if this guy was my agent, by now I'd be a superstar.*

The only thing that was unclear was what Vince actually *did*. Everyone else seemed to know. Oblique references were made to this project, that concern, or such-and-such initiative, but little of it made much sense to Hal. Just one thing was clear: whatever Vince did involved a lot of money and probably a good deal of power. In this pond, and likely well beyond, Vince Smithson was a very big fish indeed.

After chatting a while and having been recognized by several people—the rich were as fascinated by showbiz as anyone—Hal once more felt Vince's hand on his arm. He was led away from the throng, out onto a side balcony. When they were alone, Vince said, "God, that's better. Sometimes these circuses of mine depress the hell out of me."

Hal laughed. "Really? Seemed like you were having a ball. All those fat cats eating out of your hand."

The small man grinned, "Yeah—well—you know, I've always liked to run the show, And I guess I'm good at it. But—I dunno—meeting you after all this time . . . It's got to be thirty years, right?"

"That's what I figured."

"It made me realize just how quick the time passes. Suddenly, for a minute there, I actually got to feeling old."

Hal looked out into the night, where the stars and the far-off city formed a continuous pattern of light. "My guess is that 'old' for you is how most people feel on their best day. Doesn't seem like you've slowed down one bit since school. But—tell me . . ."

"What, buddy?"

"You're obviously well off, with a lot of influential friends who seem to hang on your every word. So—I've been trying to figure—just what is that you *do*."

"Not living here any more, I guess you *would* wonder that. Okay—come on, I'll show you."

Vince led the way to the opposite end of the balcony, where there was another door. He entered and a light went on, revealing a medium sized room. Hal followed inside as Vince put on more lights. There was a desk, a sofa, a couple of easy chairs, and two walls lined with books and file cabinets. Evidently Vince's study, the place actually *smelled* rich: wood, leather, and cigar smoke. Not a sound of the party made it through the paneled walls. The single window had curtains, which Vince carefully closed. He went to the desk and from a drawer produced a bag of white powder, a portion of which he expertly arranged in two lines on the desktop. Producing a straw, he inhaled a quantity into each nostril, following this with a long-drawn sigh of satisfaction.

Hal gave an astonished laugh. "*This* is what you do? You're a drug dealer?"

Vince broke from his moment of bliss to stare. "What? Drug dealer? *Fuck no!* Man, you can't be serious! This is strictly recreation! Speaking of which . . ." He indicated the cocaine. "Y'wanna bite?"

"Ah—no, thanks. Bad for the voice, I've found."

"Yeah, right!" Vince grinned. "Still old Holy Hal, eh? Seems I never *could* tempt you into anything. Okay, more power to you, bud. But the reason I closed the curtains wasn't this." He put the bag away and crossed the room to the bookshelf, pulling out a map that came down like a blind. "It was *this!*"

"This" was a large scale rendition of Victoria and surrounding suburbs. Apart from the size, the only thing unusual was a number of blocks of color: red, blue, and yellow, sprinkled over the map like confetti. "You see," Vince said, making no attempt to keep the pride from his voice, "red areas are projects completed, blue are work in progress, and yellow are ones I'm negotiating, or have my eye on. A lot of assholes—competitors and speculators—would give anything to know about those little yellow babies, and some of them are right here in this house . . . which is the reason for the secrecy."

"I see . . . but *projects*? What exactly to you mean?"

Vince raised his eyebrows. "Man, you always were in a world of your own. Okay, I'll spell it out. This is real estate, Hal. I'm a property developer, for chrissake!"

Hal laughed. "Ah!"

"Not so exciting as being a Don of the Medellin Cartel, but a lot safer, I'd guess."

Hal moved closer to the map. The little colored blocks ran to the dozens. "All this is yours?"

"Nah—some I own, or co-own, or lease, or have an interest in. But *all* of them I had a major hand in developing. That's what really intrigues me—the building bit. You understand?"

"Actually, I think I do—it's like rehearsals,"

"Come again?"

"When I'm working in the theater, the thing I get the most kick out of is rehearsals: opening night is great, and a few performances, but then it starts to get boring."

Vince nodded vigorously, indicating the map. "That's it!" When a project's finished, I'm happy, but it's a yawn." He indicated a blue area. "These are what keep me occupied most days. But *these* . . ." His hand seemed almost to caress one of the yellow dots. ". . . These are what I *dream* about. I guess it's like when you guys get to act Hamlet or something."

Hal chuckled. "Point taken."

"It's the new projects that really get under my skin. When they're working out—when the property is coming under my control and I'm winning, I feel like the king of goddamn creation. But when I'm taking shit, being crossed up; when I can't get my parcels together, or I'm having other problems . . . well, what can I say? Life ain't quite so sweet."

For the merest moment, Vince's expression was surprisingly grim, then he grinned, snapping the map so that it rolled back up and vanished. "You asked what I do, so now you know. Sorry, buddy!"

"What for?"

"For hustling you away from your quiet supper to come to my circus."

"You kidding? Vince, it's been cool. What you're doing is quite something."

"Yeah? I guess you're about the last guy I've got left to impress." He laughed. "Running into you like that, I just couldn't resist the opportunity. How much longer are you going to be in town?"

"Not long—a couple of days."

Their youthful friendship had been a product of circumstance, created by their differences from the herd rather than in any real affinity for each other. So Hal was neither surprised nor disappointed when, without further ceremony he was ushered back to the party. Almost immediately a man approached and took Vince by the elbow. The newcomer was a fit-looking fifty-year-old who seemed somewhat out of place amongst the classy guests. He had the physique and appearance of a tough outdoorsman, this image enhanced by a U-shaped scar high on his forehead. But his voice and manner were unobtrusive. After a few muted words, Vince turned back to his old schoolmate.

"Hal, this is my associate, Lyall Penney. He always seems to need to talk business just when I'm having fun." He clapped Hal on the back and it was as if their short time of intimacy had never happened. "Parties are okay, but they're just grease for the old wheels of commerce, eh? Enjoy, old bud: eat, drink, and all that shit. You've got some admirers here, I'll bet. Maybe you can find one who *really* wants your autograph—if you catch my drift? See you later."

Vince winked and, already deep in conversation with Penney, vanished into the crowd. Hal finished his drink but declined another. He stayed a while, chatting easily but in no mood for adventures. He didn't catch sight of his host again. Before 10:00 PM he was heading back down the mountain.

TEN

Stephanie was doing a final clear away when the phone rang. At this hour, with the café closed, the chef gone, and Fran in back cashing out, there was only herself to answer. Since it was unlikely to be a customer—nobody in Duncan would dream of dining after nine—this would probably be a personal call, and on her way to pick up, Stephanie thought of Trent's brother. Had he come up with some ideas already? Her heartbeat quickened as she picked up the phone. "Fran's Restaurant: good evening."

"And good evening to *you*, sweetface," her fiancé's voice said.

With just these words, Stephanie could tell that Trent was feeling better. Earlier, when she'd confronted him with the folly of the stunt at the house, he'd seemed genuinely ashamed. Now, his tone made her worry that he'd convinced himself he didn't care. She was sure that deep down he did. But the swiftness with which he'd slipped back into denial made her see that convincing him to sort out the mess was going to be harder than she'd thought. Her heart sank, but she didn't let this show in her voice. "Darling, hey! I'll be leaving in five. Did you want me to pick up something on my way home?"

"No," his cheerful voice said, "That's why I'm calling: Don't *go* home."

"Oh—why not?"

"Because, kiddo. I'm at *my* place. I want you to come here."

Though they'd been going together a year, and were definitely—

albeit without the formality of a ring—engaged, this did not yet include a permanent living arrangement. Stephanie had a little house on the outskirts of Duncan, where she'd lived, with her son Gary, for the ten years since her divorce. Trent often stayed over—almost always on weekends—but they'd not taken the final step. Ostensibly, Trent needed to maintain a presence at Shawnigan Lake for his care-taking duties. In fact, had they really wanted, something could have been worked out. "Why the change of plans, hon?" she said.

"I realized you were mad at me. You know, for playing that little game with Hal . . ."

"Darling, my only concern is why you think you have to impress him. Anyway, it doesn't matter right now. Why do you want me to come there?"

He gave a conspiratorial chuckle. "Terry doesn't get back till Monday. We could sleep up at the big house."

"You know I don't like to do that."

"Whatever. Anyway—what I *do* have is a surprise for you. I've been working on it all night. So you have to come here to see it. Okay?"

"Sure. So—is there anything you need?"

"No. Just bring your sweet self."

"Okay—see you in a bit."

She hung up and quickly finished her cleanup, changed out of her uniform, and popped her head into the office to say goodnight to Fran, the owner. Her old VW was parked out back. This late, she was hardly enamoured of the prospect of a half-hour drive to Shawnigan Lake, but resignedly started out. Trust Trent to come up with a mysterious "surprise," a diversion, no doubt, from his embarrassment of the earlier charade.

She loved Trent, no doubt of it. Though ten years her senior, he was the most exciting, passionate man Stephanie had ever known. He was also brilliant, with a wonderful imagination, fantastic memory and math skills that made her feel humble. Though he'd taken to business rather than the arts, the richness of imagination that had served his brother so well was evident in him too. Finally, he adored her—he was capable of making her feel happier and more desirable than anyone ever had—the snag being that he was also a bit of a flake.

Apparently, the fortune he'd recently lost wasn't the first. According to his friend Terry Bathgate—who'd told her this in confidence—Trent had been up and down several times over the years. Undoubtedly a whiz-kid, he had trouble staying focused and was easily bored, the final problem being that, though an astute market analyst, he had trouble taking his own advice. His present predicament was the result of just that.

So why had she committed herself to such a man? He had come by chance into her restaurant, a charming but obviously adrift guy, and he'd returned again and again, chatting her up until finally she agreed to go out with him. A year later, she'd come to believe she'd found someone just one small misstep from extraordinary. If he'd just sort himself out and try to be a bit more mature, she was sure that the rare soul she sensed beneath the slightly wacky exterior would one day emerge in triumph.

Or was she just a sentimental fool?

Whatever! She loved the man, which was all that mattered. As for the drive to Shawnigan he'd sprung on her, after the bustle of work she found it soothing. Fifteen minutes from Duncan, she left the Island Highway at the south end of tiny Dougan Lake, heading in the direction of Shawnigan Village. The road was dark and winding but still quite busy. The blinding lights of oncoming cars began to give her a headache. Traffic started to pile up behind, and at one point a giant pickup overtook her with a roar. By the time she reached the village, she was feeling exhausted and somewhat less benign toward the instigator of this late-night odyssey.

The last couple of kilometres around the lake, though even more winding, were less busy. Stephanie reached the familiar entrance to Lake Haven and turned down the drive with relief. The light was on in the lower courtyard, Terry's Bathgate's convertible parked off to the left near the rear entrance to the house. Stephanie turned her VW in the opposite direction, on a track that led through the trees to a cabin. Outside there was just room for two vehicles. Trent's battered Landrover was parked there, and Stephanie edged in beside it. The only way out was to reverse all the way back to the courtyard—but she wasn't going anywhere tonight.

The porch light was off, making the normally cheery guest cabin look a little mysterious. It was built of logs, with a steep-pitched, shake roof. There were windows to right and left of the front door, one side being the kitchen-living room, the other the bedroom. The bedroom curtains were closed, as—surprisingly—were the drapes to the living room. No light showed behind either, which was odd; Trent usually kept the place bright and cheerful. Stephanie gave a small toot on the horn to announce her arrival, gathered up her handbag, and moved to the front door.

It was locked.

That was odd. She'd never known Trent to lock his door. Stephanie gave it a sharp rap. "Trent!" she called. "Honey?"

No answer. From the lakeside a couple of houses away came a girlish shriek and the sound of high-pitched laughter. A voice cried. "Hey—no way—too fucking *cold!*" The sound of a splash was followed by more laughter.

Stephanie knocked more loudly. "Trent—it's me—open up!"

Silence—then the sound of footsteps. Finally, Trent's voice, muffled and low. "Are you alone?"

"What?"

"I said, are you *alone?*"

His voice actually sounded nervous, which was absurd. "Of course I'm alone. What else, you nut? Open the damn door."

Lights came on in the living room. There was the sound of a key turning, then the door opened. Trent stood there, a dark figure silhouetted by the glow beyond. Stephanie couldn't see his face, but his stance told her that she hadn't mistaken the voice tone. Something was wrong. "Trent—what's the matter?"

"Shhh!" he whispered urgently. "Get in!"

She did as requested and Trent quickly closed and locked the door. Stephanie felt her unease growing. "Honey, what is it? Why are you locking the door?"

"I've got to! To stop him?"

"Stop *who*, for God's sake?"

"Terry, of course!"

"Terry Bathgate?"

"YES!"

"Stop him doing *what*?"

"Throwing me out!"

Trent's voice was no longer just afraid, it was growing angry, and Stephanie began to feel more than a little nervous herself. "Why would Terry want to do that? Oh, Trent, you two didn't have a fight . . . Hold on, he's not even *here*. Did he just come back? What's going on?"

Trent put his finger to his lips and hustled her away from the door. His grip was none too gentle, and Stephanie felt her nervousness increase. Half an hour ago her fiancé had been chatting on the phone, sounding perfectly cheerful. Now he seemed to have become totally paranoid. "What's going on, Trent?" she repeated, trying hard to keep the panic out of her voice.

Trent led her into the kitchen area, and only then did he loosen his grip. "We didn't have a fight," he said. "Terry's not here. But he'll be coming—coming to throw me out!"

"Darling, why would he do that?"

Trent laughed: the sound was impatient, exasperated—and chilling. "You must know! You must have worked that out!"

"Worked out *what*, for heaven's sake?"

Her fiancé's expression suddenly changed, becoming sly and—yes—suspicious. "Unless you're in on it too?"

Whatever had happened since they'd known each other, Trent had never shown the smallest negative attitude toward herself. She forced her voice to be calm when she said, "In on *what*? Hon—please tell me what you're talking about?"

He looked at her squarely, his eyes dark and—was this possible?—dangerous. "The conspiracy that Terry and my brother are cooking up."

"What are you talking about? Terry and Hal have never met!"

"The minute he arrived I knew."

"Knew *what*?"

"That I was really on my uppers. He was just testing me, taunting me, seeing how far I'd go with my pathetic shit—so he could report back to Terry how crazy I am!"

"Trent, that's ridiculous. You may exaggerate a bit from time to time—tell a few harmless fibs—but one thing you're definitely *not* is crazy." She finished lamely, "Anyway, as I said, Terry doesn't know your brother."

Trent chuckled. "That's what you think."

"Darling, how *could* he?"

"Very simple." Trent began to pace. "All those clever bastards know each other. That's how they get where they are. I've been figuring it out and now I understand: oh, yeah!"

"Trent—*really*!"

"It's fucking *true*! If you can't see that, you're either stupider than I thought—or you're in on it."

There was no answering this. She knew it very well. She also understood that, if she could believe what she was hearing, she was witnessing something entirely new: Trent was becoming delusional. She was both astonished and afraid—and her immediate concern was not to show it.

"I'm not 'in' on anything," she said swiftly, in as reasonable a voice as she could muster. "Come one, hon, you know that."

He paused, took a deep breath—and finally smiled. "Yes—I do. So now—I want you to help me."

Relief washed through her. "Of course I'll help you. Any way you want. So—why don't we just relax. Put on some more lights and I'll put on the kettle—"

"No, no, *NO!*" he blurted savagely. "That's not what I meant! What I need is for you to help me to get *away!*"

"Away?"

"From *here!* I'm going to fool them! Do what they'd never suspect. I'll escape. Go where no one can ever follow, or make me look stupid again. Then I'll have the last fucking laugh on the lot of them!"

In the light from the single lamp, Trent's face was drawn, rigid, his eyes aglow with excitement and triumph. Whatever was going on, whatever strange country her fiancé had entered since his mind had apparently become unhinged, he now seemed beyond influence or diversion; Stephanie understood this, and felt real fear. "Darling," she whispered, "I just don't understand."

"Of course you don't!" Trent shouted. "But you *will*. Come on— it's time!"

He grabbed her arm, pulling her across the room. "Trent—what are you doing?" Stephanie cried.

"This is why I brought you here. I want you to be the witness!"

They had reached the bedroom. Trent snapped on the light, and flung back the door. The room was neat and tidy, bed made, everything as usual—except for a single item.

Suspended from a beam in the high ceiling was a hangman's noose.

Stephanie gasped, stumbled sideways as Trent released her and strode ahead. In a single fluid movement, he leaped on a chair, stretched up, and put his neck in the hideous loop.

The other end of the rope had been securely tied off, unreachably high, so that once the noose had begun its work, nothing could be done to stop it.

Head in the noose, Trent looked down at his almost swooning fian-cée. His face was now serenely calm. One of his legs lifted, poised to kick away the chair. "Goodbye, darling," he said softly. "Remember me."

Stephanie stumbled forward, wanting but not daring to clutch the chair, terrified of precipitating the very action she desired to prevent. "*No!*" the word echoed like a rattle from the grave. "Trent—sweetheart!—*please—DON'T!*"

"But I must!" His raised leg shifted, hovered in front of the chair back, pausing before its final, fatal thrust, "You can see I must."

Her insides convulsed in a frenzied effort not to scream. Agonizingly, she rammed sobs back into her throat, forcing her mouth to make the words that likely would be the last her fiancé would ever hear.

"Oh, Trent," she whispered, "if you love me—*please don't do this dreadful thing!*"

Stillness. Dead silence.

The suspended foot, waiting to perform the last life-ending shove, paused—hovered . . .

Then planted itself firmly back on the chair.

Trent's hands rose, deftly removing the noose from his neck. He flipped it aside, leaped to the floor—and executed a broad, theatrical bow.

"End of performance. Applause, applause!" He said with a goofy grin. "So—what do you think? Aren't I as good an actor as my famous brother?"

ELEVEN

On Sunday morning, Mattie woke feeling a lot better. The angle of the sun, dazzling through the east-facing bedroom windows, showed that the hour was more than decent for rising. So she got up, feeling a lightness of spirit which, considering recent events, was remarkable. She headed downstairs and had barely reached the kitchen when the telephone rang.

Sylvie! Mattie thought, the idea scarcely intuition; her friend had been due to return from a trip, and often called on Sunday mornings. "Hello?"

"Good morning, darling girl," drawled Sylvia Skeffington's grand English tones. "Is the coffee on?"

After all these years, Mattie's heart still warmed at her friend's voice. "Hi, Sylvie, I thought it might be you."

"Oh, the joys of being anticipated. Just called to say I'm on my way—but I'm sure you knew that? See you in ten. Ciao, dear!"

Mattie put on coffee and it had scarcely brewed when there came the sound of a vehicle approaching fast: Sylvie piloted her minivan like a rally driver. Then the screen door thwacked and Sylvia appeared, striding in as if concluding a brisk hike. She was five years younger and five inches shorter than Mattie, built like an athlete, brown-limbed and sturdy, with curly blond hair, rosy cheeks, and a perennially cheerful countenance. As usual, she wore a flowing dress and stout boots, a combination she somehow managed to make appear both sensible and stylish. She threw her potter's well-muscled arms about Mattie and hugged until her friend gasped.

"Whew!" Mattie laughed, as she was released. "It's good to see *you*, too, Sylvie. How was Arizona?"

"New Mexico," Sylvia corrected. "The pueblo potters are something else. Didn't learn much I didn't already know, of course. But just being around them was an inspiration."

From a pocket of her dress, she produced a tiny, beautiful pot, two inches tall by three wide, jet-black, with a sheen so deep it seemed almost to have an internal fire. "For you!"

Mattie took the pot, eyes bright, caressing the delicate surface as if it were alive. "It's beautiful. Oh, Sylvie—you shouldn't."

"Don't I know it, ducks," Sylvia grinned. "Scandalously expensive, actually. Those Navajo ladies are scary business women. I only wish I was as good at marketing *my* old tat."

Sylvia's "old tat" was fine and very original pottery. She had great talent and considerable reputation. Working like a slave, with only one assistant, she made a healthy living. "Oh, come on," Mattie said laughingly. "Your work's terrific, as everyone knows. But thanks so much for this. It's lovely."

Mattie poured coffee and they sat. After a few minutes' chat, Sylvie rose and refreshed her own cup. Plunking herself back down, she said without ceremony. "All right darling girl, now we've done the bullshit. Time to tell mama what's been going on."

Mattie raised an eyebrow. "Is it that obvious?"

Sylvia sniffed and laughed simultaneously, an oddly expressive combination. "Darling, how long have we known each other? Have I suddenly grown blind? I think not. Out with it."

Without further argument, Mattie obeyed. Sylvie already was familiar with her father-in-law's obsession with his property and the mini-saga that had been going on regarding outside attempts to acquire it. She also knew something about the old man's history of drinking. But when Mattie got to the part in her story when, just thirty-six hours previously, she'd stood staring down the barrel of a shotgun, then had it go off almost in her face, Sylvie's face was slack with horror. "My God, Mattie," she breathed. "How terrifying. What did you *do*?"

This being the first time she'd told of the experience, Mattie was unprepared for the severity of her reaction in reliving it. Cathartic it might be, but in retrospect its effect—no longer shielded by the numbness of shock—seemed even more distressing than originally. Tears welled up in her eyes and her hands shook by the time she reached the conclusion. "Oh, God, Sylvie, I've never been so scared in my life. Luckily, I *did* realize that Fitz wasn't mad. Just drunk and half asleep. And in the glare of the lights he didn't recognize me. After the first shot—so close I swear I felt the wind—instead of running, which probably would have been fatal, I managed to stay still. And finally I made him understand that it was me."

"Thank the Lord. What did he do?"

"Oh, you know—gasped, swore—dropped the gun. It was all over so quick, it was almost like a bad dream. I was so shocked I didn't even get angry. Just put him to bed—would you believe?—like a naughty kid."

"Gracious! I bet you gave him hell when he sobered up next morning."

"Not really. If fact, we've hardly talked about it. I don't know how much he remembers. Enough that he's pretty mortified, I think. And he *has* apologized in a general way. But I don't believe he's aware of how near things came to—you know."

"But that's no good, ducks. What if he gets smashed and tries it again?"

"He can't. I've buried the gun."

Sylvie gave a surprised chortle. "Really? Good for you. But what's to stop him getting another?"

"Unlikely. Despite what happened, guns aren't Fitz's thing. That one was an heirloom he'd only recently dug out of the attic. Also . . ."

"What?"

"In spite of everything, in his own way he cares about me. He's certainly wild about Jennifer, though not too thrilled that she's—as he puts it—'run off to Froggieland.' But he's already lost a son and . . ." There was a small pause, which was not lost on her friend. ". . . and his only grandson. I'm sure he doesn't want to add to the toll."

At some time during the narrative, Sylvie had taken hold of Mattie's hand. She gave it an encouraging squeeze and let go. "Darling, of *course* he doesn't. Stupid of me to suggest otherwise. Fitz may be a cantankerous old fart occasionally, but he's also a sweet man who'd be lost without you." Sylvie rose and administered a swift peck to her friend's cheek. "As would we all, my lamb. So it's over and everyone survived. We must just thank our lucky stars and carry on. Actually—funny as it may seem, after what you've just told me—it was also Fitz I came to see."

"Oh?"

"On my way through Phoenix, I visited some super galleries. One of them had an exhibition of animal carvings that reminded me of Fitz's work, though not nearly so good, I might say. And I suddenly thought, why on Earth doesn't Fitz *show* his wonderful work? And then later I thought, hey, maybe Fitz and I could have an exhibition together. In Victoria. Vancouver, even. What do you think?"

"*I* think it's wonderful. Not enough people see his stuff. But what *he'll* think is another matter."

"I know. I had this idea I might use my feminine wiles to try to persuade him." Her enthusiastic expression faded. "But, after what you've told me, I can see that today isn't the best time. So . . . what else has been happening?"

Before Mattie could reply, the telephone rang. It was an old landline handset, situated on a shelf at the far end of the kitchen, with a harsh bell that could be heard all over the house. When the racket commenced, both women jumped. "Lawks, my heart!" Sylvie laughed.

Mattie headed for the phone. "I don't know who it could be. No one but you ever phones on Sunday morning."

"Probably a telemarketer. They're getting bloody shameless. I'd tell him to go to hell."

"I bet you would," Mattie smiled, picking up the phone. "Hello."

"Hi," said a voice Mattie instantly recognized. "I hope you really *did* want me to call."

TWELVE

Hal turned off the Trans-Canada Highway at Duncan. This was the second time in two days he'd made the trip up-island: yesterday to see his brother, now to visit with someone who, somewhat more surprisingly, had managed to turn up again in his life. Having prodded himself into finally making that phone call to Mattie, he'd checked out of his Victoria hotel. Whatever happened, later that day—not much later, if the meeting turned out to be a disaster—he'd be taking the ferry to Vancouver, to get on with things in the real world. Strangely though, the thought of the forthcoming gig didn't fill him with the usual buzz of anticipation.

The road to Maple Bay was pleasantly winding, with a lake off to one side and some new-looking subdivisions clustered on the hills nearby. Hal felt that he must have been out this way in the old days, but he had no memory of it, which was hardly surprising considering the elapsed time. Passing yet another development, where many large homes could be glimpsed under construction, on level after level ascending the flank of a steep rise, he began to realize just how much money must be pouring into this favored island. That put him in mind of the visit to his old friend Vince's Malahat mansion. No wonder the clever bastard was rich; Vancouver Island seemed to be in the process of huge expansion. This was no surprise, since it had a great climate, low crime rate, and relatively unspoiled natural beauty. *Not for much longer*, he thought glumly, then sighed resignedly. A paradise such as this could hardly hope to remain undiscovered forever.

The directions Mattie had given him were pretty simple. Shortly before reaching the coast, he turned south toward Genoa Bay, passed a marina, then swung onto a side road that skirted the ocean. Presently he came upon an unusually large section of undeveloped land sandwiched between the road and the water. A little later he spied a gate with the name TRAIL on a tipsy mailbox. Hal swung into the drive, which meandered through a stand of densely packed fir and coast maple, giving no hint of what might lie beyond. The approach was in the shape of a lazy S. After the completion of the second bend it emerged from the trees and there, on the far side of an expanse of parched lawn, was a house.

After all Hal had recently witnessed of new construction, this was like stepping back into another era. The building was large, solid, in a broad-gabled style which in the late nineteenth century would have been considered modern. Hal had seen such places in the venerable streets of Rosedale in Toronto, pampered and valued in the millions. This house, of no less grand lineage, was nonetheless in need of some TLC. And though it commanded an ocean view of breathtaking beauty, it also had an aspect that was more than a trifle forlorn.

The driveway curved around in front of the building, ending in a parking area that contained several vehicles. The nearest was a minivan with the words SYLVIE'S POTTERY WORKS painted in bold letters on the side. Hal parked beside it and walked back to the house.

The veranda, under the overhang of a second-floor balcony, was broad and cool. To the right, it was enclosed with mesh, giving it a tropical feeling; to the left, it was open, stretching the length of the building. The front door, of oak solid enough to repel Viking marauders, sported an iron knocker. Hal was in the act of reaching for this, when the door was opened by Mattie.

Prepared as he was, Hal nonetheless experienced a reprise of the shock he'd previously felt when, sprawled on his rear end, he'd first spotted his old friend. Momentarily, it was if he was transported back in time, looking at someone who'd been frozen, waiting two decades for his return. Then the illusion dissolved as Mattie smiled and reached for his hand.

"*Hal!*" Mattie said. "I'm so glad. I was such an idiot the other day, running off like that, I wouldn't have blamed you if you'd given up on me entirely. But you're here. Come in."

Briskly she ushered him inside, and led him through a paneled hall, past stairs that climbed to upper regions and a large dining room, finally into a bright kitchen. Through high windows, Hal could again see the spectacular sea view. Mattie indicated the room's other occupant, an attractive women who, he discovered, was surveying him with frank amusement.

"Hello, Hal!" The woman said, in a plummy English voice, at once aristocratic and earthy. "I've been hearing a lot about you. And my-my! Aren't you the pretty lad."

"This is Sylvie," Mattie laughed. "My oldest friend. No tact at all, but a wonderful artist."

"Crafty old craftsperson, actually," Sylvie responded. "But I manage to keep busy."

Mattie poured coffee and they sat around the big kitchen table. In contrast to the awkwardness he'd feared, the talk was as easy and light as if they were at a cocktail party. Hal wondered if Mattie had perhaps invited her friend for moral support. In any case, the exuberant Sylvie monopolized the conversation. She claimed she saw few movies, but nonetheless was familiar with most of his own, her comments critical, witty, and admiring in almost equal proportion. She asked him questions about show business, his career, and—with complete lack of embarrassment—his personal life. Hal was starting to think that she was coming on to him, when he tumbled to what was going on. This was a sort of set-up. Mattie was cleverly using her friend as a buffer, while extracting information in a way that was easy and painless. Hal didn't know whether to feel amused or embarrassed. But one thing was sure: for her to have gone to all this trouble, his reappearance must have created something of a stir.

He hoped it wasn't one they'd both regret.

Then, as effortlessly as she'd performed her inquisition, Sylvie broke it off. If she'd been booked as the opening act in this show, her performance was apparently concluded. "Well, duckies, I really must run," she chirped, clapping her hands together and rising briskly. "Sunday it may be, but the potter's wheel never rests. Mattie darling, thanks for the tiffin. Hal, you hunk, as my Cockney nanny used to say 'it's been corker.' And when you and Mattie get tired of reminiscing—*please* get her to send you along to me. Cheery bye!"

With a brisk buss on each of their cheeks and a swish of her long dress she was gone. Presently there came the sound of an engine, revving high then fading fast.

"So that was your friend Sylvie." Hal grinned.

"That was Sylvie. She's—helped me through some hard times."

"This being one of them?"

Mattie colored. "You noticed."

"Did you think that talking to me would be so difficult?"

"I didn't really know how it would be. Anyway, that third degree of Sylvie's wasn't exactly planned. It's sort of what she does. I just took advantage, I guess. Do you mind?"

"As long as you now know that it's not necessary. All I wanted was to say hi and chat about old times. The thing I said the other day, being guilty at how we broke up, that was stupid. You've had a whole life since then, and it was pure ego for me to think you'd even remember me well enough to be mad. I'm sorry."

Mattie grinned. "Apologizing again?"

"So I'm sorry for being sorry, too," he laughed. "Okay?"

"Okay, peace. Hal, I'm just glad you're here. Let's start again. Do you want some more coffee?"

"No, thanks." He sat looking at her, Mattie who—he now

admitted—had been quietly waiting in some back alcove of his heart. Not that he still loved her, of course. But now it was possible to admit that there was perhaps something unfinished between them. And here they were, at last face to face again, in a house where she'd spent much of her life—and he still knew next to nothing about what that life had been. "What I *really* want," he said, "is to hear about you!"

"Me?"

"Well, of course. You realize I don't know anything: whether you're married, if you have kids, what it is you do. Mattie, the only clue I have right now is that name on the mailbox. Trail—is that your name now?"

She nodded, smiling. "Yes, and it's my turn to say sorry. I wasn't trying to be mysterious. I've always been a bit shy, remember? So, where do I start? All right . . . I'm a widow. My husband died twenty years ago. We had two children, a girl and a boy, who were one and three at the time. This house belongs to my father-in-law, Fitzgerald Trail, whose family has owned the property forever. Fitz is in his seventies and is off somewhere, probably fishing, but you'll maybe meet him later. My daughter, Jennifer, is twenty-three and teaching ESL in Toulouse, France. I teach English too, but literature, at Cowichan High, in Duncan, where I also—this will hardly surprise you—do some theater. Now and then I direct plays for the local dramatic club, and sometimes help out with sets and costumes—but never act. That's just about it."

"Looks like you keep busy. And your son?"

"My son?"

"You said you had a girl *and* a boy, What does he do?"

Mattie didn't immediately reply. She rose and drifted to the window, gazing out at the water. At last she said, "It was really quite maddening."

"Come again?"

Mattie's head turned slowly from left to right, as if she were searching for something in the distance. Hal had no idea what was happening, but it had something of the feeling of a ritual. He stayed quiet and waited. After a while Mattie said, "I told him not to go."

"What?"

"He was an accountant, you know. A real quiet guy, nothing like the theater people I was used to. He was sweet, and dependable, and he really did love us all very much. But a stickler, not cheap or mean—but such a stickler: for details, you know, and what he thought was *right!* God . . . Anyway, we'd rented this video. I can't remember what the movie was or if we even liked it, only it was due back and somehow we'd forgotten. Then, at the last minute, *he* remembered. If he got in the car right away, he said, he could just get it in on time. I told him not to bother, I'd take it back tomorrow. But he wouldn't hear of it. So off he went, and he made it. Video back, no fine, everything dandy. The only trouble was that on the way home some drunk ran a light and hit him, broadside, right at the driver's door. The car was nearly cut in half. The only way they could identify him was—through our dentist."

Shock and horror kept Hal silent a long time. At last he said, "Mattie, I'm so very sorry. How long ago did this happen?"

"As I said, twenty years."

"Twenty . . . ? Then—we're not talking about your son?"

Mattie shook her head in apparent surprise. "No, My *husband*. I was telling you what happened to Will."

Hal gave a whistle of relief. "Whew, I thought . . . That's terrible, of course. But I thought you were talking about your boy. What's his name?"

"Brian."

"Right. So what's he up to?"

Mattie turned back to the window. "He's out there."

"You mean he's at sea."

"I mean *in* the sea. Somewhere in the sea. Five years ago he vanished and we never found him."

Mattie's head was slowly turning again, in that searching way.

Stunned, Hal watched her, this once-regular girl who'd come back into his life as what seemed like a genuinely tragic figure. He had a sudden urge to leave her like that, to hurry from the house and bolt off the Island, back to his life of professional make-believe, where hearts, though teased, were seldom long discomforted.

But he swiftly dismissed that first gutless impulse. He knew his real need was to be right here. To discover, at very least, what it was between them that felt unfinished—or if indeed there was anything at all. So he sat quietly and after a while Mattie said, "I *will* tell you about Brian—if you really want to hear—but not right now. Okay?"

"Of course."

"Do you think you'll be staying for lunch?"

"I'd very much like to."

"Good."

She remained at the window, watching the sea. After a while he joined her. Though as yet he had no idea what this was all about, being part of it felt unusually important.

THIRTEEN

When Trent arrived at Stephanie's he found her door locked. It was well before the time when she had to leave for work and her car was in the drive, so that didn't bode well. He knocked tentatively, but there was no response. Then the door opened, but it was not his fiancée. Her twenty-year-old son Gary—known as Gat—appeared, clad in his bike leathers. Instead of holding the door for Trent, he shut it firmly and moved off. Trent tried the door but found it still locked. "Hey, Gat!" he called after the departing figure. "What's up? Why'd you lock the door?"

Gary barely turned his head. "Orders, man."

"What do you mean 'orders?'"

"Duh! She doesn't want to see you."

"Why not?"

"What do you think? She's mad as shit. Some stunt you pulled? Sounds like you really fucked up good."

Gary's motorbike was parked besides his mother's old vw. He got on, donned his helmet, and started up. With a wave, as sardonic as if he'd lifted the middle finger, he was gone.

Trent winced, sighed, then knocked on the door again. "Steph," he called. Then louder, trying not to sound melodramatic. "Stephanie, *please!*"

After a minute a voice drifted from the direction of the kitchen. "Go away!"

Trent felt sick to his stomach. Gary's description of his position, though crude, had been all too accurate. "Fucked up good" was exactly what he'd done. What in heaven had he been thinking? Yet at the time the charade had seemed—God help him—like a neat idea. He stood on his toes and peered in the kitchen window. Yes, there she was, sitting at the table with a cup of tea and the newspaper. She didn't look up when he tapped on the pane, but just seeing her there gave him a sliver of hope. If she really didn't want to see him, she'd be in her bedroom. This silent treatment was maybe just a statement, a sign that he was being punished, but also part of a possible dialogue. His job now was to move the communication to the next stage.

He tapped again, not expecting her to look, but just hoping to get her attention. He put his face near the window, close enough that he could speak in a normal voice and still be heard through the glass. "Look, Steph," he said carefully, "I'm truly sorry I frightened you last night. If you'd stayed around, instead of rushing off, I could have explained. What I did was stupid, I can see that now, but—you've got to believe me—I'd no idea you were taking my act so seriously. I thought you were just playing along. I was only trying to have a little fun. And—okay, I'll admit it—the reason I wanted to show that I could do my brother's job is because I've recently made such a fuck-up of my own. But it was an asinine idea and scared the hell out of you, which was unforgivable. But listen, darling, I love you. And though I may be a moron, I'd never hurt you on *purpose*. You must believe that."

He stopped, waiting, hoping. After a pause that seemed interminable, Stephanie rose and, without looking in his direction, left the kitchen. His heart sank, but presently there came the sound of the back door unlocking.

Trent felt relieved, at least face to face he'd have some chance of getting back into her good graces. When he got inside, however, he wasn't so sure. Her expression told him that he'd underestimated the depths of her outrage. Stony faced, she gestured toward the kitchen. "Trent, go in and sit down, please."

He extended a placating hand. "But, darling . . ."

"Don't fucking 'darling' me, you callous asshole. Either do as I say, or get out now and don't come back."

Alarmed, he backed off. This was bad. He shut his mouth, and hurried into the kitchen, sitting opposite where she'd been at the table.

This room, like the rest of the fifties-style bungalow, was small and compact, saved from dreariness by the yellow walls and bright ceramic floor tiles which Trent himself had laid. (And damn skilfully, if he did say so himself.) On the table were a brown-Betty teapot, Stephanie's cup, and the Sunday *Times Colonist*, open to the Arts section. Prominent was a review of a local theater production, and Trent considered discussing this as a diversion. But before he could begin, Stephanie said curtly, "Trent, *look* at me!"

Since she'd not looked at *him* directly since he'd arrived, he considered this somewhat unfair, but he did as he was bid. To his surprise, her expression was no longer angry but sorrowful and very calm. Quietly, she said, "You *do* know I love you, right?"

He hadn't been prepared for that opening, but rallied. "Of course, darling, And I love . . ."

"*Shut up!*" she snapped, with an intensity that was scary. "Trent, this is not a discussion or a silly little making-up drama that's going to end in sex. This is serious—and could be the last talk we ever have. So just can it, okay?"

Purse-lipped, he nodded.

"All right, now listen carefully. I've been awake all night working this out, and I'm only going to say it once. That fake hanging scene last night—just like everything you do when you put your mind to it—was brilliant. So good you succeeded in making me more terrified than I've ever been in my life. And why? Because you're embarrassed at what you see as your failure. Which was also the reason for that rich-guy charade with your brother. But what you did last night wasn't just a charade. It was horror. Trent, that sick little scene you staged was plain crazy."

Trent opened his mouth to dispute this, then thought better and closed it again. She continued, "Look, I know the troubles you've had: the bad luck, disappointment, and lost fortune. I also know that, despite everything, you can be wonderful, brilliant, and more fun than anyone I've known. You also can be a flake with the attention span of a flea. But that's okay, I guess it's part of your charm. Whether or not you make it back to being a success, I've never much cared. Still, I *had* thought that being with me was helping you to grow up a little. But last night has opened my eyes. I finally get it: the only thing you *really* care about is your own selfish ego."

He finally broke in. "Steph, that's not *true*."

"Well, I believe it is," she continued relentlessly. "Trent, don't you see? It doesn't matter that you don't own that house by the lake, or that you've fallen on hard times. Your real trouble is that deep down you don't give a damn about anyone. And here's the thing: I really can't see myself spending the rest of my life with someone like that."

Stephanie turned her face away and stared at the table, as if she'd already withdrawn to some achingly unreachable place. Fortunately, Trent was smart, which stopped him sinking himself entirely. Instead of arguing, he said quietly, "Does this mean you're breaking up with me?"

She sighed, staying behind the wall she'd built. "Yes, I suppose it does."

"Christ, Steph—just like that?"

"Did you hear—*understand*—anything I said?"

"Yes, And I agree. Really! I was stupid and selfish and—everything. You're right, I am an asshole. But I can change!"

"Oh, Trent!" she cried in exasperation. "People don't change, You know that."

Love can make them change, was the cliché that came to mind, but he dismissed it before it could spew out and do him in. Instead he said, "I guess not. But I *do* love you. And I promise never to do anything stupid like that again."

"It's not just that . . ."

"But I can't just walk away. Not until you've given me a chance to show you that—even if I can't change—at least I can *grow*. Can't you think of a single thing I could do to show you that? Please, I'm begging you."

Stephanie sat very still. Finally she said. "Well . . ."

"Yes?"

"This is all about your stupid ego. You do know that?"

He gave a sickly laugh. "Man, *do* I."

"If you really want to show you can grow, it has to begin there. So, right now, you need to do something that may be very hard."

"Okay!"

"You may not like it."

"Never mind. What?"

Stephanie's voice was quiet, but its tone was of stern finality. "All right, Trent, you should set the record straight with your brother."

FOURTEEN

Penney found the man he was looking for at a booth at the very back of the dimly lit restaurant. It had taken the best part of an hour to drive up from Victoria on an unseasonably wet night and reach this out-of-the-way spot. He slid into the booth, doing nothing to conceal his foul mood. "Jesus Christ, boss," he snapped. "Why did you have to drag me all the way out to the boonies at this time of night?"

His companion kept his eyes on the rare steak he was carefully carving. "Keep your voice down," he said quietly. "And don't call me boss."

"Why in hell not?"

Before the diner could reply, a waitress appeared and the newcomer ordered a beer. Only after it had been served and they were alone was the question answered. "Because," the small man said crisply, "it's a bad habit. I'm not your boss. I don't give orders. I simply make you aware of my interests, which you help me with, as you see fit."

"Meaning, if I'm rumbled it's my ass?"

"Take it how you like. Anyway, meeting *here* is part of the same strategy. Delicate things are going down, so it's best we're not seen together anymore."

The other shrugged. "As long as the cash keeps flowing, who cares? But why schlep all the way over the friggin' Malahat? We could have done this on the blower."

"That sort of thinking," his companion sighed, "is a perfect illustration of why I want our association at arm's length from now on. You should know that phones are never one hundred percent secure. Meaning, incidentally, you will no longer call me."

The other man nodded sourly. "If that's the way you want it."

"When we need to meet, I'll get instructions to you. Now—business! The property in Maple Bay."

Penney sucked on his teeth glumly. "I figured that was what this was about."

"What else? You swore that by now the old fart would have folded."

"Yeah, well he's stubborn as a blind mule. Seems the family has been squatting on that miserable patch since five minutes after Captain fucking Cook sailed by."

"Who cares. I must have that land. Money and persuasion haven't worked. Your scare campaign has obviously been a bust—and I'm running out of time."

"How much is left?"

"I can renew my options on the surrounding properties, but the investment capital won't hang about much longer: realistically, a month."

"Shit!"

"Tell me about it. So . . . ?" He looked hard at his companion, who sipped on his beer and waited.

"So?" Penney repeated finally.

"Must I spell it out? We need to move to the next level. That—er—barbecue you arranged when there was a similar problem in Nanaimo is best not repeated, however."

"Why not?"

"Once is coincidence, twice might seem like a pattern. Use your head. Whatever goes down, it's most important that there should be no—*no*—perception of irregularity. Understood?"

"Yeah, you bet."

"Good. So that's it. I'll look forward to hearing, very soon, that the climate in Maple Bay has unexpectedly improved. When I do, you can look forward to an equivalent boost in your own fortunes. No need for further contact until it's over. Okay?"

"You got it."

"Fine! Then good night—and thanks for coming all this way in the rain."

Penney nodded, finished his beer, and left. The diner busied himself with his meal, in his quiet corner, respectable and neat—as if never in a million years would he ever be connected with anything so uncivilized as murder.

FIFTEEN

At Mattie's place, Hal had done a good deal more than stay to lunch. After their first awkward start, he'd spent a most pleasant afternoon and evening at the old house in Maple Bay. When he thought of it later, he realized that as mature adults their connection had seemed even better. Physical chemistry was still present, but something more subtle had been added, powerful yet unthreatening. Hal's earlier concerns, guilt about the past, nervousness at how he might now appear, fear that they'd simply have nothing to say to each other, all turned out to be groundless. And if the occasional cloud came over his heart, prompted by the suspicion that all those years ago he might just have abandoned the best thing in his life, he pushed it resolutely away, and concentrated on enjoying the moment. As the day wore on and they wandered the beautiful property by the bay, exchanging histories of half a lifetime, Hal felt wonderfully content. As for Mattie, slowly her aura of sadness had seemed to fade. They didn't speak again of the tragic disappearance of her son; somehow Hal knew that the appropriate time for this had not arrived. Nor did he get an opportunity to meet Mattie's father-in-law. The legendary Fitz—whose ancestors had acquired the Maple Bay land and who now apparently was involved in some sort of tussle to retain it—never appeared. So Hal and Mattie spent the day alone. Not until evening did he realize how swiftly the time had fled, and only by luck did he make the last ferry. A day and a half later in Vancouver, having settled in and prepared for his new gig, the meeting with Mattie still lingered warmly.

As usual, however, all else receded when he started to work. The movie was a computer-animated tale about a bunch of eccentric farm animals who, faced with being put out to pasture—or worse—had run away to make their own circus. Hal's character, a horse with a secret passion for being a high-wire performer, was one of the main instigators of the plot. Creating a comic voice for the creature was great fun, but also tough and exacting work.

Much of modern cartooning is achieved by recording voices first and building animation around the vocals, a process easier on the actors. But in this case the visuals were complete, so it was necessary to fit tricky post-synchronized dialogue while still creating an engaging character. Hal's horse—whose name was also Hal—was an ancient, sway-backed nag with a tendency to fart while attempting ballet pirouettes on the trapeze. In no time, Hal became so immersed in bringing this fellow to life that all else faded. It was as if the drama of the previous week was a fiction and this comic fantasy the reality. He was back where he belonged, happily immersed in his own world.

It all came to an abrupt halt on the third day.

They'd been running a long scene, a chase involving all the major animal characters. Each of the voices could be dubbed individually on separate tracks—which would be done anyway—but for the sake of pace and comedy, the director had decided to try a mass take with everyone putting in their lines on cue: probably unusable, but much fun and, at very least, a good way to rehearse. They'd just started the second take on this when, although the movie clip kept running, there was a sudden silence in the studio. Hal looked up from his script to see the actor whose line it should have been staring open mouthed across his mike. All the performers turned to gaze in the same direction and several more jaws dropped.

The control room was empty.

Astonished, everyone started to talk at once and mill about. Then the studio door banged open to admit the director. Mat Margasen, who'd been calm and amiable throughout, was now purple with fury. In his hand he held a paper, which he began to wave and flap.

"Fucking court injunction," Margasen croaked. "Just fucking delivered. Whole fucking production's stopped till further fucking notice. FUCK!"

It was all to do with copyright. Out of the blue, someone had come up with a claim that the script had been stolen. The complainant had gone to court and somehow obtained an order to halt production. It didn't matter what the merits were. Until things were sorted out, everything was on hold.

Hal talked to his agent briefly. Apparently ACTRA, the performer's union, was aware of the mess-up. Meanwhile Danny was negotiating a fat holding per-diem for his client. It could be several days before things were settled. Meanwhile all the performers could do was cool their heels and wait.

The first evening of enforced idleness, Hal was in his hotel wondering what to do, when he was provided with an answer. His cellphone rang, on the other end was a familiar voice.

"Hi," Trent Bannatyne said. "What do you know, bro—I didn't go to India after all."

SIXTEEN

As he did most Wednesday mornings, Fitz was sitting in the boathouse, scanning the paper for news of upcoming property developments and smoking his usual chain of cigarettes. This latter was an activity he relished, despite the modern stigma surrounding an act that, in saner times, had been considered no one else's business. Mattie wouldn't let him smoke in the house anymore, one more reason he spent so much time in his own domain. But the boathouse, with its profusion of smells, tar and fish and freshly carved cedar, its ancient ambiance of creaking timbers and soothing sea-sounds, was where he felt most comfortable anyway. But after seventy years on this property, struggling to keep it intact, as was his duty—or perhaps curse—and seeing his family vanish one by one, something had happened that he'd never have believed possible: the struggle was beginning to seem pointless. His resolve to thwart the bastards who were trying to get their paws on the place—hadn't weakened—it had assumed the proportion of a sacred mission. But later, when he'd croaked, the others could do as they pleased. He didn't care any more. Meanwhile, in the boathouse he felt some small measure of peace, the least bother to the living and most connected to the dead. This last applied less to his son, who'd been gone a long time. But his grandson Brain, whose vanishing had snatched so much light from the world, here seemed just that little bit less sadly absent, which made the boathouse a good place to be.

Soon, he put the paper aside and moved to the window to work on his latest carving. About mid-morning, he glanced down at the beach, and spotted a man sitting on a rock near the low tide line. Fitz didn't pay much attention, people came by on the beach all the time. But when half an hour later he glanced up again, he was surprised to see the guy was still there, completely immobile, with the tide coming in around his feet. *Some sort of dreamer*, Fitz mused. *Better move your buns, old buddy, or you're gonna get 'em wet.*

As if he'd heard Fitz's thoughts, the figure *did* move. He stood up slowly, then clutched his back and abruptly sat again. Fitz couldn't actually hear a cry, but everything about the action made him sure there'd been one. He put down his chisel and moved closer to the window.

The rising water was now washing around the man's ankles. Slowly, his pain now obvious, he looked first at his soaked feet and then at the sea. With great effort, he hoisted himself up again, managing to stay on his feet, but still precariously bent. Then, with his upper body as stiff as a ship's figurehead, he began to shuffle gingerly toward the shore.

It didn't need Fitz's own slightly arthritic seventy-year-old frame to tell him what was wrong. The guy had badly damaged his back. If in his precarious retreat from the rising tide he now should fall, he probably wouldn't be able to get up again.

Without further thought, Fitz was up out of the boathouse, down the short flight of steps and hurrying across the rapidly disappearing flats. He was sloshing ankle-deep by the time he reached the tottering fugitive. Quickly he moved to the man's side. "Here, mister!" he said briskly. "Take my arm. Hold tight and lean on me."

With a grateful grunt, the man did as he was bid. His grip was surprisingly strong. But that was good, showing that despite his crippled state he still had reserves of energy. "Shitty disc!" he muttered. "Always pops at the worst times."

"Sonofabitch!" Fitz said. ""All right, look—move slow—keep walking as best you can. Don't panic and don't hurry. Okay?"

"Sure. Thanks."

"You're welcome. If you just don't fall, we'll get you out of here. Ready?"

"Yeah!"

It took several minutes to reach the shoreline, where the surface became a sharp incline, mud replaced by the stones of the beach proper. This was the hardest part, climbing through the unstable, rolling gravel. It was all Fitz could do to keep supporting the man's heavy weight. He longed to stop and rest, but the boathouse steps were only yards off. Somehow he managed to maintain his support until, at last, the weight was transferred to the stout handrail. The man leaned there, breathing hard, then lifted his head to peer at the boathouse.

"Your place?"

"Sure."

"Somewhere in there I could get flat?"

"I guess so."

"Dandy." With gritty determination he started to climb the steps. To Fitz, who was catching his own breath, it appeared that the man's movements were a trifle stronger. Halfway up he called over his shoulder. "By the way—the name's Bill Iverson."

"Fitz Trail."

"Hi, Fitz." Iverson heaved himself up another step. "You sure saved my bacon, there."

"Yeah—let's get you inside."

At the top of the steps the railing ended and again Fitz had to lend his support. But the level dock made progress easier and soon they were at the boathouse door. Once inside, Iverson peered briefly about, then adjusted his grip on Fitz arm. "Okay, Fitz—think you can help me down?"

"Where?"

"This back of mine—I need to get it flat. Can you help me down on the floor?"

"Oh. Sure!"

Fitz steadied Iverson as the big man lowered himself to his knees, carefully transferred his weight to his arm, then to his elbow, finally getting his shoulder down and at last—despite the accompaniment of a heartfelt groan or two—successfully deposited his heavy frame prone upon the boards. Settled, he gave a great sigh.

"That feel better?" Fitz said anxiously.

Iverson grinned crookedly up at it him. "It will. I have to wait."

"For what?"

"The muscles to relax and release. Then whatever's out of kilter down there seems to slip back into place. Generally takes half— maybe three-quarters of an hour."

"This has happened before?"

"A few times."

"You seen a doctor?"

"Guess I should—but so far I've found that this works." He sighed. "Bleeding Jesus, what a relief. I always forget how good it feels when it's over. Don't worry, Fitz, I'll be out of your hair pretty soon."

"No sweat. If my messy old floor can help your back, you're welcome. And I'm not going anywhere."

"Terrific! You're a great guy and I'm a lucky stiff. *Stiff* being the operative word, eh? Listen, Fitz—as if you hadn't done enough already—you wouldn't have such a thing as a cigarette?"

"Sure thing." Fitz got out cigarettes, lit two and passed one down to his prone guest. "Here you go. Maybe later I can even find you a beer."

Iverson laughed. "A smoke *and* a beer! Man, and to think that a while back I thought I might be going to join the fish. You're not just a good Samaritan, Fitz, you're a damn saint." As well as he could from his prone position, he took in the boathouse. "And, by the look of it, a man after my own heart."

"Oh?"

"I mean, wow! Look at this place. Anyone can see it's a piece of history. And it's still *here*. So often great old stuff like this gets junked to make room for garbage that won't last a dozen years. Don't you agree?"

Fitz shrugged, making a noise meant to be gruff, but which came out sounding almost affable. He placed an ashtray where Iverson could reach it and settled in the nearby armchair. Pretty soon the two were chatting as if they'd known each other forever.

SEVENTEEN

The phone rang on Thursday evening just as Mattie got out of the tub. Being alone in the house, she walked naked along the hall and picked up the extension in her bedroom. "Hi! Me again." It was Hal, sounding a trifle over-cheerful, which meant he was nervous.

Mattie, while being pleasurably surprised, also felt embarrassed. "Hello, Hal—just a minute," she said, feeling foolish as she donned her old robe. "Hi—this is a surprise."

"Did I catch you at a bad time?"

"No, the time is fine," she replied, feeling a ridiculous urge to tell him the real reason why she'd been momentarily flustered. Of course, Hal had seen her naked countless times, but in another life. "It was really lovely seeing you again the other day. I just didn't think I'd be hearing from you so soon."

"I didn't think to be calling. But a couple of unexpected things have happened." He explained about the court injunction that had left him with time on his hands, then mentioned the call from his brother. They'd talked of Trent on his earlier visit, but only in passing. Now he explained all that had happened since their surprise reunion. "Trent's brilliant and entertaining" he concluded, "and such a bullshitter he managed to convince me he's still rich when actually he recently lost everything. His girlfriend, Stephanie—who set me straight about his real situation, incidentally—seems like a great girl and really loves him. But she's sick to death of the tricks he's been getting up to lately.

Apparently he scared her so badly with some hair-brained stunt that she gave him an ultimatum: either grow up or they're through. He swears he will, and to prove he's serious he's promised to start by coming clean with me about his real situation. God knows, that's not something I want, but it's apparently what he needs to do. So tomorrow I'm coming back to the Island to meet him."

Mattie hadn't asked for this explanation, but he'd evidently felt the need to give it. When he'd finished, she said, "I'm sorry about your brother, Hal. But I'm glad you're going to try to help him." Rather fatuously she added, "Does that mean I'll get to see you again?"

He gave a mildly embarrassed cough. "If that's possible—yes."

'Of course! It'd be . . ." she'd been about to say wonderful but, not wanting to sound girlishly effusive, modified it. ". . . *really nice* to see you again. When are you coming?"

"Tomorrow. I don't know how long I've got. A few days, I'd guess. As soon as the injunction's settled they'll call and I'll head back. It's sort of open ended."

"I see," Mattie said, surprising herself by what popped out next. "So why don't you stay here?"

There was a pause, in which Mattie bit her lip, thinking she'd been really stupid. But then Hal said, quietly but with enthusiasm. "Really? Are you sure?"

"Of course. As you must have noticed, we're not exactly crowded."

"Then—I'd like it a lot, Thank you."

"You're welcome."

"I've still got my car. And I'm keeping my room here in Vancouver, so I'll be traveling light. What'd be a good time to arrive?"

"It doesn't matter. I'll be at school tomorrow, of course. But it's Friday, so I should be home by five."

"I'll try to make it by then?"

"That'd be fine."

When the call was over, Mattie realized her hair was still wet from the bath. Catching sight of herself in the mirror, she thought, *Damn,*

I really must get rid of this ratty old robe. She removed it and, for the first time since she could remember, began examining her body in the mirror. Her slim figure was not too bad, though gravity had been a little unkind to certain areas. Looking at her breasts, she realized with embarrassment that she'd been wondering what Hal would think of them now. Then she laughed aloud. Who the hell cared? They were both middle-aged people, if not exactly old fogeys, certainly well started in that direction. Anything concerning the allure, or otherwise, of body parts was half a lifetime away.

Nevertheless, if only to get ready for company, she began to search through her wardrobe for a few non-fogey things to wear. Though she'd previously planned to go to bed early with a book, she dressed and went downstairs to start bringing the old house to life.

EIGHTEEN

He was in. Fitz Trail was anything but a pushover, but neither was he as difficult as had been believed. All that had been needed was the right entree. And now he was perfectly positioned to get the job done.

For a couple of days he'd scouted the area, keeping an eye on his target to get the pattern of his movements and habits and trying to figure the best way to proceed. Having lived in Maple Bay all his life, the old fart doubtless knew everyone within miles. So the sudden appearance of a stranger would be bound to evoke suspicion. Yet, it was necessary to get close, to become a buddy. If he could just break the ice and get chatting, that would do it; he had a real talent for that kind of con. But how to get a foot in the door?

By the end of the surveillance, he realized an interesting thing: when Trail wasn't out fishing, he spent most of the time in his decrepit old boathouse. That, he decided, was the ideal place to start the ball rolling. His first idea was to simply stroll up from the beach and knock on the door, pretending to have lost his way. But that was dangerous; if the crabby old bastard gave him the brush-off before he could work his charms, that'd be it. He wouldn't get another chance. As he sat on a log just out of sight and tried to work out a plan, his back had started to ache—the result of an old injury—which gave him an inspiration. Introductions weren't necessary: all that was required was to make the mark come to *him*.

Next morning he set his trap. There was a spider, he recalled, that hunted by pretending to be injured until its victim was put off guard, then pounced. He'd established that Trail would be in the boathouse, so all he needed was a little patience. Sitting on a rock on full view, he waited till he was sure his presence must have been noted, then he went into his act. He did a powerful performance, rising, falling back, staggering around. Then, at the climax, as he did his pathetic and desperate-escape routine, came the payoff: his quarry arrived on the scene.

Within minutes he was being "helped" into the boathouse itself, where the last and cleverest part of the drama took place: the old guy was given the chance to do a bold act of healing. If that didn't set the stage for a buddy-bond, nothing would.

It had all worked perfectly.

He now understood why his earlier efforts to scare up a sale hadn't worked. Apparently the Trail clan had been on the place for generations. But the good news was that they were dying off like flies: a son had been killed years ago and a grandson had been lost in some kind of sailing mishap. Apparently only orneriness was making the granddad cling to the land now. But if he ceased to be a factor—with just two women remaining—it would become a brand new ball game.

By the time he and Trail had talked for half an hour, consumed a couple of beers and some cigarettes—he'd recently quit but, hell, this was for a good cause—the entree was made. This was one lonely old dude, a pushover if handled right. Using all his skill, he even worked it so that worries about his own—mythical—son in the service in Afghanistan appeared to be wormed out of him. Oh, yes, he knew all the moves.

He'd not yet decided how this new friendship would be brought to its sad and premature end. But now he was in, rigging an "accident" wouldn't be hard. After all, the boathouse stood beneath a useful looking cliff. Alternatively, there was the nearby ocean, with all those currents and icy water. And of course lots of mishaps occurred in the woods . . .

Whatever plan evolved, in good time the job would get done. No big deal. No questions asked.

His boss would have no cause for complaint.

In his motel room now, a safe distance from the action, he relaxed with a Scotch and *Survivor* on the TV. Everything was well under way. And tomorrow, he and his buddy were going fishing.

NINETEEN

As Hal once more negotiated the steep drive down to the house by Shawnigan Lake, he found himself undergoing an odd shift in perspective. Part of his mind still retained the image of this luxury villa as belonging to his brother. Seeing it again, he shook his head, in admiration as well as annoyance. "You cheeky bastard," he muttered, as he pulled in beside the Mercedes—which of course wasn't Trent's either. "So, where exactly *do* you hang out?"

The opportunity for the question to be answered arose at once. As Hal got out of his car, a woman appeared from the house, approaching across the courtyard. She was petite, late-thirties, trim and tanned, plainly dressed but with—from her coiffure to her slender shoes—a definite air of money. With the distance between them half covered, coming into sunlight, she stopped, turning her head away and blinking. "Whoops!" she called over her shoulder. "So sorry! With you in a minute."

Bemused, Hal waited, The woman shook her head back and forth several times, blinking. Finally she turned back, with what looked like tears on her cheeks. Has was just thinking he must have interrupted some sort of domestic drama, when she rubbed at her cheeks, laughing. "Oh, don't be alarmed, I'm not crying." She indicated her eyes. "Just put in my contacts. They give me fits if I come into bright light too soon. Hello, I'm Jill Bathgate. And I think I know who you are."

So here was the real owner of the house, the wife of the actual millionaire his brother had pretended to be. After they'd made introductions, and Jill's eyes had settled enough to get a good look at him, she must have sensed his discomfort, for she put a friendly hand on his arm. "Don't worry. Your brother's not really our caretaker. I mean, we do sort of pay him—though he insists it's a loan—and he does look after the place while we're away. But he's more of a guest, really."

Hal frowned. "But I thought . . ."

"I know. It *is* a little confusing." Jill glanced conspiratorially over her shoulder. "To tell the truth, Trent's a bit short of money right now. But he's a sweet man, a very old friend of my husband's. After his big bust he sort of came out here to lick his wounds, and Terry's been trying to persuade him to—you know—get back on the horse ever since. He's even thinking of . . ." She looked embarrassed. "But that's another story: I'm sure Trent'll tell you when he's ready. He can be a bit—well, *unfocused* I suppose is the best word. But he's also extremely clever. And he thinks the world of you."

"Mmm—so his fiancée told me."

"Ah, yes, Stephanie—wonderful woman," Jill said, with no hint of condescension. "Certainly the best thing that ever happened to Trent. I do hope if he goes back to Toronto she goes along."

"Why wouldn't she?"

"West Coast folk often don't like it. I'm from here, so I know . . . which is why I persuaded Terry to buy this place. If I couldn't get back to sanity every now and then I'd go squirrelly." Jill laughed. "But you don't want to know about me. It's your brother you came to see. He's a lovely man . . . and perhaps seeing you again will . . . well, who knows. And now I'll stop bending your ear." Jill pointed to the far side of the courtyard. "Down that little drive is the guest house. We've come to think of it as Trent's place. Go on down."

Hal thanked her and watched her head back to the house. At the door she turned. "Oh, and if you can persuade Trent to bring you up to the house later, I know Terry'd just love to meet you. 'Bye."

A minute's walk brought Hal to his destination, a well propor-
tioned cottage standing in its own tree-shaded yard. Parked in front
was a battered Jeep. The cottage had two sets of windows on either
side of a central front door, the left ones covered by drapes. As he
knocked, Hal peered through the right side and saw a cozy kitchen,
which showed no signs of life.

Getting no reply, he banged louder and then called. Still nothing. But Trent's vehicle—he assumed it was his brother's—was here,
and chatty Jill Bathgate had thought he was home. Hal knocked a
third time, then tried the door. Soundlessly, on well-oiled hinges, it
swung open.

"Trent?"

Unconsciously, he'd used stage projection, his voice bouncing
richly off the back wall of the kitchen, but evoking no hint of a
response.

"Hey Trent? It's me, Hal."

Still nothing. He closed the door and backed off, looking round
about. A short walk took him through the trees to the lake. Here was
sparkling water, boats, distant sails. To the left, a path followed the
shore back to the main house. Nowhere was there a sign of life. Hal
retreated, deciding to have one more try at the cottage.

This time he went right in, calling as he went. Greeted by silence,
he put attention on the one place still unchecked, the next door room
with the curtained windows. Maybe Trent was in there sleeping. Hal
knocked on the door.

"Trent?"

With still no answer, he went ahead and opened. Inside was dim,
but he could make out a bed with a telltale hump in the middle.
Entering, he immediately tripped on something on the floor. He
lurched clumsily, saved himself by clutching the wooden bedstead,
then recovered and moved carefully around the bed.

The commotion had caused no reaction from the bed's occupant.
Of course it was Trent. Even with his head half buried in the pillow,

and a bird's nest of silver hair obscuring much of what was visible of the face, there was still no mistaking his brother. He was on his side, arms and leg crookedly splayed, absolutely still.

He looked dead.

The hair on Hal's neck stirred. With sickening vividness, he recalled once discovering the body of a colleague who'd taken a drug overdose. The guy had looked exactly . . . Appalled, Hal thrust aside the vision and gripped Trent's shoulder—vastly relieved to discover it was neither cold nor stiff.

"Hey, brother?"

Trent's head turned and his eyes squeezed open a fraction. After a moment's puzzlement, the lids snapped wide and he sat bolt upright. "Shit—Hal! What time is it?"

"Afternoon."

"Yeah? Wow!" He scrambled out of bed and stood, swaying and grinning. "'Fraid I was up all night. Didn't hit the sheets till sunup and I entirely forgot you were coming. Sorry."

"Don't sweat it, man."

Trent, who was in his underwear, began to pull on clothes, his movements becoming more coordinated as the task progressed. Whatever had kept him up, it was seemed not to have been revelry, because as the sleep dropped away he seemed fresh and lively. Nevertheless, Hal couldn't contain his curiosity. After the exchange of a few pleasantries, he found himself saying, "So what were you doing up all night?"

"Oh—what else?—the computer!"

"Doing what?"

"On the Web, bro! Checking world markets: London, Frankfurt, Tokyo—you know the drill."

Hal smiled. "I don't, but I'll take your word for it. Hey, does that mean . . . ?"

Trent, who by this time was dragging a brush through his mop of hair, shrugged. "Don't know what it means yet. But we'll see. You hungry?"

"No! But I could use coffee."

"You got it!"

Moving with a snap and energy in contrast to the laid-back character he'd presented at their last meeting, Trent hustled to the kitchen and got busy. As he filled the coffee pot he said, "First thing I have do, bro, is thank you."

"Yeah? For what?"

"Not calling me a stupid asshole. But I *was*—as I already told you on the phone—and I deserve to be called out on it."

Hal grinned. "Maybe so. But its understandable. I mean, a place like this . . . I guess I might be tempted to pretend I owned it too."

In the act of putting bread in the toaster, Trent winced. "Don't patronize me, Hal, okay? I may be broke, but I'm not stupid. I mean, pretending to be lord of this manor was ridiculous, but I'm not fool enough not to *know* that."

"So why did you do it? Am I such a shallow bastard you couldn't tell me you've had troubles?"

Trent shook his head violently. "No, no, no! If anyone's shallow it's me. Anyway, I hadn't meant it to go that far. It started as a joke. Then I was sort of over my head, and I was too chicken to fess up."

"But why start in the first place?"

"Oh, come on! You're my big brother. And this great honkin' success. I just hated to have to start out admitting I was a loser."

"Oh, come on! All you've lost is money, isn't it?"

"*A shitload!*"

"But it's not the first time, is it?"

"Maybe not," Trent replied. Then, in the act of removing toast from the toaster, he looked around sharply. "How did you know?"

Realizing that Stephanie must not have told Trent that they'd talked, Hal was saved by the memory of his meeting with Jill Bathgate. "I met your buddy Terry's wife on the way in. She . . . sorta mentioned it."

Trent gave a resigned flick of the brows. "Yeah, I guess she couldn't resist."

"It wasn't like that. They obviously think a lot of you. And she— Jill—was saying that Terry hopes you'll—how did she put it—get back on the horse."

"Probably want me the hell outta here," Trent laughed, then sighed. "No, that's bullshit. Terry's a great guy. I've lost some dough for him over the years, but I've made a hell of a lot more."

Having poured them both coffee, Trent was now buttering his toast, following up with dabs of thick, black Marmite. Their English-born grandmother had introduced both boys to the esoteric—and to most North Americans, disgusting—concoction at a young enough age to ensure lifelong addiction. Traveling as he did, Hal hadn't seen Marmite in ages. It not only made his mouth water but, absurdly, did more than anything else to reawaken ancient reflexes of kinship.

Noticing Hal's gaze, Trent broke off to chuckle. "Hey, of course— another Marmite man. Takes you back, eh, bro? Want some?"

Suddenly sharing toast and Marmite with his brother seemed like the best idea in ages. Hal nodded and, as Trent fixed more toast, found himself wishing that their mother could be there. How long was it since the three had actually been together? Appalled, he realized that it was actually more than a decade. God, how the ways of the world pulled families apart. No point feeling guilty about it. The centrifugal forces generated by differing personalities, talents, and lifestyles often made the sundering inevitable. But it was sad all the same, and this little domestic scene brought home that fact with unexpected force.

Moments later, as they were munching in silence, Hal said, "Do you by chance remember Mattie, that girl I was going with at UVIC years ago?"

Trent frowned. "I think I once met someone you were with back then. What about her?"

"I ran across her while I was working on the film—or rather, she ran across me. Anyway, we sort of—reconnected. I'm going to stay with her."

Trent's eyebrows raised. "Renewing a conquest?"

"Nothing like that. Just catching up with an old friend. In my line I lose touch with too many people."

"But doesn't being—you know—this famous star, make up for that?"

"Trent, I'm not famous. I'm just a working stiff who's been lucky and done okay. To be a real *star*—as you call it—I'd have to move down south, forget about being a proper actor—or a *Canadian*, come to that—and play the Hollywood game. Apart from anything else, that'd bore me senseless."

Trent whistled. "Wow! And here's me thinking you might be too stuck up to want to know your old bro."

"Jesus, Trent—that really *is* stupid."

"Yeah, sorry!"

"But it also shows what losing touch can do. Which brings me to what I really wanted to say: wherever we are, or whatever happens, from now on we've gotta make sure that we never do that again."

TWENTY

"We made real progress," Hal said. "It was great. I didn't realize how much I'd missed seeing the guy all these years. My fault as much as his. But at one point I nearly let the cat out of the bag: I didn't realize you hadn't told him we'd talked."

He was sitting in Stephanie's small, bright kitchen, having left Trent in order to catch her before she left for work. Haste wasn't necessary, but he'd wanted to give her the good news as soon as possible. Now, however, Stephanie's relief turned to concern.

"I'm so sorry." she said. "I didn't want him to think I'd gone behind his back. What happened?"

"It slipped out that I knew more about his troubles than he'd actually told me. But it was okay. I'd already met Jill Bathgate—so I said it'd come from her."

"Thank goodness. What did you think—of Jill, I mean."

"Seems like a nice lady. She and Terry really like Trent, that's obvious."

Stephanie looked surprised. "You met Terry? But I thought he was—"

"Just got back today. After Trent and I were done, we went up to the big house to meet him." Hal shook his head. "That Terry, wow!"

"What?"

"Well, I thought Jill was chatty but, man, old Terry was a dynamo. Gave me the third degree for an hour. If I hadn't needed to get away to catch you, I reckon he'd be talking still."

Stephanie laughed. "Yeah, that's Terry all right."

"Don't get me wrong, he's obviously a neat guy. From what I can see, Trent's been so embarrassed about what he sees as his failure he's forgotten how much his buddy respects his real ability. When Terry wasn't picking my brains about showbiz—and when Trent was out of the way—we talked a lot about that. Anyway, they haven't given up on him, that's for sure."

"I'm so glad. But I'm even happier about what you did for him."

"For me too,"

"Good. But I think he needed it most. That awful hanging scene, for instance: now I've had more time to think, I believe it was actually a cry for help."

"Really? How do you figure?"

"It needed something really bizarre to make him see how ridiculous his life was becoming. Anyway . . . I'm sure that now's the start of better times. So thank you for being there for him."

"You're welcome."

"And it was so nice of you to let me know so quickly."

"My pleasure." Seeing her glance at the clock, Hal rose quickly. "But I've made you late for work."

"Who cares. I'm just so glad you came. Are you going back to Trent's now?"

"Not today. I left him busy on the computer."

"That's a good sign. But where will you go?"

"Actually, I've arranged to stay with an old friend. Someone I knew years ago and just got reacquainted with."

"That's nice, What's his name?"

"*Her!* Mattie Trail."

Stephanie nodded, then frowned. "That name's familiar. She's not a teacher by any chance?"

"Yes, as a matter of a fact. I believe she teaches English at Cowichan High. Do you know her?"

"Not personally. But she did teach my son."

"Really? Small world."

"Also . . ."

"Yes?"

"*Her* son was one of Gary's friends: Brian Trail. But the poor boy was . . ."

"Drowned? Yes, I heard."

"Mrs. Trail told you?"

"Well, yes—not the details."

"Such a terrible thing. It was a couple of years ago. Everyone was devastated. God, you have to wonder how you'd feel if your own . . ." She didn't finish.

This seemed to be a good time to make an exit. As he said good-bye, she came to him and delivered a solid hug. "I must confess I've no idea what kind of actor you are, Hal," she said quietly. "But one thing I *do* know: you're a real good man."

THIS TIME HE drove unerringly to Mattie's address and turned in at the battered mailbox. As he bumped down the drive, he got a good look at the woods through which it wound. The trees were huge, Douglas firs hundreds of years old, which was remarkable; though Vancouver Island was still clothed in a thick blanket of green, most of the old growth had been logged off generations ago, at least in the south. The giants here were a testament to the length of the time the land had been in the Trail family and the zeal with which it had been protected. No wonder Mattie's father-in-law was so passionate about it. By the time Hal was approaching the big old house—itself a piece of history, by the look of it—he was feeling pretty impressed by the spirit that had kept this rare property intact.

An old pickup, which Hal didn't remember from his first visit, was in the parking area. Mattie's car was absent. As he pulled in, Hal checked his dashboard clock: 4:40. Mattie had said she'd be home at five. He was early.

He got out of the car and stretched, breathing deeply of the breeze that wafted up from the water. Here, on the ocean side of the house, the ground was clear, with only lawn, some perennial beds and a low stone wall to distract from the dazzling view. To right and left, framing the seascape, were thrusting headlands and, in the distance, the steep swell of Salt Spring Island. Having grown up on the coast, Hal was not over inclined to be impressed by scenery. Nevertheless, standing quietly on this sweet afternoon, with the old house nearby, the great trees behind, and his eyes taken prisoner by the grand panorama, it was hard not to smell at least a passing whiff of paradise.

"What in hell are you doing?"

Hal's heart leaped. He whirled to confront the owner of the voice, a wiry, tanned fellow with a shock of white hair, who seemed to have appeared from nowhere. Then Hal recalled from his earlier tour that there was a path leading down the nearby cliff. Simultaneously he realized who the newcomer must be. "Hello, Mister Trail," he said, holding out his hand, "I guess I should introduce myself . . ."

That was as far as he got. The man used a dismantled fishing rod he was carrying to deliver a sharp slap across Hal's wrist. "Don't bother," he snapped. "You can tell the crooks who sent you that the answer's still 'no.' Now get off my land."

Hal hastily withdrew his arm "Look, you don't understand," he began, then stopped as yet another man appeared.

This one was younger, hardly more than a teenager. He was carrying a brace of fat salmon and half-running, drawn by the commotion. Seeing Hal, his expression also became angry. He stepped up and stood shoulder to shoulder with the old man. "You heard him, asshole, fuck off!" he cried—then abruptly drew in a breath, frowning. "Hold on! Don't I *know* you?"

Mystified, beginning to feel exhausted, Hal shrugged.

"I know him all right," the old man snapped. "It's another of those land-grabbing bastards."

Before Hal could protest the younger man shook his head. "No he's not," he cried. "I've got it. This guy's from the TV." He tossed the fish into the back of the pickup and came forward, wiping his hands on his jeans and grinning. "Am I right?"

"Don't be a fool, Con," the old man began, but was interrupted by his companion chanting an inane little jingle.

"'The man from the West,'" Con sang, in a mock-country twang, "'His heart is the best.' That's you in that old TV ad! It *is* you, eh?"

Indeed it was: a rare on-camera appearance in a TV commercial, which in a moment of weakness (encouraged by an obscene amount of money) he'd agreed to years ago, and which had haunted him ever since. Despite his vast array of professional credits, a certain segment of the public remembered him only as the corny old Man from the West. Young Con was evidently one of the tribe. "Yeah!" Hal sighed. "I have to admit it is."

"Right on!" Oblivious now of his peevish companion, he came forward, cheerful hand extended. "Dude, I must have seen that ad a zillion times. Could I get your autograph?"

WHEN HAL'S REAL identity was finally established, the transformation of the old man was so radical as to be almost comical. From being an angry curmudgeon, Fitz Trail became a picture of amiability, and touchingly apologetic for the earlier misunderstanding. Having heard something of Fitz's struggles against developers, Hal dismissed the apology. "That's perfectly okay," he said warmly. "When you first appeared I mistook you for my brother. We all make mistakes." He grinned and rubbed his wrist. "I'm just glad you didn't have a gun, is all."

This quip provoked a hoot of laughter from Con, who elbowed Fitz in the ribs. The old man looked even more embarrassed. Apparently there was some significance to this that Hal didn't know about. He resisted the urge to ask what it might be.

Mattie didn't return at five, as promised. A note, discovered in the kitchen, explained about Hal, and asked Fitz to entertain him till she returned. "There you go, Fitz," Con laughed: he seemed as at home in the house as if he lived there. "If you only came inside once in a while, instead of chippin' away down in the boathouse, you wouldn't have attacked Miz Trail's guest."

"That's enough from you," Fitz said, mildly. "Don't you have some place to go?"

"No, sir," Con grinned. "Not every day I get a chance to meet a TV star. Reckon I'll stick around."

Fitz snorted, "Young pup! You think you can do what you like around here."

This was evidently a well practiced routine. Fitz and Con were as familiar as family. It came to Hal that Con must be somewhat the age of the strangely vanished Brian. Had Con been one of his buddies? Childhood friend, maybe? That would explain his familiarity with the place. Interrupting his thoughts, Fitz said, "Okay, Mattie's going to be a while, so we can relax. Care for a beer, Hal?"

Hal said he would. Con went to the fridge, discovering only milk. "Hell," Fitz said, "There's plenty down below. And I could use a smoke."

Hal didn't mention that he'd already had a tour of the property with Mattie, happy to do so again. The old man was an enthusiastic guide, proud of his family's tenure of the land. The steps down the cliff were steep, winding precipitously, so they took a while to navigate. By the time they reached bottom, Hal knew a surprising amount about the Trail family's history in Maple Bay.

This also included background on their destination, the boathouse. It had been built by Fitz's grandfather in the 1920s, the tradition being that during US Prohibition it had been used for rum-running. "Probably bullshit," Fitz added. "My dad was pretty obsessed with getting his hands on cash, but I doubt he'd have had the guts to smuggle whisky to the San Juans—let alone the smarts. Later on, he sold off most of the land we used to own, then lost the money playing the market. Damn fool. But he made a decent enough job of this." Fitz indicated the boathouse, to which the path had finally brought them. "Older'n me and still rock solid. Thirty years ago, this part of the bay silted up and you couldn't float boats in anymore. So I closed off the sea end, and it's been my second home ever since."

"Mostly for goofin' off in," Con quipped,

"Maybe so," Fitz chuckled. "But I reckon you're pretty good at helping me with that."

Con laughed and threw open the door.

The three of them moved inside.

TWENTY-ONE

The inside of the boathouse was much as Hal might have expected. The semi-gloom, the result of the place being shielded by the cliff from the westering sun, receded as his eyes adjusted. Revealed was a barn-like interior filled with ropes and tools, fishing gear and miscellaneous junk, plus something unexpected: a collection of remarkably fine wood carvings. Some, such as the figure of a leaping salmon, in progress on the bench, were realistic, with a skilful economy of detail and line; others were more abstract, clearly influenced by native ceremonial art. Hal was impressed. "Chippin' away," had been Con's description of Fitz's activities. Was this just teasing? Or didn't they realize the considerable talent that was on display here? Yet another question, in a list that seemed to be growing.

But what got to Hal was the atmosphere of the building itself. As soon as he entered, it settled on his mind like a chord from a great organ. Oddly, at first he couldn't make out whether the mood was threatening or benign, but it was very powerful. The nearest he'd ever come to the notion of "feeling" in a structure was in old theaters; on occasion, he'd sensed a residue of the hurly-burly of emotions that had been invoked in those places. But that had been pale compared to what crowded in on him here.

Hal glanced quickly at the others. Con was threading his way through the clutter toward an old fridge. Fitz had drifted to the workbench and had idly picked up a chisel. Neither seemed aware of what

Hal was experiencing—and almost immediately it was gone. The place must have reminded him of something, he decided, a movie, maybe, or an old dream, which had prompted this somewhat melodramatic response.

However, the boathouse did have one truly unusual feature: a large bay window overlooking the ocean. Seeking distraction, Hal took the beer that Con offered and said, "This window's kind of different. Not what you'd expect in a place like this."

Fitz now had a chisel in one hand and a beer in the other. "Picked it up in a junkyard years back. Stuck it there when I walled in the sea end. Bit out of place, I guess, but it gives decent light. And a good view of the comings and goings."

Con grinned. "Fitz keeps a real close eye on the *comings and goings*."

"Good thing I do." Fitz snapped. "Like just yesterday. I noticed this fella down on the flats in a real bad way. Might even have drowned if it wasn't for me."

"What was wrong with him?"

"Hurt his back. I fetched him up here and got him straightened out. Pretty scary for a while. But he was okay. Afterwards we had a good chat."

"You're kidding!" Con turned to Hal. "He *never* lets strangers in here. You getting soft in your old age, Fitz?"

"Not too soft to kick your cheeky butt."

"You and whose army?" Con laughed. "Seriously, you *talked* to this guy?"

"Sure. Name of Bill Iverson."

"Never heard that name round here."

"He's not from here. Just retired and bought a place up the bay. Tomorrow I'm taking him fishin'."

Con looked astounded. "Wow, cool. Hey, Fitz, looks like you got yourself a buddy."

"Wouldn't go that far. But the guy's heart's in the right place."

"What makes you say that?"

"Well, for a start, he's real pissed about all the development around here."

"Sounds like a regular soulmate."

"Don't be an ass. He's just a fella."

For all Fitz's attempts at diffidence, Hal could see he was excited. Since his only companions, apparently, were his daughter-in-law and someone young enough to be his grandson, this was hardly surprising. Con seemed happy too. Likely he was relieved that Fitz had found another companion. Young people needed their own kind. Even if Con was an old friend of Brian's, he could never replace him. But then, Hal thought, who knew what was really going on here? He'd only just met them, so what did he know?

One thing he was certain about, however, was the quality of Fitz's carving. Having examined several pieces, his attention finally centered on a remarkable rendering of a sailboat. Carved from a single block of fine-grained yellow cedar, it stood in the bay window, sleek lines of hull and sheets wrought with an unerring sense of the raw power of the sea. Hal had never been on a sailboat and had little interest in things nautical, but this creation—so evocative that one could almost feel the wind lashing the shrouds and the figure of the lone helmsman—had an effect that was almost hypnotic.

"That's my grandson's boat, *Orca*."

Hal gave a start. The old man had moved in beside him and was contemplating the carving meditatively. "Young Brian was a damn fine sailor—though that doesn't seem to have helped him in the end."

Startled by the sudden introduction of a subject that until now had been avoided, Hal said, "Oh? What happened?"

"Hey, Hal!" Con said suddenly. "You want another beer?"

"I'm fine, thanks." Hal replied, not taking his eyes off Fitz.

"Hit you again, Fitz?" Con said

"No, boy. What happened, Hal, is that my grandson went sailing one day and—"

"Aw, jeez, Fitz," Con interrupted. "Hal doesn't want to hear about all that."

"Con doesn't like to talk about Brian," Fitz said quietly. "Best buddies since they were shrimps, so in a way it's understandable. But, I keep telling him, you can't fix things by being afraid to talk."

"Aw, shit, old man," Con muttered. "It just depresses me, is all."

"Brian's mum's the same," Fitz went on, apparently oblivious. "But you know what I say? If folks aren't talked about, they're not properly remembered, which is like a sort of double death. When my son, Will, got killed, I clammed up for years, hardly let myself think about him, let alone talk; which maybe helped a bit, but made things worse in the end. Now I can't hardly remember his face. I'm not going to let that happen with Brian."

Hal was taken aback. This confession was not what he'd have expected from the taciturn old fellow. But the mood was swiftly broken as Con banged down his beer bottle. "Yeah, well—it's late and I gotta get movin'. Nice talkin' to you, Mister TV star. See you, Fitz."

Con strode to the door and was gone.

Fitz shrugged. "I guess I shouldn't be so hard on the kid—but he's got to learn. Another beer?"

Hal said okay. Fitz fetched fresh bottles, then settled in the rocking chair. Hal was drawn to the bay window. The sky was taking on the deeper tones of evening. Though the water glowed bright, the enclosing headlands and distant island were beginning the long slide into dark. A far-off tugboat moved at a pace that indicated it was under load, the distance too great to reveal what that might be. Nearer to hand were several drifting sails. At water's edge hovered a motionless heron. It was a magically peaceful scene, but Hal's curiosity would not allow him to be lulled. Once a story was begun, he had to know the end. Knowing he might regret it, he said, "So what *did* happen to Brian?"

Fitz stared out at the bay for so long that it seemed he wasn't going to answer. Finally he said, "There was no place he was happier than out there. He had this little sailboat, which I built for him. Not so big a good sailor couldn't easily handle her alone. And that boy was good: a better feel for wind and weather than most grown men. That's what made it all so strange . . . "

Fitz's voice drifted off, his gaze consumed by the ocean.

"He and Con were best pals," Fitz continued. "Pretty much inseparable since they were kids. Did most everything together too, except for the sailing, Con wasn't so much into that. Oh, he'd crew for Brian now and then, even handled the *Orca* by himself well enough. But he never had the passion. When Brian was older, most often he went out alone. There he'd be in all weathers." Fitz pointed to a cap on the window ledge. "And always wearing that crummy old Cardinals cap. Sailing meant as much to Brian as this land means to me. He just couldn't get enough . . ."

The old man fell silent again. Hall watched and waited.

"Now his dad—my son—was quite different. Will never liked the outdoors at all. He was a good man, but I've no idea how he happened in this family. Nor what Mattie saw in him, if you want to know. But *Brian* . . . it was as if everything that got left out of Will came back in the next generation. And where that really showed was on the water.

"His mum was real proud of him. She was no sailor, but she'd often watch through binoculars as Brian went out. Because of that, we know how his last day began. It was a Saturday morning. Five years ago last May. Brian was in his last year of high school. It was the end of exam week, so the first thing Brian needed was to get in the boat and—as we used to say—blow the stink off. His sister, Jennifer, was away, Con was in Vancouver. I was up-island at an ecology conference that turned out to be a lot of hot air. So Mattie was alone when Brian went off. After he left, Mattie kept busy in the kitchen, waiting for the *Orca* to appear from below. It didn't leave right away, but that's not unusual; there's always something to fix before a boat is ready to go. But finally there it was. Mattie watched the *Orca* sail off. There was a decent breeze, so she went out fast. The binoculars we've got are strong, Zhumell 20 x 80s that can see halfway to China. Mattie could still make out Brian's red cap when he was almost to the headland. But he didn't come about then as usual. The boat kept on into the Sansum Narrows, luffed around the point out of sight—and that was the last she saw it."

"Until when?"

"Until *ever!* The *Orca* never returned. When I got home that night, Mattie was almost crazy with worry. The coast guard had been called and the police alerted. By Sunday we were all half out of our minds. Our only hope was that Brian had got stranded on some little island and was unable to let anyone know. But by Monday there was still no word. It was another twenty-four hours before we got a call from the RCMP. A boat matching the description of the *Orca* had been found, wrecked, on the rocks near Sooke."

"*Sooke*? But that's . . ."

"Yeah, to hell and gone up the west coast of the Island. Half a day's sail for a small boat. But we checked it out, and it was her all right. How it got there we'll never know, because there was no trace of Brian. And only one clue as to what had happened: the boat's tiller was lashed."

"Lashed?"

"Secured, so it could sail without someone at the helm. Apparently, while Brian was out in the strait, there was some kind of mishap. Maybe he just wanted to fetch a drink or take a leak, something stupid and simple. He secured the helm, went to do—whatever—but somehow tripped and fell overboard. It can happen. So the boat would have continued on by itself until it piled up on the Sooke rocks. Of course Brian would have been wearing a life jacket, but he'd have been carried out into the strait. If no one spotted him, eventually he'd have died of hypothermia. That's only theory, of course. But we had to believe something like that happened. Because the only trace ever found of my grandson—caught up in the wreck of the *Orca*—was his old red Cardinals cap."

The view of Maple Bay had undergone a slow transformation, mirroring the dark narrative with its own somber trek toward the night. When the story ended, both men were very still. From the ocean came muted gull-sounds and the faint whine of a speedboat. After some time, Fitz said in a quite different tone, "You're *him*, aren't you?"

"Who?"

"The one who got away."

"*What*?"

"The fella Mattie's been holding a torch for all these years."

Hal did a double take, feeling his face redden like an adolescent's. "What makes you think that?"

"Just a guess," Fitz said mildly, then grinned "Though by the way you look right now, I'd hazard it's a pretty fair one."

Hal shrugged resignedly. His only option, if any dignity was to be retrieved from this situation, was to tell the truth. He said quietly, "I'd hoped it hadn't been as bad for her as that."

"I wouldn't call it bad," Fitz replied. "In fact, it may have been one of the things that's kept her going. I told you I didn't know what she saw in my son: he was a decent man, but not exactly . . . her sort of person, it seemed to me. And though she was always caring and loyal, I couldn't shake the feeling she married him on the rebound. After he died, she was properly devastated. But deep down . . . ? Brian, of course, was something else again. For all of us. But what Mattie's always had—long before any of the troubles came into our lives—is a sort of *alone* thing. In the last few days that's changed . . . and now maybe I see why."

Hal stared. "You think because of *me*?"

"Nothing else has happened around here to perk up her spirits."

"Christ!"

"Don't look so alarmed. I didn't say she expects to marry you. She's just happy you're here, is all. You've taken her mind off the past, my stupid carryings-on, and the life—I won't say lonely but maybe a bit dull—that she leads round here. That's all I'm talking about."

"Okay—then—I'm glad."

"Oh, there you are!" a cheerful voice said. Both turned as Mattie came through the door. "Goodness—I might have known."

"Known—what?" Hal said nervously.

Mattie laughed. Fitz was right, Hal thought, she *did* look happier. "Why, that the first thing Fitz would do is bring you down to this stinky old boathouse."

TWENTY-TWO

The café closed early, so Stephanie was able to get away sooner than expected. She was less tired than the last time she'd driven to her fiancé's place—the visit that had terminated in the horrific hanging scene—so the journey didn't seem so arduous. In fact, considering all that had happened lately, she was feeling remarkably upbeat. The stunt Trent had pulled, his so-called "acting," had been spectacularly ill-conceived. Yet, as she'd tried to explain to Hal, a mistake as extreme as that probably had been necessary, if only to demonstrate just how much he'd let the notion of failure warp his thinking. And though he'd scared her badly, she didn't doubt he loved her. The breakup threat had been an overreaction, but some sort of ultimatum had definitely been in order. So it was a vast relief that the meeting with his brother had gone so well. Trent had already phoned her at work with his version of the good news, so there'd be no need to pretend surprise.

She arrived at her destination just before nine-thirty. As she drove down the steep drive, the sky to the west of Shawnigan Lake was showing the last hint of afterglow. The big house was lit up, but when she turned in the direction of the cottage she saw that the only light there was a dim glow from the kitchen. That was unusual, since Trent always left the porch lamp on when he knew she'd be late. A sour memory arose of her earlier visit, the house in darkness, and the chilling events that had followed. She resolutely pushed it aside.

Nothing like that was ever going to happen again.

She parked beside Trent's Jeep, gave the usual toot on the horn to announce her arrival, and headed for the front door. The residual feeling from last time was strong enough that she half expected it to be locked, but the handle turned and it opened easily.

"Trent?"

She stopped, taking in the scene inside. The light in the living area was dim because it issued from just two sources: a small lamp near the fireplace and a laptop computer, open on the dining table. Sitting at the computer, very still, his profile illuminated by the ghostly monitor glow, sat Trent. He was staring at the screen, transfixed, a tableau broken only by the tiny, staccato clatter of keys.

"Trent—*hello*!"

Her fiancé's head twisted in her direction. He nodded a greeting and his right hand lifted from the keyboard, beckoning, yet somehow managing to command both patience and silence.

"But Trent—"

He made the gesture again, this time accompanied by a slight scowl, after which came a positive explosion of key clattering.

Stephanie's heart sank. God, what kind of game was he playing now? With a sigh, she closed the door. Pausing to switch on the over-head light—which at least had the effect of making the place feel more normal—she threw down her coat and bag and moved into the kitchen area, intending to fill the kettle. Whatever Trent was up to—she prayed it was not just some little charade to convince her that he was getting his mojo back—she'd give him a few minutes and then . . . well, then she'd see.

There were a few dirty dishes on the draining board. She piled them in the sink and began washing, completing the task as the kettle boiled. Its whistle made Trent glance up sharply. But instead of look-ing annoyed, he gave a big grin and snapped the laptop shut.

"Ah, tea!" he said cheerfully. "Just what we need to celebrate!"

A WHILE LATER, as they sat drinking tea, Stephanie said, "How did you find out about all this?"

Trent, who had a day's growth of beard and looked as if he hadn't showered in a while, was nonetheless in fine spirits and, considering the hour, bubbling with energy. "Simple enough," he replied. "The information's all right there on the Web, for anyone who can put it together. Look, the biggest need in the world is energy, right? The recession we had hasn't changed that, just dampened the demand for, like, half a minute. And right here in Canada, in Northern Alberta, we have some of the biggest oil reserves in the world. Though it's trapped in the tar sands and expensive to get out—and the environmental lobby hates it—extraction methods are getting more efficient all the time; and—most important for the West, it's a safe source, free of all the political shit that's plaguing much of the world."

"I can see that," Stephanie interjected. "But what's that got to do—?"

Trent cut her off with the same silencing gesture that had greeted her arrival. "Give me time," he snapped, then softened the moment with an apologetic smile. "*Please!* I'm getting there, okay?"

Mollified, she nodded.

"One of the things I was always good at," Trent continued, "was speculating on futures: oil futures particularly. But, shit, who could have known that the world oil price would drop from a high of a hundred and fifty bucks a barrel to a quarter of that in less than a year. It's a historic fluke, but it killed me. If I'd only taken my own advice—like Terry Bathgate did—and got out when things started to slide in '08, I'd have been okay. But no, I just hung in—as the housing market nose-dived, banks teetered, and commodity prices tanked—thinking that this couldn't be happening. But it was, it did, and I was ruined. And after I'd been out here a while, living like a bum on Terry's handouts—the only thing making life bearable being *you*, incidentally—I came to see, finally, that I might be a real clever-ass—but I had this fatal flaw."

"What?" Stephanie couldn't help interjecting.

Trent shook his head glumly. "That I'm too much of a gambler for the securities game. Which is why, though I've made heaps of money, I always lost out in the end. And why, since the last bust, I've been mooning around out here. You see, I knew if I returned to investing—got back on the horse, as Terry likes to say—the same old thing'd happen."

"But now something's changed?"

"Yes! In *me!* I guess it's been coming a while, But meeting Hal again—after that first idiotic charade, or maybe *because* of it—sort of speeded up the process. I realized I didn't want to be a bum, trying to impress my brother and my girl with stupid tricks. I really *did* want to get back to work, but not as a gambler any more. So then I got to thinking about oil again—which has always fascinated me—but not futures: oil *production*. Specifically, *Canadian* production! With all that enormous potential in the tar sands, it's obvious that whoever figures out how to get the stuff out most efficiently is gonna clean up. *Someone's* got to be trying to do that, I thought. And, after an Internet search: science articles, news items, oil company reports, I came up with a candidate. This small outfit, CANTSO—Canadian Tar Sand Operations—has come up with a brand new process of extraction which is cleaner, cheaper, and more efficient than anything yet. They'd proved their method with a prototype plant and had a full scale plant built and ready to go into production when the poor buggers got slammed by the worldwide collapse. Their massive debt, which could have been easily handled with the proceeds of pending extraction, went sour when prices tanked. CANTSO was taken over for cents on the dollar and its patented process—which at anything over sixty bucks a barrel is like a licence to manufacture gold—has been languishing in a limbo of shock and inertia ever since. But now the recession is over and oil prices are climbing. Suddenly the CANTSO process is back on the radar. In the last few days I've been following the reports, the rumours and the numbers, in the States, in Europe, and the East. All the indications are that a lot of big hitters are getting ready to try to get control of the company that owns CANTSO. No one wants to show their hand too strongly yet: you can't make a big buy without waking everyone else up. But, believe me, this is going to happen. I've been watching all week, and every instinct I possess tells me that when the markets open on Monday the demand for CANTSO is going to explode!"

Trent stopped, eyes aglow, and Stephanie had the urge to applaud. Unlike the hanging fiasco, however, when he'd actually requested such a response, Trent obviously wasn't looking for praise. But his certainty was unmistakable—and very convincing.

"That sounds wonderful." Stephanie said finally. Then, since he said nothing more. "So, what are you going to do about it?"

Trent's excitement abruptly faded. "I don't actually know."

"What do you mean?"

"Well . . . I guess I hadn't got that far. First I wanted to make sure I was right, I guess."

"And now you are?"

"Of course! But . . ."

"What?"

"Steph, as you well know, I'm flat broke—"

"But Terry Bathgate isn't, for God's sake!" Stephanie all but exploded.

"Yes, but—"

"You *must* know you've got to tell him!"

"But I've already lost him a fucking fortune."

"*Trent!*" Stephanie was so exasperated she sprang to her feet. "Is all you've just told me just a fantasy? Just another *game*?"

Trent scrambled up, too. "No! *No*! *NO*!!!"

There was a long silence as they stared at each other. Finally Stephanie, her insides aquiver, reached out and took her fiancé's hand. Using it to pull him in close, she lifted her face to his. "So listen to me," she said quietly. "When I drove down, I saw the lights were still on in the big house. If you truly believe you're onto something—but also if you believe in yourself, and in *us*—you really need to go up and see Terry right now."

TWENTY-THREE

It had all worked out perfectly. Trail had walked right into his trap. It was comical really, the way the old fart considered himself to be a tough, hard-nosed protector of his pathetic realm. Yet, when it came down to it, he'd been a pushover, buying the bad-back routine like a widow falling for a phone scam. But, instead of his life's savings, what this bozo was about to lose was his life.

The man Fitz knew as Bill Iverson appeared bright and early for his rendezvous. True to his claim to have rented a place up the coast, he arrived at the boathouse on foot. The tide was low, so the journey along the beach had been easy. The expanse of sand and exposed flats that ran below the cliff was deserted—not even any early dog-walkers—so it had been private too. Not that he was concerned about being observed. Once the job was done, which would be quickly, he would vanish, never to be seen again. Still, it was good to be discreet. It was always wise that a death should appear to be accidental, and in this case it was a requirement.

The ocean was the perfect place for fatal accidents.

Iverson put down the rod he'd purchased for the occasion, sat on the boathouse steps, and calmly surveyed the scene. A slim but solid dock ran a hundred feet out into the water. At the end was moored Fitz's motor launch, a modest affair with a forward cabin and two sturdy outboards, small but seaworthy. Iverson found himself wishing that he had a nice little set-up like this: some land by the sea, a cool old workshop and a boat to while away the hours. Then he chuckled cynically. *Oh, yeah!* he thought, *And how long before you got bored with that shit? Get real, man. Stop fucking dreaming and get it together.*

He did just that, concentrating on the boat itself. The cabin was quite big enough to conceal two people for the length of time needed for what he had to do. Once they were out to sea, trolling in the fishing lanes, there would be no witnesses anyway. From the encounter the other day, when he'd feigned the back-injury, he'd ascertained that the old man was wiry and strong. To make sure that there were no signs of a struggle, he'd need to take Fitz completely by surprise. A single sharp blow on the head would do it, in such a position that it'd seem to be the result of a fall. Then all that would be needed was to let a little water into the bilges and hold the old man's face in it till he drowned. Finally, he'd head in to a quiet beach, disembark, put the trolling motor on cruise and aim the launch into the bay, to be found by whomsoever. Ah, what a tragedy. Poor old guy. But such things happened. Sad—and perfect.

Iverson was just putting the finishing touches to his plan when he heard sounds from above. He moved down the beach a little and stood clutching his rod, like a happy and expectant fisherman. After a moment, Fitz appeared. Despite the early hour, he looked fresh and sprightly, descending the path carefully, but with fair agility. As a seasoned professional, Iverson reminded himself not to underestimate the old coot for a single minute.

Fitz reached the bottom and saw the other man. "'Mornin', early bird," he said cheerfully. "Keen to get at those coho, eh?"

Iverson laughed. "Couldn't wait. Sure appreciate the invite, Fitz."

"You're welcome. Least I could do for a new neighbour. They'll be running good, I reckon. How's the back?"

Iverson said it was okay and followed Fitz into the boathouse. There were rods in a rack by the door. The old man selected one that was already set up. He put it aside and fetched a tackle box. "How you set for lures?"

Iverson shrugged. He supposed it inevitable that they'd have some ritual fishing bullshit before setting out, but he hoped it wouldn't last long. "Dunno. Got a silver spinner thing, but I'm not sure what's good around here."

"Spinner's okay, but I maybe got somethin' better you could try. See when we get out."

"Yeah—thanks."

But they didn't leave right away. Just when it looked like they would go, Fitz put down the tackle box and took out cigarettes. He offered one to Iverson, who reluctantly accepted: too many of those and he'd get hooked again. He couldn't wait to get the job done, but it was even more important that things remain cool, that the prey be relaxed and unsuspecting until the hammer fell. So he lit up, hoping the nicotine would calm his impatience. But then, rather than leaving, Fitz became interested in the carving on the workbench—apparently a work-in-progress—and started whittling away. Iverson would dearly have loved to grab the chisel and insert it in the old fuck's brain, but he listened with a fixed smile as he was regaled with a long dissertation on old-growth timber, its benefits for carving, and how development and greed had stripped the Island of all the best trees. *We'll strip this little paradise double quick when you're history*, Iverson thought, but continued to smile and make inane comments, while half an hour passed and the asshole chattered and whittled and smoked and carved and chattered some goddamn more.

Then, just as Iverson had begun to think that the idiot had forgotten what they were supposed to be doing—and his own fingers had begun a near-irrepressible twitch—Fitz glanced at his watch and put down his chisel. "Okay!" he said cheerfully, "Tide's turning. We should go."

"That's it? We've been waiting for the *tide?*"

"Sure! Coho always strike better when it's on the flow. Some folks don't agree, but that's my opinion."

He grabbed his rod and tackle box and Iverson followed him onto the dock. Fitz in the lead, they headed at last for the boat.

Iverson allowed himself a long, silent sigh of relief. His fingers had ceased to twitch. Instead, a satisfying calm began to infuse his body, plus the anticipatory tingle of the coming kill. All gain aside, this was the part of the work he enjoyed most, the satisfying act of termination. Better than food or sex or any kind of drug, the raw power of offing a human being made every other sensation seem pale, while making him feel immortal. Ah, sometimes life was so good you could taste it.

They arrived at the launch. At close quarters, Iverson could see it was perfect for his purpose. There was even a little wooden club lying in the gunwales, no doubt for stunning the catch. The big man had to restrain a chuckle: sometimes you'd think the fools were just asking for it.

Fitz climbed aboard and stowed his rod, then reached out to Iverson, the meaning obvious. Iverson handed across his rod and it was stowed too. "Okay," Fitz said cheerily. "Cast off, will you, then climb aboard. There's a coho out there with your name on it."

Iverson did as he was bid. He let go the forward line, but when he went to unhitch the other, he got a surprise. A young man was coming fast down the cliff path. Even as Iverson spotted him, he reached the dock. On the boat, Fitz also caught sight of the newcomer.

"Well, better late than never," Fitz said. "That's my young friend, Con. Often comes fishin' with me. Good kid, but finds it hard to get up in the morning. Hey, Con," Fitz bawled. "Thought you weren't coming. Get a move on! Meet the fella I told you about."

Stone faced, Iverson watched as the newcomer approached—and his careful plan disintegrated.

TWENTY-FOUR

They had a near-perfect day together. It started when Hal awoke in Jennifer's room to find sun pouring through the windows overlooking Maple Bay. The light had a soft, coastal quality that reminded him of long-gone summers. But instead of waxing nostalgic, he felt pleasantly exhilarated. Moving to the window, he realized why; working in a patch of garden, some distance away between the forest and the cliff, was Mattie. She was wearing sandals, shorts, and a droopy old sweater, her hair in a ponytail down her slim back. At this distance she looked about twenty.

He didn't still love her: to have imagined otherwise would have been pathetic and juvenile. Yet, when he looked down at the earnest figure toiling in the morning sun, he realized that what he *did* feel was more intriguing than anything he'd known in earlier years. It was like a family attachment, but more complicated: the gentle affection one might have for an old friend, yet with a physical attraction which, though strong, was perfectly containable. In other words, while enjoying the sight of her still-lovely bones, he didn't feel compelled to jump them.

They had breakfast alone, her father-in-law already having gone fishing. It being the weekend, Mattie's day was free. They spent the morning on the patio overlooking the sea, talking about old times. She didn't mention her son, nor did Hal reveal that he'd learned the sad history from Fitz. He had the feeling she knew he'd been told, though maybe this was wishful thinking. In any case, the shadow that, to some degree, had hung over her since their first meeting, seemed to have lifted. Was this because of his presence? He hoped so, and Fitz had certainly believed that his arrival had done her good. If so, what would happen when he left? Surely, nothing of consequence. Pure egotism to imagine otherwise. After all this time, he must be no more than a diversion for Mattie. What he'd earlier mistaken for melancholy was probably no more than boredom, to which his visit was a mild antidote. Or perhaps he was just giving too much thought to the whole damn thing. He determined to stop thinking, to simply enjoy this unexpected time. To live in the moment.

But turning off his head was not easy.

After lunch they walked by the ocean. The afternoon was bright and hot, with a sky of unbroken cobalt; not uncommon summer weather, but a revelation to those who imagine a West Coast of endless damp. Mattie still wore her sandals and shorts but had exchanged the sweater for a light T-shirt. Hal had to content himself with city attire and rolled shirt sleeves. Though the tide was rising, there was still ample room to walk. They ambled for miles, passing beaches, tree-hung cliffs, and occasional marinas, sloshing through mud flats and scrambling over rocks: all of which was accomplished in leisurely fashion, as they either chatted or ambled along in companionable silence.

Later, when the tide had risen too high to allow either going on or returning by the same route, they climbed a cliff path and entered the woods. By now, Hal had no idea where they were, but Mattie was an experienced guide. Unerringly she found a path, leading back in the direction they'd come. The Island, Hal knew, was festooned with hiking trails, but being a city kid he'd paid them little mind. Though the trees here were not the old-growth giants of Fitz's domain, they were still impressive; Douglas fir and cedar, coast maple, and orange-barked arbutus, the undergrowth deep-green salal, holly, and crinkly Oregon grape.

Here also it was refreshingly cool. As they walked side-by-side along a broader section of path, Hal realized that they were holding hands. The contact had happened so naturally that he didn't know when it had started. It didn't feel sexy or romantic, just quietly *right*. Recalling, by contrast, his recent romp with the uninhibited Juliet Jeffries, he realized that this near-sisterly contact with Mattie meant more—and would be longer remembered—than anything that had happened in a long time.

They arrived home, hot, tired and content, about five-thirty in the afternoon, and Mattie went off to take a shower. Preparing to do the same, Hal went to his room. As if on cue, his cell, which had been abandoned on the dresser, began to ring.

"*That'll be Vancouver,*" Hal thought. "*They've probably been trying to get me all day. Damn!*"

But his annoyance was not because he'd missed the contact, but that it was happening at all. Somehow he'd assumed that this break would last longer, and only now did he realize how much he wanted it to.

"Damn!" he said, aloud this time. Then, in resigned tones as he answered the phone. "Hello?"

"Hi, Hal," his brother's voice said, "I've been trying to get you all day."

"Oh, sorry!" Hal replied. "I've been out on a hike, and I didn't take my phone."

Trent chuckled evilly. "A hike, eh? Is that what they're calling it now?"

"No, it's nothing like—"

"Forget it, bro!" Trent cut in. "I'm just a crude asshole. The lady's pure and you've been a perfect gent, I'm sure. Look . . . I just want to thank you."

"Thank me? For what?"

"Well, just being here, for a start. And for not calling me a complete ass after I acted like one."

"Trent, we already went over that. Enough said, eh?"

"Okay, but I've got another reason for calling. To sort of give you a heads-up."

"About what?"

"I can't reveal details yet. Don't want to jinx it. I just had to let you know that in a short while—a day or two at most—I may have some *very* good news."

TWENTY-FIVE

The phone was answered on the first ring—which at least was something. "Yeah?"

"Penney?"

"Yeah!"

"You know who this is?"

"Sure, boss . . . Yeah!"

"How are things going in Maple Bay?"

There was a barely perceptible pause. "Okay. Contact has been made and—er—I'm in a good position to get the job done."

"But it hasn't happened?"

"No! But almost!"

"What does that mean?"

"I was all set to conclude arrangements. Then something came up that forced a change of plans."

"Yeah, yeah, whatever! Look, here's the bottom line—you've got to move real soon."

"But you said . . ."

"A month, I know. But the situation's changed. Unless I can give some kind of commitment very soon, a big chunk of my capital is all set to fly."

"*How* soon?"

"A week at best."

"Jesus!"

"That's how long I can hold off. But I need to hear good news by then."

"I get it."

"So what are you saying to me?"

"That you'll *get* your news."

There was a pause. Then the voice on the other end of the line, soft in pitch but ice-cold, said just one word. "When?"

"Call me in two days!"

"Really?"

"I've already infiltrated the target and got the lay of the land. One plan didn't work out, but I've got others."

"You sure?"

"Depend on it!"

"Believe me, I am."

The man who'd initiated the call, known to the Victoria community as the respectable developer, Vince Smithson, hung up and went to rejoin his business meeting. The man who'd received it, known to his potential victim as good ol' boy Bill Iverson, poured himself a drink and sat thinking hard.

TWENTY-SIX

It was Monday evening and Trent was in a slump. Although the CANTSO holding company stock had done exactly as he'd predicted—which certainly made him feel good—his own position hadn't changed at all.

Or if it had, it was likely for the worse.

Since Trent had access to no funds himself, Stephanie's insistence that he take his findings to Terry Bathgate had seemed sensible. It was a pity that his old buddy had been sound asleep—still on the Toronto clock—when he'd gone up to the house. But since time was of the essence, he'd been roused anyway. Trent had then given his big news, thereafter spending an hour presenting a case so closely argued yet so intricate and exhausting that finally Terry had almost literally thrown him out.

Without giving a reaction.

The next day, Trent had returned to discover that his buddy had gone back Toronto.

What did that mean? Trent had no way of knowing, since Terry had neither left a message nor, apparently, said a word to this wife about what had transpired. Jill had seemed bewildered—and not a little put out—that her husband had so suddenly departed again. Though she didn't put it in so many words, it had seemed to Trent that she believed he must have messed up yet again.

He decided it was useless to try to explain.

Now, over two days later, alone in his borrowed lodgings, with still no word from the man with whom he'd entrusted his last great hope, Trent was beginning to sense that the bottom was finally about to drop out of his world. Stephanie had declared that she didn't care if he thought himself a failure, or even if he *was* one, which no doubt said a lot about her feelings for him. Unfortunately, he was now sure he couldn't live with it himself.

Early on, before his good feelings had started to evaporate, he hadn't been able to resist phoning his brother, not exactly giving details of the big break, but hinting broadly. That, he now realized, had been yet another mistake.

Meanwhile, during the period of increasingly agitated waiting, he'd naturally been glued to his computer, skipping around the markets, watching as his CANTSO predictions began to move into reality. The share price was rising rapidly, but it had been impossible to see whether Terry and the companies he represented had been in on the surge. With the sun setting and the Tokyo exchange set to close in hours—for them, Tuesday—and still no word from Terry, Trent could sit still no longer. He slammed shut his laptop, rose, and with stiff limbs and heavy heart stalked through the cottage and flung open the front door.

Jill Bathgate was approaching down the drive.

"For heaven's sake, Trent." Jill snapped, as soon as she saw him. "Terry's been trying to call you for ages."

"Yeah? I've been *waiting* for him all day." Trent cried indignantly.

"Well, *he* says all he gets is your damn voice-mail. He just phoned *me* to come find out what the hell's going on."

Trent hauled out his cell. "That's ridiculous," he said—immediately discovering that it wasn't: somehow, in his agitation, he'd managed to turn the thing off. "Jesus, fuck!" he breathed.

"About what Terry said," Jill said more mildly. "Well, no harm. He'll be calling back soon—and you look like hell. Come on! While you're waiting you may as well come up for a drink."

A SHORT WHILE later, when they had settled in the spacious living room—which not long ago, in a moment of folly, Trent had pretended to be his own—with drinks between them and his phone, now turned on, sitting nearby, Jill said. "Trent, remind me, how long is it that you've been with us now?"

Bemused, managing to sip his drink but hardly able to keep his eyes off the phone, Trent said, "About a year, I guess."

"That's what I thought," Jill replied. Then, after a pause. "Don't you think it's maybe time you moved on?"

She had his attention. "What do you mean?"

Jill took a careful swallow of her drink, watching him over her glass. "I mean . . . I know where you're living's supposed to be a guest house. But, well, after a while, guests can become something else."

Trent was very still. "*Freeloaders*, you mean?"

Jill shrugged. "I wouldn't put it that strongly. Still, it'd be nice to have a place to offer business associates Terry might wish to entertain. His *partners*, for instance."

In shock, yet filled with a sense of inevitability, as if this moment of final casting-off had been preordained, Trent nodded numbly. He also realized that, of course, Jill must have known all along about the grand scheme he'd put to Terry. All this shit about taking a powder, leaving him in the dark, then letting his wife put in the knife, had been Terry's cowardly way of avoiding what he'd obviously seen as a huge embarrassment. Whatever the merits of Trent's plan, Terry hadn't taken it seriously. Coming, as it had, from a demonstrated flake and loser, the whole thing must have seemed preposterous—and now it was too late. He'd better accept that and get the hell out of there.

And—God—this time with a little dignity.

All this went through Trent's mind very swiftly. Gritting his teeth, he forced himself to take a deep breath, then swallowed the last of his drink and rose.

"I understand, Jill," he said quietly. "Okay, then . . . I reckon I'll pack up and get out of here tomorrow."

His cellphone rang.

Trent didn't move. He just stood staring at the thing, letting it go on and on. After all, what was the point in answering now. Finally, Jill picked it up.

"Oh, hi, sweetie," Jill said. "Well, I must have found him, mustn't I, because this is his phone. Would you believe he had it switched *off?*" She laughed. "Neither could I, but you know Trent. What? No, of course not. I've been teasing him a little, but I knew you'd want to do *that* yourself."

Trent had been staring, appalled at the callous manner in which his old friends were discussing him. To cap it off, as Jill pushed the cell into his hand, he saw she wasn't even trying to hide what appeared to be a triumphant grin.

Feeling sick, but knowing he must do it, Trent took the phone "Hi, Terry," he said, in hardly more than a whisper.

Terry's response, was anything but quiet. In fact, almost a bellow. "Jesus, buddy, I was starting to think you didn't want to hear the news."

"What news is that?"

"Shit, what else, man? That we're rich! Oh yes, and the other thing—I want you to be my partner."

TWENTY-SEVEN

Trent was scarcely aware of leaving the big house, but sometime later he found himself back in the cottage, with his cell still in hand, gazing like a zombie at the computer he'd used to extract the information that had given him back his life.

A partner! A goddamn PARTNER!

How was a man supposed to get his head around a life-change like that. Yet this wasn't one of his high-flying fancies. Not the result of gambling, either. Through his own real smarts and hard work, he'd come up with information that—during the tortuous time of waiting—Terry had used to get firmly on board with what was already turning into a market phenomenon. He, Trent, had made that possible, a fact Terry had freely—one might almost say *deliriously*—acknowledged. And now . . . now the world had changed entirely.

Finally noticing the phone in his hand, Trent realized he had to tell Stephanie. It was she, after all, who'd convinced him to take the plunge with Terry. But she was at work and this news was too big for a phone call; besides, when he said the magic word *partner*, he wanted to see her face. But, man, he had to tell *someone!*

Then it hit him: Hal!

God, yes, of course! Ironically, had it not been for the appearance of his brother, the idiotic charade he'd played and the worse foolishness that had followed, he'd likely never have been shamed into the evolution of mind that had made this change happen. And now, instead of hiding the shameful facts of his old life, he could reveal the brand new reality—and thank Hal for the part he'd played.

He opened the phone and called his brother. When Hal answered, Trent resisted the urge to blurt everything out. Again, he realized this revelation was too big for the phone. So he confined himself to, "Hello, Hal. Where are you right now?"

Hal was evidently surprised, but he answered with good grace. "Oh, hi, Trent . . . in Maple Bay, remember? With that friend I told you about?"

Perfect. He could get over there, give Hal the news, and be back in Duncan by the time Stephanie finished work. "Oh, right." he said briskly." Where in Maple Bay, exactly? I want to slip over and see you. It's important."

Trent could sense Hal was bewildered that he wouldn't elaborate. But he gave directions to an address at the south end of Maple Bay. By the time the conversation concluded, Trent was already in his Jeep and ready to roll.

The journey east through Duncan then to the coast took half an hour. He missed the Genoa Bay turnoff, a vital part of his directions, and lost some time backtracking. The road sign and the Trail mailbox were also difficult to spot in the dark. But he did it, at last finding himself in a driveway that wound through trees with trunks so huge they looked like towers in the headlights.

By this time, Trent was so pumped he could scarcely stop himself singing. But what he felt, when he thought of the reaction his big brother would have to his news, was not so much pride as amazement. After all the shit that had gone down recently, what was happening seemed truly miraculous.

When he reached the house, Trent cut the motor and lights and sat staring. It was large and old, looking slightly out of place in the rural setting, with a couple of lighted windows, plus a dim lamp on the porch. Even in the gloom the house appeared in need of some renovation, yet it stood on its perch, overlooking the water, with the dignity of an ancient castle.

Also—surprising to Trent, who was not used to thinking in such terms—the building had an aura of peace and civility. A perfect setting, he realized, to begin spreading the news of his good fortune.

Trent got out of the Jeep and closed the door quietly, not even pocketing his keys right away. Such was the serenity of the night, he wanted to create as little disturbance as possible. He headed for the lighted porch, walking slowly, now consciously prolonging the magical moment of anticipation.

He arrived at the porch and was about to knock when something caught his attention. The walk around the house had brought him into full view of the bay. A three-quarter moon had risen from behind a distant headland, sliding its silver track across the dark water to where Trent could now see a steep cliff, just yards from the house. The night was so still that the low chug of a diesel could be heard in the distance. Trent spied faint running lights and a boat wake, cutting a delicate garland across the path of the moon.

The scene was tranquil, achingly lovely. To Trent it was like a visual celebration of the miraculous change in his life. For a year he'd lived on this island, surrounded by awesome scenery, scarcely paying it any mind, so buried in his problems that he'd missed the very real wonders that were all about.

Well—all that was over.

Trent felt something rare, not a buzz now but a true lift of the heart. He drifted toward the ocean, trying with all his senses to absorb the moment. At cliff's edge was a low stone wall, beyond, a sheer drop to the rocks below. Trent smiled. The place might be dangerous, but it didn't bother him. In his present mood, he could almost imagine himself taking off and flying, though of course he felt no urge to try. But for the sheer hell of it, he stepped on to the top of the wall and stood with the breeze ruffling his hair and a hundred-foot drop at his toes. He wasn't nervous, or dizzy. He just felt alive—peaceful in a brand new way. He was finally getting his life together.

Then, as he stood at the world's edge, drinking in the night, he got a small surprise. He realized he could see lights at the foot of the cliff. There was some sort of building down there, a shed or a boathouse. Trent was taking this in when something else caught his attention. Off to his right, where the cliff bulged out and became less precipitous, was what looked like a path: something had come from there, a sound or a movement, he wasn't quite sure. Trent concentrated on the place, but whatever it was wasn't repeated. Or nothing had actually happened. A trick of the light, or of the imagination.

He opened his mouth to call. Then didn't. The idea seemed silly. Anyway, it was time he was going in. Time to start spreading the good news.

He turned to step off the wall.

Something came fast out of the dark, a movement that became an impact, that became a wild, hard, unstoppable plunge.

His last thought was, "Oh, no—not *now!*"

Then he went down.

TWENTY-EIGHT

"This brother of yours seems like a pretty strange character," Mattie said. "Are you sure he's coming?"

"That's what he said."

"To give you some sort of news?"

"Apparently. But he wouldn't say what. A couple of days ago he hinted about something big going down, so maybe it's that. I just hope . . ."

"What?"

"That this time its . . . well, *real*."

"You mean not some sort of trick, like when you said he pretended to own his friend's house?"

"Yeah, I guess so. But I'm sure he's not likely to try anything like that again."

"I certainly hope not. Poor man.""

"I can see how the guy might want to hide the fact that he was broke. But there's no need for that anymore. Anyway, I know his fiancée, Stephanie, wouldn't stand for him playing any more tricks."

Mattie smiled. "This Stephanie seems quite a gal."

"She is. Just what my brother needs. Fortunately he seems to know it."

Hal and Mattie were in the living room of the big house. A pleasant evening of talk and good wine had been interrupted by Trent's phone call. Since then they'd been waiting over an hour. Mattie was looking ready to turn in. Similarly Hal, who after a weekend in the company of his friend felt more relaxed than in years, was anxious to get to bed. Not, it must be emphasized, that that they contemplated doing this together. Though in many ways they'd never been closer, the notion of a physical reunion had not seemed appropriate at all.

Not yet anyway.

The conversation had wound down and both were trying to suppress yawns when, finally, there was the sound of the front door opening. But it was Fitz, not Trent, who appeared a moment later.

"What's going on?" the old man snapped. "Who's here?"

"No one *yet!*" Mattie said mildly "But we're just waiting for . . ."

"Then who the hell owns that Jeep?"

"*What?*" Hal and Mattie said together.

"I just this minute came up from the boathouse, and there's this junky old Jeep sitting out front."

"*Trent* owns a Jeep," Hal said.

"He must have arrived," Mattie replied.

"Who the hell's Trent?" Fitz demanded.

No one answered. The others were already heading for the door.

THEY FOUND THE Jeep sitting dark and silent in the parking area. It was empty of life, but Hal recognized it immediately.

There was no sign of Trent.

They called and searched. They checked the house, thinking perhaps he'd circled around and come in from the rear. Finding no one, hearing nothing, they re-emerged, and now Mattie had a flashlight. They called again, searching fitfully. There seemed nowhere Trent could have gone. Then, as Mattie's light swung by the cliff, Hal caught a glint of reflection from the top of the wall. Getting her to shine the light there, he walked quickly to the place. What had been a glimmer became recognizable form. Sitting on the top of the wall was a bunch of keys.

Hal picked them up. Adrenalin surged into his gut and, feeling as if he'd been punched, he leaned out over the wall, looking down.

He could see nothing below in the darkness, but that didn't allay the fear that was taking hold. "Here!" he called. "Over here!"

As soon as Mattie arrived, he grabbed the flashlight. The powerful beam had no trouble reaching the cliff bottom—nor picking out the figure lying there.

Running, scrambling and sliding, they descended the path, somehow without themselves becoming casualties. Fitz knew the terrain best and was in the lead. Hal and Mattie followed closely. The place where the body had been spotted was several yards back along the beach. Covering that last distance across the sand and rocks seemed to take an eternity. Not that it really mattered, for surely no one could have survived such a fall.

They all reached Trent at the same time. He was not lying on the ground but across a huge arbutus branch. The tree from which the limb had snapped was directly above. Trent must have hit it, substantially breaking his fall, for when the light hit his eyelids they scrinched open.

"Jesus Christ!" Trent muttered. "What happened?"

HE HAD NOT come off completely unscathed. After the shock of finding a survivor rather than a corpse, the next thing discovered was that Trent's left leg was bent under his body at a grotesque angle. It must have absorbed what remained of the impact, for it was badly broken. The smallest attempt at movement caused agonized yells. He was very much alive—though how he'd managed to fall over the cliff was quite another matter.

Fortunately, Hal still had his cell on him. A 911 call brought help, ambulance and paramedics, within half an hour. Before midnight, the sedated and stretchered warrior was on his way to Cowichan District Hospital.

Hal followed the ambulance in his car. Although Mattie looked exhausted, she insisted on coming along. Still numbed by shock, they headed into Duncan, but not until they were entering the near-deserted town did Mattie put words to what was on both minds. "Hal, I can't understand it. How could your brother have fallen? I mean, in the history of the house there's never been an accident like that."

They were waiting at the Trans-Canada Highway intersection for the light to change. Since it was no longer an emergency, the ambulance was not using its bells and whistles. When they got going again, Hal said, "One thing, anyway: at least we know it was an accident."

Mattie looked surprised. "What else might it have been?"

"Well, in other circumstances—the way Trent's life's been going lately—I guess it's remotely possible that in a moment of anger or depression he might . . . you know . . . But he was bringing good news, I'm sure of that."

"So how come he fell over the wall?"

"God knows. He doesn't know your place. Maybe he was just so excited he tripped over the thing in the dark. Anyway, the main thing is the poor guy survived."

In a few minutes more they reached the hospital. The ambulance stopped at the Emergency entrance and they pulled up nearby. Stephanie, who'd been contacted earlier, was already waiting. They stood back as Trent was brought from the ambulance and Stephanie anxiously followed. At the admitting desk there was a mild kafuffle, but it was soon sorted, and Stephanie vanished into the interior, following in the wake of her battered prince.

Feeling the enervating release of tension, they simultaneously subsided onto the hard waiting-room chairs. Trent was in good hands and wouldn't be going anywhere. There was nothing more to be done. But, at well after midnight, even the short walk back to the car seemed like a chore. They sat, resting briefly, and Hal again found himself holding Mattie's hand.

But sitting like winded geriatrics wasn't going to bring Maple Bay any closer. They rose, and were just debating on how to leave a message for Stephanie, when the lady herself emerged from the rear, looking distraught.

"What's happened? "Hal said quickly. "He's not worse, is he?"

Stephanie shook her head. "No! But I'm so confused. I don't know what to say."

"I'm just so sorry," Mattie said. "I've no idea how such a terrible thing could have happened."

The other woman seemed to be searching for words. At last she said, "Actually, I think I *do*."

"What do you mean?" Hal said carefully.

Stephanie's eyes were blinking tears. "Trent didn't just fall over that cliff—he says he was *pushed*."

TWENTY-NINE

From the darkness, Iverson watched as the ambulance bore the charmed-life idiot away. By that time his earlier frustration had turned to relief. The instant he'd pushed the guy he'd known he'd made a mistake. Only night, the fact he'd no idea there was any other man but Fitz around, plus the haste of what had seemed a fortuitous moment, could have made the error possible. Still, as things had turned out, the blunder had an upside. Had it indeed been the intended victim—the old man, rather than this freaky stranger—his survival would have presented a worse problem: with Fitz merely injured and safely ensconced in hospital, finishing him in time would have been next to impossible. As it was, he'd been given another chance.

This time, there would be no slip-ups.

His error, he admitted, had been impatience and too much dependence on improvisation. Now, with the deadline drawing ever closer, a more careful strategy was required. Ironically, the less time left for doing the job, the more was needed for proper planning.

Okay, so he'd just better get his act together.

After the ambulance departed and the old man went back in the house, Iverson waited patiently. After a while a light came on upstairs, then went out again. It seemed Fitz had hit the hay, a more prosaic end to his day than had been intended, but never mind. Iverson waited a while longer. The house remained dark and silent. The others, who'd left following the ambulance, would no doubt eventually return. It would have been nice if, before then, he could have crept into the house and finished the botched job. Unfortunately, nothing so obvious could be contemplated.

So, when he was ready, Iverson carefully descended the cliff path, back the way he'd come. Reaching the boathouse, he tried the door. Locked, which held him up for about two minutes. Inside, he was tempted to put on a light—surely it would not be noticed—but nixed that idea; considering the errors of the night, even the smallest risk was no longer acceptable. His little flashlight would have to do.

But before he got to work, he stood in the dark, waiting, listening, making extra sure that he was alone. It was then that he was overtaken by a quite uncharacteristic sensation: for a brief moment, it felt as if this creaky old junk pile was somehow aware, and that it housed some dark and dreadful secret.

An instant later, the feeling was gone. "Shit," he muttered to the shadows, "What was *that* about? Must be getting fucking senile."

However, unused to such flights of fancy, he quickly forgot it. Taking his time, he drifted quietly about, examining every detail of the messy hideaway; tools and beer cans and carvings and fishing gear and books and ashtrays and piles of wood-shavings: all the detritus of one eccentric old man's life.

Here also was the key to what would come to be regarded as his natural death.

All Iverson had to do was find it.

THIRTY

Hal awoke, feeling shocked and amused and embarrassed and aroused in about equal parts. He'd been dreaming he was back in the past, making love to Mattie. They were having a fine old romp, until he looked across at a mirror and saw, grinning nakedly back at him, the reflection of his father. He instantly understood that the "parent" was in fact himself, but *that* made him remember his true age. And when he looked back at Mattie, she was not only still just eighteen, but looking at him in horrified disbelief. "Oh, God, Hal—where did you *go?*" Mattie whispered, and vanished in the dazzle of waking morning.

What a crock, Hal thought. If my subconscious was a script writer, it'd be doing soaps. Why must dreams be so damn corny?

Clichéd or not, this one unsubtly hinted at things he didn't want to think about. So he rose and dressed and ambled, yawning, through the big old house, finally ending up in the kitchen. Its sole occupant was Fitz, who was slumped over a mug of coffee.

"Want some?" the old man said without preamble.

"Thanks." He went to the table and sat facing the window, with a clear view of the cliff and the wall from which Trent had taken his extraordinarily non-fatal plunge. Bringing his coffee, Fitz followed Hal's gaze. "So how's your brother? They get him patched up okay?"

"We left them at it. I guess he'll have his leg in a cast. But otherwise . . . Some kind of miracle he wasn't killed. Thanks for all your help, by the way."

Fitz grunted. "Least I could do. But how he went over beats me. Drunk, you reckon?"

That possibility had occurred to Hal, but it didn't seem likely; for all the high drama of last night, Hal hadn't got the feeling—or the smell—of liquor being involved, despite the possibility that Trent might have been celebrating the good news he had, as it turned out, been bringing.

Then, of course, there was the *other thing*.

He didn't know what to make of his brother's claim of being pushed. Was it a true belief, or an invention to cover his own stupidity, or klutziness? Hal didn't know. But since Fitz would hear about it soon enough, he figured he might as well be the one to tell it.

"My brother is an unusual guy," he began carefully, "with a really vivid imagination—so I don't take him seriously . . ."

Fitz glanced at him sharply. "Meaning?"

"Last night, Trent seemed to have the idea that the reason he went over the cliff was because he was—er—pushed."

The old man's eyes narrowed. "No kidding."

"I can't say I believe it. My feeling is that Trent was making it up because he's embarrassed . . ." He stopped. Fitz's expression, far from being dismissive or amused, was of intense interest. "*What?*"

Fitz didn't reply right away. He went to the window and stared at the cliff. Finally he swiveled on the balls of his feet, a movement surprisingly agile, and returned to Hal. "Who knew your brother was coming here last night?"

"No one. He just phoned out of the blue. We didn't even know he'd arrived till you found his Jeep."

"Exactly!" Fitz went back to the window, continuing to look thoughtful.

"Fitz, what's going on?" Hal said.

The old man's expression was now an unnerving mix of horror and triumph. "Of *course!*" he whispered. "I should have known!"

"What, for God's sake?"

With a sigh, Fitz fetched the coffee pot, refilled both their cups and told him.

"DID HE ALSO tell you," Mattie said later, "what happened the night I came home after meeting you in Victoria?"

Unprepared for her bitter tone, Hal spoke carefully. "Not specifically."

"All right, *I'll* be specific. Lately, Fitz has been getting more and more angry about PacificCon—"

"*PacificCon?*"

"Pacific Construction: the company trying to get their hands on this property. Didn't he tell you?"

"Yes, but he just called them 'the bastards.'"

"That figures. Granted, they've been a pest. Worse than that, I guess. But he's let it get to him beyond reason. For instance, the night we met in Victoria, he was up here getting plastered, convincing himself that company thugs were going to appear any minute and burn the house down—as he thinks they did to someone else in Nanaimo."

"Yeah—he did tell me about that."

"What he obviously didn't tell you is that when I returned home, he nearly killed me."

"What? *How?*"

Visibly shaking at the recollection, she told him everything: the drunken challenge; the roar of the gun, so close she could feel the wind; the terror that the next shot would end her life. Then the sickening aftermath: maudlin apologies, sleepless hours, the burying of the hateful weapon—and the niggling fear that maybe, sooner or later something similar might happen again.

"And all for what?" Mattie concluded. "So Fitz can preserve his precious heritage: these goddamn trees and oh-so-special view, which no one ever gets to see but us. The story is he's holding it for the family. But half of us are dead. Fitz is old, Jennifer will never live here again, and I . . . just don't care. But you know the real reason he won't let PacificCon have this place—and they've offered a fortune—is pure old-man cussedness. They've kicked him around—so he believes—and rather than give in he'd rather drive himself and everyone else mad with his damned obsession . . ."

Mattie stopped, breathing hard. "Goodness," she said, after a pause, "I'm sorry, I didn't mean to sound so extreme. Poor Fitz isn't as bad as that. And he does love us, I know. But after all the sad things that have happened to this family, to have this stupid land business on top of it sometimes gets too much to bear. I've tried to persuade him to sell, but nothing will make him part with the place. And now, just when it seems I might get some peace . . ." She smiled without embarrassment. ". . . and some nice time with you, along comes your damn brother—excuse me—and we have another great drama on our hands."

Hal nodded glumly. "I'm afraid Trent's accident—whatever the cause—is my fault in a way. I'm as happy as you about our time together. But if I weren't here neither would *he* be. You seem to have got us as a package. I'm sorry."

Impulsively, she reached across the table and took his hand. "Don't be! This visit is the best thing that's happened to me in ages. It's very special, Hal. Not just because we're old friends and were once lovers, but because of how we both are *now*. Meeting you again has made me realize that, though our parting was hard, it really did allow us to become the people we were meant to be. Since you arrived, I've felt . . . released from something: a pouty little dream that has nothing to do with the real me. Seeing you"—she grinned—"*grown up*, has made me realize how truly changed *I* am too; and, despite everything, mostly happy. Does that sound weird?"

He shook his head emphatically. "No, I couldn't have put it better."

"I know you'll soon have to go back to work, that this is probably the only time we'll ever have. I'm content with that, but I don't want it to end just yet. I've even started dreading the phone will ring and drag you away . . ." She colored. "Whoops! I probably should have left out that bit."

"That's okay. I've been thinking the same thing. Anyway . . ."

"Yes?"

It had been in his mind to say that the end of the visit needn't mean the end of their renewed relationship. But that seemed glib—and perhaps too committing—and he was old enough to know the damage that careless words could do. So he said, "By the look of things in Vancouver, I've probably got a little time yet."

"I'm glad," she said simply. "But of course, you'll want to spend some of that with poor Trent."

Hal smiled. "Not so poor anymore, apparently. I don't know what this partnership thing with Terry involves. But it's got to help getting his life on track. When I called Steph, she said she's taking him to her place. I guess I'll call on him there, see how he's doing." He realized they'd circled a long way from where the conversation had begun. "But what about Fitz? I'd certainly have thought twice about telling him Trent's *pushing* idea if I'd known what he'd make of it. But it's done. So what do we do?"

Mattie sighed. "I haven't the least idea."

"You don't think it possible, by the smallest chance, that someone *could* be trying to harm your father-in-law?"

"If I'm honest, I must admit I don't know. I mean, Fitz *is* the only one standing between PacificCon and their big development. So it's not beyond the realm of possibility, I suppose. But, Hal, this isn't the movies. Surely, stuff like that doesn't really happen, at least not around here."

Hal shrugged. "This is no longer the quiet little backwater it used to be. Anyway, these days it doesn't seem to matter where you are; when big money's involved, there's always likely to be some kind of scam."

"That sounds a bit cynical."

"I suppose it does. Maybe I'm wrong. I sure hope so. Anyway, apart from Trent's fall, and your near-thing with Fitz, nothing bad's happened yet. I guess all you can do is hope it stays that way."

They continued talking in this vein for a time. Hal began to realize something was niggling at the back of his mind. He tried to ignore it, but it kept popping up, all the more annoying because he couldn't put a handle on it. Then finally, after Mattie had gone to prepare lunch, and he'd walked out to examine Trent's Jeep, to try to figure the logistics of getting it back to him, the niggle finally found form.

It concerned the development company that Mattie had mentioned: PacificCon. Something about the name was oddly familiar.

THIRTY-ONE

The discovery of Trent's car keys, which had in turn led to the rescue of their battered owner, had another less dramatic consequence: they made it possible to return his Jeep. Hal drove it, followed by Mattie in her own car, the small convoy arriving at Stephanie's place in the mid-afternoon.

Stephanie met them at the door. When she and Mattie were introduced, she said, "Oh—yes, of course, Miss Trail!"

"Oh, heavens," Mattie said. "*Mattie*, please!"

"No, I mean, you're *the* Miss Trail—the English teacher at Cow' High, right? You taught my son, Gat: Gary Tremblay?"

Stephanie smiled. "Ah, yes, Gary. How is he? Quite grown up, I guess."

"He's twenty. Regular big lug, and mad about motor bikes. But a good kid. Doesn't give his mum too many worries. But don't you have a boy the same age? I seem to remember he and Gat were . . ." Stephanie stopped, growing red as the realization hit her. "Oh! Yes! How awful of me. I'm so sorry. I'd forgotten that he . . ."

Mattie laid her hand gently on Stephanie's arm. "It's okay. If your boy was a friend of Brian's, I'm glad to hear about it. It makes it all the nicer to meet you."

Stephanie looked relieved, and any further embarrassment was forestalled by Trent calling from the living room. "Is he here? Hey, bro—that you?"

Stephanie grinned. "That's my man: one busted leg, but still kickin'."

She started to lead them through the house, but Hal stopped her. "What about that—*other thing*? Does he still think he was pushed?"

Her response surprised him with its casualness. "I really don't know. He was pretty bummed out last night. I guess we all were."

"Hey!" Trent's voice hollered. "What's going on?"

"Just coming, hon!" Stephanie called. Then, to the others, "And really, unless he brings it up, I think we should just forget it."

They entered the living room to find Trent on the sofa. His left leg, encased in plaster, was propped on a footstool. Beside him on a tray was the remains of lunch. Trent himself—apart from the cast and a few bruises—looked remarkably unscathed. The real difference in him was more subtle. Ever since their first meeting, Hal had been aware of an underlying resonance to his brother's personality—a kind of *gloom*—which today, despite the physical trauma, was quite gone. Replacing it was an inner animation which could only come from the knowledge that his life was quite spectacularly back on track.

"Hi, 'Partner.'" Hal grinned. "How are you doing?"

Trent said he was fine, considering he'd apparently tried to perform some sort of crazy circus act. Mattie was introduced as Hal's friend, and resident of the property where the incident had occurred. Trent's reaction was one of embarrassment.

"Listen, I'm sorry for all the trouble I caused," he said, contritely. "Really, I don't know what happened. When I arrived at your place, the night was so beautiful—the moonlight on the water, the cool view—and I was so excited, you know, because of my news—I became sort of giddy. Why the hell did I climb on that damn wall? Just felt a bit crazy, I guess. You know, the way you do when something really terrific has happened. Anyway, I got so carried away I must have slipped. After that—wow—who remembers? But here I am, still alive. Largely thanks to you guys. That's even luckier than the big break I was coming to tell you about."

And that appeared to be that. Stephanie made coffee and they sat around for a while, chatting. The happenings of the last days had obviously moved Trent's relationship with his fiancée to a new level. Although not mentioned, it seemed unlikely that they would ever be living apart again.

A while later, as they were preparing to leave, Stephanie's son Gary arrived. He recognized Mattie instantly and, unlike his mother, was not embarrassed to talk about her son. "Brian was a real cool guy," Gary said simply. "What happened was a bummer, Miz Trail. We miss him a lot."

"Thanks. Gary," Mattie smiled. "I miss him too."

"I didn't know him as well as some of the guys. Con Ryan was his best bud. And I was more a friend of Con's. But we all kinda hung together. I haven't seen Con in ages. You see him at all?"

Mattie nodded. "Yes. Actually he often goes fishing with my dad."

Gary's eyebrows raised, leaving little doubt what he thought about that. "Well, say 'hey' to the dude from me." He grinned. "And tell him, if he's ever stuck in Sooke again, he knows who to call."

"What does that mean?" Mattie asked.

"Nothin', Miz Trail—just a little joke—he'll know."

"All right, I will."

"Okay—well, gotta fly." He stuck out his hand. "Nice to meet you again. Good times at ol' Cow' High, eh? Seems like a long time ago."

"Yes," Mattie said quietly. "I suppose it does. Goodbye, then."

Then Gary Tremblay, after a nod to his mum and a wink at Trent, was on his way.

Soon afterward, taking the young man's exit as their cue, Hal and Mattie prepared to depart. As they were getting up, Trent gave a meaningful look at Stephanie, who took Mattie's arm. "I think Trent wants to have some guy-talk with his brother. Come on, I'll show you the garden."

When they were alone, Trent said, "Want to sign my cast?"

Hal grinned. "If you promise not to sell it on eBay."

"Sure—look . . . what I wanted to say—I'm sorry for all the trouble I caused."

"That's okay, I understand."

"Yeah, of all people I think you do. I can be an asshole, no mistake. But I do care about Steph."

"She's a great lady."

"Damn right! She's a West Coast girl, so it may take some persuading to get her to move back with me to TO, but I'm sure not going without her." He gave a knowing grin. "Hey, how about that woman of *yours*? Still a flame burning there?"

To his surprise, Hal felt himself redden. "Of course not, idiot. She's just an old friend."

Trent shrugged. "If you say so. But you might be missing out on something. Anyway—better not keep her waiting. I'll see you, bro. And thanks for everything."

"You're welcome. I'm just glad we got together again."

"Me too!" Then, as Hal turned to leave. "Oh—just one more little thing."

"Yes?"

"You may not want to mention this—probably for everyone's sake better not—but last night on that cliff, *I really was pushed.*"

THIRTY-TWO

The leaping salmon was finished. For Fitz, in the final stages of a carving, there would always come a point when, after some small adjustment—shaving a projection here, correcting an angle there—he stood back and something inside him said, *there!* He never quite knew when this would happen, and hadn't been expecting it today, which still felt unpleasantly disrupted after last night's strange happenings.

But in truth, after his strong reaction to the final revelation, Fitz had begun to have his doubts. Yes, maybe the injured man *did* look a bit like him, but he also seemed like a real fruitcake. His story of being pushed off the cliff could well be a cover for having been drunk, or perhaps even suicidal. The more Fitz thought about it, the more likely that kind of explanation had seemed. Ruefully he'd reminded himself of the near-tragedy the last time he'd got paranoid about intruders. There'd been none then or since. And the nearest thing to a trespasser had been the arrival of Mattie's old beau. Had it not been for Con, he might have made a fool of himself then too. So getting too upset about this latest incident was not wise. If he didn't want to get the reputation of a senile old fool, he'd better—as the young people said—be cool. Fitz had repeated that admonition to himself, finally relaxing enough to concentrate on carving. He then became absorbed, going through half a pack of cigarettes as he shaved, sanded and polished, and it was shortly after noon when the "*there*" moment arrived, and he knew he was done.

At the same time he felt hungry. In the fridge he usually kept a supply of basics, cheese, bread, smoked sausage, some cans of sardines, but a search showed that the larder was almost bare, just a half-empty jar of Polish pickles and a couple of lonely beers. He took out a brew, opened it, and downed half in a single swig. That felt better. He went back to the carving, stared at it for a moment, then hefted it bodily into the light of the bay window. But before he could stand back to regard his work, his attention was taken by the sight of his new friend, Iverson, down on the beach.

That in itself was no surprise. Since the fishing trip, where Con had accompanied them, the fellow had poked his head in the boat-house a couple of times. They'd just been short visits. Iverson made it clear that he respected Fitz's privacy. He was a good man, affable but not pushy, who clearly did not want to make a nuisance of himself. Fitz liked him all the more for that. In time, he figured, they might become real friends.

But now, he realized, something was odd. Iverson was sitting by himself on a rock, much as on that first day. Was his back bothering him again? Fitz was wondering about that, when the man rose, paced, looking agitated but quite fit, stopped, gazed out to sea, shook his head, then slumped back onto the rock. His head lowered into his hands and his shoulders began to heave.

He appeared to be weeping.

Fitz's first reaction was to turn away in embarrassment. To watch another man in emotional crisis seemed like ill manners. After a moment's thought, he fetched the remaining beer from the fridge and carried it, along with his own half-finished brew, down onto the beach.

He made enough noise to be sure that his approach was noticed, but said no word. He stood quietly, gazing out to sea. Finally, not looking at Iverson, he handed down the beer. Iverson reached up and took it. In a snuffled mumble he said, "Thanks."

After that the two were quiet and, except for sipping on their beers, motionless. Eventually Iverson said, "Sorry!"

"Why?"

"I didn't mean to bother you."

Fitz sat slowly nearby. "Looks like *you're* the one bothered. Something bad happened?"

There was a long silence. Fitz waited. Finally Iverson said, "Reckon I told you about my boy with the Princess Pats in Afghanistan?"

"You did."

"So—this morning—I got this call . . ."

Iverson tailed off. Fitz felt a chill. He didn't dare attach a conscious surmise to what was coming, but he knew—*he knew.*

"Yesterday his unit was patrolling this road north of Kandahar. Their vehicle hit a roadside mine. Two guys were injured—one killed . . ."

Another long silence. Fitz had no need to ask the obvious; a man didn't sit weeping because his son was merely wounded. From bitter experience, Fitz knew that there were no adequate words for such occasions. Finally, all he said was, "Reckon you could use somethin' stronger'n beer, eh?"

For a moment it looked like Iverson hadn't heard. Then he gave a shuddering sigh and stood. Only then did Fitz see the wetness on his cheeks. He grimaced, rubbed his eyes with his sleeve, grunted, then shook his head pathetically. "I feel like a fucking clown."

"I guess, you've a right. Come on. I've got some rye stashed."

Iverson nodded, then looked freshly pained. "I don't need anyone seeing me like this."

"Don't worry. If anyone comes down, I'll send them packing."

"You're a good guy, Fitz," Iverson said gruffly.

"Yeah, yeah." the old man replied. "Let's go."

Slowly the two moved up the beach, heading for the boathouse, which, in early afternoon, was already being consumed to the cliff's long shadow.

THIRTY-THREE

They arrived home to discover yet another vehicle parked outside the house. This was familiar even to Hal, who'd noticed it on his first visit: a minivan bearing the legend SYLVIE'S POTTERY WORKS.

"Oh, Sylvie's here!" Mattie said, pleased. "You remember my friend, Sylvie?"

"Hard to forget," Hal smiled, as they alighted from the car, to discover Sylvie herself emerging from the boathouse path. She was wearing a flowing outfit similar to the one she wore on her last visit, except the boots had been replaced by sandals. She came out of the cut at a fine pace, brown legs pumping. as if the journey up the cliff had required as little effort as a short flight of stairs.

"Hi, Mattie, hello Handsome!" Sylvie called in greeting. "I wondered where you two had got to."

"We *two*?" Mattie laughed. "How could you know Hal was here?"

Sylvie indicated Hal's rental car, abandoned due to the necessity of returning Trent's Jeep. "I remember *that* from last time. Don't try to hide anything from me, kiddies. Auntie sees and knows all."

Hal was amused to see Mattie blush. "Don't be a twerp. Hal's just a friend."

"You mean a *hunk!*" Sylvie said, giving Hal an unashamed leer. "I also recall telling you to send him along to me. I'm still waiting, ducks."

"Good to see you too, Sylvie. You want a cup of tea?"

"Love to, darling, but can't. Just dropped by to see your pop-in-law. To run by him my idea for an exhibition, and to get some pictures. I talked to some friends in Vancouver, and they're really keen on the idea."

"Terrific! What did Fitz say?"

Sylvie looked awkward. "Actually—I didn't get to talk to him."

"Wasn't he there?"

"Yes he was. Down in the boathouse, as I expected . . . but . . . we didn't talk. Didn't seem much point really."

"Was he in a bad mood?"

Sylvie grimaced. "No, I fear old pops was pretty sloshed."

"Really?"

"Yeah! When I knocked, I thought at first he wasn't there. Then he came weaving out. Wouldn't talk. Wouldn't even let me in to take pictures of his stuff. Said he was busy—though God knows at what. The state he was in, I hardly think the old dear would be fit for carving, or anything else much."

"Damn!" Mattie said, with a vehemence that surprised Hal and evidently astonished Sylvie.

"Oh, shit," Sylvie said. "Did I let the cat out of the bag?"

"No. It's something I needed to know. It's just . . . after what happened last time he got drunk, I would have thought . . ." She glanced at Hal. "I guess that thing last night must have affected him more than he let on."

"Last night?" Sylvie said. "What happened?"

Hal and Mattie eyed each other. Words weren't needed for agreement that an explanation was next to impossible. Mattie said, "Oh, we had a bit of an upset. Not Fitz's fault, but I guess I took it too much to heart. I hope he wasn't too rude to you."

Sylvie shrugged. If she sensed that they were holding something back, she gave no sign. "It was fine. I'm a big girl. I can take a little brush-off. And my gallery idea will keep. Look, dears, I'd love to stay awhile, guzzle tea and ogle Mister Wonderful, but I'm on my way to Vancouver. That's why I wanted pictures of Fitz's carvings. But they'll keep." She gave Mattie's hand a squeeze. "Sorry about pops, dear. But don't let it worry you. He'll be okay, I'm sure. Anyway—you said you'd buried the gun, right?" She smiled at Hal. "Bye, Gorgeous."

With a casual wave she strode to her van, which roared to life and exited the property like a rocket. When they were alone, Hal said, "'The *gun?*' You told her about Fitz and the gun?"

Mattie shrugged. "I guess I tell Sylvie everything."

"Was that wise? She's a great girl, but she looks as if she might be a . . ."

"What?"

"A bit of a blabbermouth."

"Not about anything that matters. All right, she's a bit of a flake— and she's certainly taken a fancy to you—but Sylvie's as loyal as they come."

"Of course," Hal said hastily. "If she's your friend, I can't imagine anything else."

Mattie grinned. "Thanks. Listen, on the way home, I was thinking it was time we got out of here for a bit. We need a change of air. So what say I take you out to supper?"

"Sounds terrific."

"Good. But right now, I want to relax. I'm going up to take a bath." She headed for the hall, but turned back. "Hal, I'm not really too worried about Fitz. If he's tied one on, he'll just sleep it off down there. But since we're going out, I would like to make sure he's okay. But the thing is . . ."

"Yes?"

"I really don't want to see him drunk. Not today. It'll just make me angry again and spoil our evening . . ."

"Would you like me to check on him?"

"*Would* you?"

"A pleasure."

Mattie smiled ruefully. "I very much doubt it'll be that. But thanks. You'll take a weight off my mind."

ONE THING THAT Hal had found surprising about the boathouse was how completely its aspect altered with the time of day. Until early afternoon, the cliff was bathed in warmth and light. But as soon as the sun swung into the west, the path and the deep cleft in which the old building nestled fell first into shadow, then, by slow stages, into a shade so deep that, in contrast to the still-glowing bay, it seemed quite mysterious.

This was the situation as Hal went to carry out his task. By the time he was halfway down the cliff path, where it curved under the overhanging rock and the thick canopy of arbutus, it was as if he'd slipped forward in time to the onset of night. Reaching the bottom, where the path ended at the dock and the boathouse door, Hal found himself not only in semi-gloom but aware of an uncomfortable feeling of oppression. What was it about this place, he wondered. On his first visit, he'd had a sensation which, though brief, was of almost brutal intensity. Now here it was again, the sense of being—what?—in an almost physical presence.

Damn! Hal thought. *This is stupid. Let's just get this thing over.*

The boathouse door was ajar. Approaching, he became aware of music. It was jazz, funky New Orleans stomp, almost a dirge, low and soulfully sweet. This music, Hal mused, had seen its first incarnation at the time the old place was built and certainly fitted it well. But rather than darkening the boathouse's somber mood, the music leavened it, transmuting menace into something more like melancholy.

Instinctively, he kept quiet. Almost on tiptoe, he slipped through the door. The barn-like structure was very dim. Had it not been for the bay window, scooping reflected rays from the luminescence of the bay, he wouldn't have been able to see a thing. Then his eyes adjusted, and the first objects that came into focus were Fitz's carvings.

Several of these stood in a row, in a grouping that was new since Hal's last visit, silhouetted by the light beyond. There were animals and birds and, at the far end, the leaping fish Fitz had been working on. The cumulative effect of these images—stylized yet eerily lifelike—was so compelling that Hal sucked in a breath. In the background, the jazz slouched along, sweet and mellow, and if Fitz's creatures had begun to sway to the antique rhythms, Hal would not have been completely surprised.

The moment passed as the field of his vision broadened. Hal then saw that to one side was the tableau's creator. He was sitting in the rocking chair, a glass in one hand, a cigarette in the other. His eyes were half closed, his head nodding in time to the music. If he was drunk, as Sylvie had asserted, he didn't seem very bad, just sitting quietly, listening to music and contemplating his handiwork. The picture looked not only harmless, but very civilized. After all the turmoil, it was good to see at least one person taking it easy. No wonder Fitz didn't want to rattle on to Sylvie about her grand plans for his career. He looked like he was content with things just the way they were.

Hal had no intention of intruding. He'd verified that Fitz was okay, which was all Mattie wanted to know. Quietly, Hal started to turn away . . .

And stopped.

At the last moment his eye had been caught by an extra detail: another shape on the far side of the tableau, slightly apart and so still as to have remained unnoticed. It was a man, leaning casually and gazing out into the bay, a heavy-set fellow, perhaps in his fifties. He too was holding a glass and a cigarette, the smoke of which rose in a tiny unbroken stream into the rafters.

Then, as Hal watched, Fitz sucked in a breath and took a drink from his glass. The movement caused the man by the window to turn and glance around at his companion. For the first time, Hal got a look at his face. It was broad and wide, rugged in a slightly coarse way. The squarish skull was covered by a brush of dark hair, receding at the temples, one of which bore a quite pronounced scar. Something about him was vaguely familiar.

Then the man turned away, looking back at the bay. With the withdrawal of the face, the feeling of familiarity evaporated. Anyway, Hal thought, at least the old man wasn't drinking alone. So that was a good thing.

He backed off, leaving the boathouse without a sound. As he started up the cliff path, he could still hear the music of New Orleans, a sweet lament for a time long departed.

THIRTY-FOUR

Lyall Penney, known as Bill Iverson to his new buddy Fitz, was very pleased with himself. Having surveyed the boathouse the night before and developed a meticulous plan of action, he was now carrying it out to the letter.

The vitally important thing was that the death should appear purely accidental; no reason for questions, or investigations delaying the disbursal of the estate. Once the old man was out of the way, Iverson's boss needed to know that a clear and legal path was open for the acquisition of the vital parcel of land. In that way the investment capital could be kept on the hook, and the facilitator of all this—his worthy self—suitably rewarded.

So this operation was going to be immaculate and based on two factors.

The first was the character of the man. He was a heavy smoker. That and the fact that he was also a drinker formed the basis for a scenario all-too familiar to fire investigators. The second factor was the character of the fire itself: it must not only do the job, snuffing out Fitz for good, but be seen to be accidental and entirely the old coot's fault. So traditional accelerants such as gasoline were out; they'd been okay in the Nanaimo job, but wouldn't do here. Of course, he'd been told not to use fire at all, but that was too bad. Time was short and he was running out of options. A fire would do fine—just so long as there was absolutely no hint of foul play.

As for accelerants, nothing artificial was even needed; the tinder-dry building was practically knee-deep in wood shavings. With minor encouragement, they could promote a fine inferno. Should there be enough evidence left to investigate, it would be clear that the starting point of the fire was where the old man had dropped his last cigarette before drunkenly passing out.

Now, in the early evening, most preparations were complete. Sucking Fitz in with a tale of a mythical soldier-son had been—if he did say so himself—a stroke of pure genius. Considering Fitz's own history of loss, hitching a ride on that emotional roller coaster had been the perfect way to go. Letting the old fuck come to *him*, as he had with the bad-back scenario, had been elegant in its simplicity.

But since this opening gambit was fluid, requiring Fitz to discover and approach him in his own time, an early start had been needed. As it turned out, that stage was quick. He'd been safely and secretly ensconced in the boathouse by early afternoon. That was good, but also left a small problem: though the fire itself was unlikely to be noticed down below the cliff, the smoke certainly would. To avoid the risk of premature detection, it was vital that nothing happen until after dark, which meant there was a whole lot of time to fill.

Once they were alone, it would have been simple enough, of course, to knock the old guy out and wait till the appropriate time to roast him. But that left hours in which anyone might appear, so Fitz needed to be compos mentis to ward off busybodies. This precaution bore fruit in late afternoon, when a mouthy Limey broad had dropped by. Fortunately, folks were well used to getting the bum's rush from the grouchy woodcarver, so that had worked out okay.

All through the long afternoon they'd talked and drunk rye. Comfort for Iverson's "loss" had been the starting point for this charade and he had to admit, had the farce been real, Fitz's brusque camaraderie would have been effective. As it was, Iverson let himself be fed booze—which he mostly disposed of—while making sure his companion maintained just the right degree of intoxication: not too much to render him incapable of repelling visitors, but enough to hold him comfortably until it was time for the ax to fall.

When the talk ran down, Iverson kept things moving by getting Fitz to show off his carvings. Iverson didn't give a shit about such junk, but it didn't take a brain surgeon to concoct the kind of baloney that would appeal to the old fart. Then there was the music. At one point Fitz had plunked on some old jazz and Iverson was surprised to find it was something they actually had in common. Well, wasn't that funny as hell; they might have shared some good times, had it not been necessary to fry the old goat's ass.

After the departure of the Brit bitch, no one else had appeared. It was still too early to complete the next phase: that would involve getting Fitz passed out, then in the right location for his immolation. Next would come the delicate task of arranging and distributing the shavings to maximum effect. Finally—the fatal match.

But, now that they were unlikely to be disturbed, things could start to move. Iverson drifted from the window where he'd been appearing to drink while he really *did* smoke up a storm. (Sadly, he'd probably rekindled his old addiction, but if all went as planned it would be worth it.) Feigning a slight stagger, he went to the old man, smiling, his eyes moist with what looked for all the world like real tears.

"You're a good guy, Fitz," he said, with a slur so believable that even he was impressed. "Let's have another drink, ol' buddy. I just can't tell you how grateful I am for all you've done for me today."

THIRTY-FIVE

Genoa Bay was a tiny haven fifteen minutes by winding road from the Trail property. When Hal pulled into the waterside parking lot, it was to find himself confronted by a scene of near-mythic beauty and peace. The bay itself was a small but deep basin, almost completely surrounded by steep hills, which reared greenish-purple in the evening haze. The water was blue-black, slashed with bronze where ripples reflected the last hurrah of a radiant sunset. In the foreground, a marina filled with yachts and snug houseboats occupied almost the entire frontage. Farther out, in the still waters beneath the cliffs, more boats were moored. To one side, perched on an outcrop commanding a fine view of the harbor, was a picturesque building. The back section was enclosed with a series of antique-looking windows. The front was a broad deck overhanging the ocean. The place was tastefully lit, with a sign indicating that it was an eating establishment.

"This is it," Mattie said, as they emerged from the car. "Great seafood. And not too crowded during the week."

"Looks cozy."

"Actually, I haven't been here in ages," Mattie continued, as they walked up the wooden approach ramp. "But Con works here now, and he says it's very good."

"Con? Your dad's fishing buddy?"

Mattie smiled. "The same. Doesn't look like the waiter type, I know. And, frankly, it's quite a comedown from what we expected. Con was one of my brightest students. I was sure he'd go on to university and end up as some sort of writer. His English compositions were that good. But after . . . what happened . . . he seemed to lose all interest. Just hung out in town or mooned around our place. In some ways, I think the disappearance of my son affected him as much as any of us. They were best friends, after all. Without Brian, Con sort of lost his way. His poor mother wasn't much help either."

"Why not?"

"She had a lot of sadness of her own, not helped by alcohol, I'm afraid. She's a really nice woman, and I know she loves Con. But—well—she's not often in the best state to show it. But I think Con's finally coming out of his troubles. Fitz certainly thinks so. And . . . here we are."

They entered the restaurant and were shown to a table. Tucked in a corner, it was near a window with an impressive view of the rich after-glow. They ordered drinks, and after these arrived Mattie said quietly. "Thank you, Hal."

He smiled curiously. "For what, exactly?"

"I don't know . . . Well, yes, I do, but it's too complicated to put into a few words—or maybe *any*. So—just—thanks for being here."

They talked of this for a time, while waiting for the meal, at first awkwardly and then later, as food and wine did their work, with more ease. Bit by bit, they were able to say that, though their lives apart had been good—and indeed the only ones possible—they'd also missed each other. This conversation was not so much confession as discovery. Not lovemaking, but the clearing away of cobwebs, of denial and perhaps regret, in preparation for what—they both would have agreed—was a more mature friendship. The fact of physical attraction, which was still strong, was something they couldn't be quite so frank about. But it was a wonderful evening, not only heartwarming but—in light of recent events—a vast relief.

Toward the end of the meal, Con, who'd been busy with tables on the other side of the room, got a break and came over. "Hi, Miz Trail," he said cheerily. "What do you think of the place?"

"Fine, Con," Mattie replied. "We had a lovely dinner, thanks. This is Mister Bannatyne."

"Yeah, we met when he first arrived at your house." Con grinned. "Old Fitz thought he was from the developers. Wanted to kick his butt! But I recognized him from the TV. Hi, again, Mister Bannatyne."

"Hello. And it's 'Hal.'"

"Sure! Hey, I hear some weird stuff went down last night. Fitz says your brother took a dive off the cliff. Almost offed himself. What was that all about?"

Before Hal could reply, Mattie cut in quickly. "A small accident, that's all. Fitz was exaggerating, as usual. Oh, I saw an old friend of yours today. Gary Tremblay."

Con looked surprised. "*Gat?* Wow, I haven't seen him in ages. How was the guy?"

"Fine. He said to say hello." Mattie smiled. "He also sent a message: if you're ever stuck in—where was it?—*Sooke*—again, you'll know who to call . . . What's wrong?"

Her question was prompted by Con's expression of what looked like dismay. But he recovered quickly. "Oh, nothin'—old joke. That Gat always was a smartass. Thanks, Miz Trail—gotta get back to work."

After he left, hurrying off to busk a table in a far corner, Hal said, "What was the matter with him?"

Mattie shrugged. "You know kids, always playing pranks on each other. Con was probably just embarrassed." She rose. "Powder my nose. Back in a jiff."

As Hal sipped on what remained of his wine, he idly watched Con bustling away. The boy never again glanced in their direction. He had been more than just embarrassed, Hal thought, more like shocked, at least momentarily. But who knew? Kids had always been cruel to each other. And what with all the new forms of harassment available—like text messaging and the Internet—things seemed hardly to have improved.

This somewhat somber train of thought was interrupted by a small commotion on the other side of the restaurant. Someone was having a birthday. The table erupted in cheers as a waiter brought a sparkler-topped cake. After the singing, laughter, and applause, someone jumped up to speak and then . . .

Hal was seized with a powerful sense of déjà vu. This had happened before. No, he'd seen something *like* this before—recently—in some place like this. Where? *Where?* Then he had it. Of course! A while ago when he'd dined at the restaurant on the Malahat, the noisy party whose host had turned out to be his old friend, Vince Smithson.

So much had happened since then that the evening afterwards at Vince's had been forgotten. Now he recalled vividly the clever guy and his mansion full of glitzy guests. Also the visit to the private office, where Vince had produced the map with all of his property developments. Hal recalled this scene with great clarity, only now realizing that at the time—apparently subconsciously—he'd noted a logo across the top: PacificCon.

PacificCon! he thought. *Now where have I . . . ?*

"Jesus!" Hal exclaimed, so loudly that a couple at the next table glanced around. The other day, when Mattie had told him about the people trying to get hold of the Trail property, she'd mentioned PacificCon. The name had sounded familiar then, and now he knew why. He'd seen it on Vince Smithson's map. Which meant his old pal owned the company that had been giving Mattie's family so much grief.

"Shit!" Hal said, this time in a whisper. But that embarrassing revelation wasn't the end of it. It had started a process he recognized from of old: a whole bunch of data would accumulate in his subconscious until a single fact created an overload and everything spewed out into the light. This final puzzle-piece, he sensed, was about to emerge. Something disturbing—*dangerous*—was coming—coming . . .

He found himself visualizing the evening at the hilltop mansion, recalling that soon after the visit to the map room, Vince had left him on his own, being called away on business. Suddenly, with brutal clarity,

Hal recalled the face of the man who'd pulled Vince aside: someone who'd appeared to be out of place at the party, a tough-looking character with a broad face and an odd scar.

Hal grew very still. The memory fused with another more recent image, the face he'd seen when, at Mattie's request, he'd gone to check on Fitz. And then, with a precision that left no room for doubt, it was all there. His old friend Vince's associate and the man who had been with Fitz in the boathouse were one and the same.

"Oh, holy Christ!"

A final memory shoved aside everything else: his own brother's words: *Last night on that cliff . . . I really was pushed.*

HAL'S CHAIR FLEW over backward as he jumped to his feet. He strode across the restaurant, intercepting Con on his way to the kitchen. As Hal grasped his arm, the young man turned, growing alarmed as he saw Hal's expression.

"Hey—*what?*"

"Fitz's friend—how long has he known him?"

Con gaped, but quickly gathered his wits. "You mean, the Iverson dude? Not long. Why?"

"He works for PacificCon!"

"You're shittin' me."

"No! And I think he's already tried to harm the old man."

Hal was hardly aware of Mattie's presence as he burst out with a barely coherent account of his revelation. But his words must have done their work, for both she and Con were galvanized. As they all raced out of the restaurant, Mattie's said only, "Give me the keys."

Hal didn't argue with her command. A lifetime on these winding roads made Mattie the obvious pilot for what was to be a desperate journey. But Mattie had barely started the engine before Con's pickup sped by. By the time they left the lot, it was already out of sight.

THIRTY-SIX

They made the journey from Genoa Bay to the house at impressive speed. Mattie astonished Hal by performing like a rally-driver, throwing his rental car around the winding curves with nail-biting precision. But still the trip seemed never-ending, and not once did they even catch a glimpse of the tail lights of Con's truck. But at last there was the Trail mailbox, a flash-picture instantly doused as the car swung into the drive. Then they plunged through the trees, almost coming to grief on the final curve before skidding to a halt in the courtyard. Save for the porch light, the house was dark. Con's pickup was stopped nearby, engine running, lights pointing at the top of the cliff path. Con was nowhere to be seen.

Hal and Mattie tumbled out of the car and raced to the top of the cliff. At first there was little to be seen. The truck lights picked out the first section of the cliff path quite clearly. No sign of Con or anyone else. But with no moon, the region beyond the cliff was a void, broken only by a faint gleam of lights in the far distance and a pale net of stars above.

But there *was* something else; as soon as they stopped both became aware of the smell of burning. Then their eyes adjusted and conveyed fresh information: the gloom below was not quite featureless. The sky straight ahead was marginally lighter. This paler column was not solid, the pattern mottled and rising—smoke.

"The boathouse!" Mattie cried. "It's on fire!"

As if on cue, from below came a dull *whump*, followed by a sharp tinkling sound. Immediately, like a fiend unleashed, an ugly orange glow infused the night.

"Fitz!" she screamed. "Oh, dear God, *Fitz*!" She began to stumble down the path.

Hal thought fleetingly about his phone, but the sight of Mattie heading into danger would not let him pause. "Mattie!" he yelled, over the growing sounds of burning. "Mattie—be careful—wait!"

But she didn't, so he raced down the path in pursuit. Without flashlights, a descent at any speed would have been hazardous. But the glow from the fire was growing with frightening speed, lighting their way all too well. Hal caught up to Mattie as they reached the curve below the overhang. He grabbed her arm, but she shook off his grip and went on. Then they were around the bend and both pulled up short, transfixed by the sight below.

The boathouse that had graced the ravine for nearly a century was an inferno. Flames were shooting from the side windows, which had blown out, and reaching like evil talons from under the eaves. The far side was even more fiercely ablaze, the ancient timbers so dry that they were being devoured like paper. Now that the fire was really taking hold, it was nearly smokeless; but the sound was a cyclone roar.

The back door of the boathouse gaped wide, the opening like an angry orange eye. Arriving there, they peered inside, shielding their faces against the growing heat. Not far back they spotted a moving figure. It was just a silhouette, but definitely Con, and looked to be dragging something heavy.

Hal knew exactly what was happening. Had there been time to reason, he might have hesitated. But, overwhelmed by the image of the struggling figure in fiery peril, he instinctively dashed forward.

It took just seconds to reach his destination, but each was an eternity. He reached the struggling figure at last, discovering Con desperately trying to drag Fitz to safety. Hal lunged forward, his foot colliding with a heavy wood carving that had fallen on its side. Pain seared through his ankle. He lurched, staggered, almost fell, only just succeeding in regaining his balance.

This mishap cost vital seconds. Unaware, Con kept dragging, but he was making little headway, then he was stopped completely by a gut-wrenching cough. As Hal recovered, there was an explosion and a blazing section of roof crashed onto an area nearby.

"Con! *Come on*!" Hal yelled, staggering in and grabbing the old man's legs, somehow surprised at the lightness of the burden. Then at last the two began to make progress, moving in a desperate sideways shuffle towards the door. Their first exit attempt was nearly fatal. They cannoned into the door-jamb and almost went over. Flaming debris was now raining down all around. Grimly they recovered, reoriented themselves and with a burst of frantic endeavor finally staggered outside.

"Thank God," Mattie cried as they appeared. "Come on—bring him out on to the dock."

With her help they carried the inert figure out of danger, setting it down at last. Mattie fell to her knees beside her father-in-law. In the glow from the fire they could see him clearly. Apart from singed hair and ruined clothing, Fitz seemed physically intact.

But was he *alive*?

Desperately, Mattie called his name and, as she leaned in to look more closely, the question in all their minds was answered. Fitz let out a healthy snore.

"Oh, Fitz. Oh, thank God!" Mattie cried, hugging her father-in-law, then looked up at the others. "Are you two all right?"

Hal scratched his head, realizing that, although out of breath and with an ankle throbbing in agony, he was in one piece. "Yeah, fine!" He turned to Con. "How are you doing?"

Con didn't hear. He was staring back at the shore. The glare from the fire threw him into dramatic silhouette as he lifted his arm with finger extended.

"*Look!*"

They obeyed, straining to see what Con was pointing at. At first Hal saw nothing—then he could make out a still figure a hundred yards along the shore, half concealed by a large boulder. At that moment, the sea end of the boathouse imploded, sending up a shower of sparks and an explosion of light. As the glare washed across the rock, the features of the figure were starkly clear.

Before anyone else had time to react, Con took off down the dock, screaming at the top of his lungs.

THIRTY-SEVEN

Standing at his vantage point, Iverson had watched with cool satisfaction as the boathouse began to burn, After he'd left, with the flames solidly established, he'd propped the back door open to encourage a draft, then made his way to where he could safely monitor the end of a good day's work. From the start it had been clear that the blaze would be a beauty. So well was the fire doing its work that all his careful cover-up plans seemed to be superfluous: the only thing left to investigate was going to be a big pile of ash and some bones.

However, as he settled down to watch, something unexpected happened: a figure came bolting down the cliff path, stopped at the boathouse, yelled out, then rushed inside. Iverson recognized Fitz's fishing companion, Con, and cursed the improbable chance that had brought the kid on the scene. But the flames were growing fast. When no one reappeared immediately, he began to relax. Two roast chickens for the price of one was okay by him.

Then other people appeared, a man and a woman, and it all swiftly went to ratshit. The man, a powerful looking bastard, followed the first fool into the flames. By now the place was blazing fiercely, yet by some improbable miracle both men reappeared, bearing between them an unmistakable burden. "Shit!" Iverson breathed, a sublimely inadequate word to express his feelings.

Transfixed, he watched all three newcomers carry the victim out onto the safety of the dock. His only hope now was that the fucking Samaritans would discover their efforts to have been in vain, that they'd risked their idiot lives to rescue a corpse. He moved from behind the cover of his rock to get a better view. His consternation grew as he watched the pantomime on the dock. Soon the woman, leaned down and hugged the old man, while the big guy stepped back with a stupid-ass grin. And then—then the kid, Con, was standing up and pointing . . .

Pointing straight at HIM.

Iverson was so dumbfounded that he froze, out in the open—he belatedly realized—standing in the firelight like a beacon.

The pointing kid yelled. It was the weirdest sound, not fear, or shock, more like a predator's scream. Then he was charging along the dock like a madman, his purpose unmistakable. The little shitbag was coming for him.

Caught between surprise and amusement, Iverson nonetheless knew he had to get out of there. There was only one practical direction of retreat, so he started jogging swiftly along the beach. Beyond that rock outcrop fifty yards ahead was plenty of cover, a mess of logs and rubble, then woods into which he could swiftly vanish.

But before he reached the outcrop, which he had to pass to be in the clear, his feet splashed into water. "Shit!" he said again. He hadn't taken into account the tide, which had risen to the full during the evening. There was no retreat this way—unless he cared to swim.

He became aware of something else: the banshee yell of the kid was increasing at an alarming rate. Turning, he could see the lunatic figure approaching at a dead run. Con's feet thrust into the pebbly sand, spurting it back with manic force. His face was a mask-like rictus. In his hand was a jagged rock.

At the sight of this apparition, a lesser man might have lost his nerve. But Iverson stood his ground. As the racing fury approached, he remained perfectly still. Then, at the last moment, he stepped aside, letting his assailant's momentum provide half the force for the vicious punch that he delivered to the side of his head.

Con spun, crashed, and lay still. Now the only sound was the background roar of the burning boathouse.

Iverson made a swift calculation. Since the others were still occupied on the dock, his best escape route now was the cliff path. The entrance to that would soon be blocked by the fall of the building, which would be dandy—but only if he got to the path first.

Iverson paused just long enough to give his would-be attacker a vicious kick, then he began to run.

THIRTY-EIGHT

Con was halfway down the dock before Hal realized what was happening. Even then it took more precious seconds to comprehend the boy's full purpose. "Con!" Hal yelled. "Con, let it go! STOP!"

He might as well have been trying to command the tide.

Hal started to run, but as soon as he put his weight on his damaged ankle, it buckled, sending a flood of agony up the leg and almost throwing him into the sea. By the time he'd recovered, Con was off the dock and sprinting along the beach. Despite his discomfort, Hal felt icy wonder at the swiftly unfolding scene: the avenger moving with uncanny speed, never letting up on his outlandish cries, pausing only long enough to scoop up a big rock.

"Oh, shit!" Hal cried. "God, Con—don't do it!"

But he needn't have worried, at least about that. Con's target turned in plenty of time, sidestepped and downed his would-be assailant with a single vicious blow. The reversal was so fast it was almost comical. After Con fell, he lay still, passion apparently no match for highly competent evil.

The entire sequence had taken mere seconds, hardly longer than it had taken Hal to recover his balance. Then, as soon as the tables were turned, Iverson was on the move again, this time toward the boathouse. Apparently, he meant to make his escape by the cliff path.

That realization fired Hal with new resolve. He was less than half Iverson's distance from the path; despite his injury, he might be able to cut the villain off. He began to hobble along the dock, going as fast as he could. The pain was bad, but he ignored it, then forgot it entirely as he neared his destination.

Soon he began to feel radiant heat. The dock was dangerously close to the blazing boathouse. By now flames ruled the entire structure, consuming the shore end that was still standing. Soon that too would crash, blocking the cliff path and destroying the nearby dock. He had to hustle.

Putting on a painful spurt, he managed to reach the interception point seconds before Iverson. The man was racing in diagonally, paying Hal no heed, intent only on reaching the path. If he got there first, it would be game over. In a last desperate effort, Hal began to hop, covering the final yards in three ungainly bounds.

Simultaneously, Iverson leaped onto the dock, ducked and twisted in a furious attempt to reach the path . . . close but not reachable.

One option remained. Planting both feet, Hal launched himself in an all-or-nothing rugby tackle. If lucky, he might just grab hold of *something*; if not, he'd kiss the deck and Iverson would be gone.

His clutching fingers snagged one of the fast-pumping knees. The legs thrashed, a heel cracked against his Hal's chest. But the quarry's forward momentum was slowed. After a wild struggle, during which Hal managed somehow to tighten his hold, the man finally came down.

The impact made Iverson's legs jerk out of Hal's grasp. A violent kick cracked his forehead, sending a shock wave down his spine. But he somehow managed to grab a foot and give it a sharp twist. That triggered a sense-memory of long-ago stage fights, which rescued him from confusion. He twisted Iverson's foot again. Then, when the man's other leg drew back to kick, Hal punched savagely at the exposed crotch.

Iverson gave a low-pitched squawk, followed by a huge in-suck of breath. In the firelight, the whites of his eyes gleamed pale above the gaping *O* of his mouth. Hal used that moment to launch himself forward, pinning the other man to the dock.

At that point, had he been as experienced—and ruthless—as his opponent, he might have finished things; some solid punches while the man was helpless could have done the job. Lacking the killer instinct, he waited too long. Iverson heaved violently, bucking off his attacker. Hal rolled away and before he could recover, Iverson lashed a bone-jarring jab at his head. The blow only half-connected, which probably saved Hal from being knocked out. But a stage fight it definitely was not: the impact sent an electric pulse from jaw to brain, causing a shower of stars, plus a roaring in his ears louder than the nearby inferno.

Before he had time to rally, Iverson was on his feet. Hal was now sprawled across the dock, blocking the escape route. As Iverson edged around him, he again tried to grab for the legs. This time the move was anticipated. A boot kicked him smartly in the shoulder. There was a crack as something parted. A red haze flooded his vision, barely allowing him to see Iverson backing off. In the glow of the fire, the man's face was an ugly mask of triumph.

Hal made to rise, but couldn't. When he tried to push himself off, his shoulder screamed in protest and he fell back.

Iverson snarled and turned away. Now he had a clear route to escape. As Hal watched helplessly, the man bounded towards the cliff path—but stopped. He picked up something and came back.

Hal's clearing vision showed Iverson holding a fat driftwood club. He gasped and began to scramble crablike away. But behind him the situation was worse. Flames had now taken firm hold on the dock. In trying to escape Iverson, he was retreating into the fire.

Hal's predicament was not lost on his attacker. Club raised, he paused, leering satisfaction. Hal could either have a roasted butt or a smashed skull, either way was fine with him.

There was a moment of absolute stillness—but what happened next was completely un-anticipated: out of the darkness, swift and silent, came an apparition.

Hal had an instant to register Con.

Iverson, however, saw nothing. Con was on the dock and launching himself before the other man knew what was happening. Under the first impact, the club went flying. Caught off balance, Iverson staggered in the direction of the boathouse. As he neared what was left of the doorway—which looked like the hatch of a furnace—he managed to stop, desperately trying to regain balance and reverse his trajectory.

He almost succeeded. But then Con came at him again, his expression as serene and empty as an avenging angel's. Then came the impact. This time Iverson anticipated. His fist lifted to defend himself, as he'd done so well before. But now he seemed to inhabit a different time-continuum—Con moving normally but he in slow motion—so he'd barely begun to move before Con connected. Strong as he was, Iverson could not withstand the momentum. He gave a grunt and staggered toward the boathouse door, seemingly fused to his assailant, who kept running and shoving, like a tough little tug pushing a liner.

Hal could no longer see Con's face, since the boy's head was buried in his opponent's chest: a last, fatal embrace. He did, however, catch a glimpse of Iverson. In the raw glow of the flames, the man's expression was of pure amazement.

Then the time-snapshot shattered. The conjoined pair catapulted through the boathouse door and kept going—back—*back*—until the fire was a corona about them, then part of them, then replacing them . . . a searing flash.

And they were gone.

A moment later, in a lava-like cascade of sparks, the last of the building came down.

Hal barely had time to roll off the dock.

Doubtless he would have followed the others into eternity, had it not been for the blessedly high tide.

THIRTY-NINE

The building might have been in Toronto or New York. Though small by comparison to structures in those cities, it was every bit as sleek, a fitting part of the mini-metropolis emerging from once-sleepy Victoria. The offices of PacificCon occupied the top floor, overlooking the Inner Harbor with its ring of new hotels and condos, many of which had been developed by that company,

Hal Bannatyne, with one arm in a sling and his free hand holding a walking stick got a few stares on his way up in the elevator. At the PacificCon reception desk, the girl gave him a look of half-recognition; as an actor, he had a familiar enough face to get that reaction often. Saving her from speculation, he said, "Hi, I'm Hal Bannatyne. To see Mr Smithson. I don't have an appointment, but he's an old friend."

"Oh yes, Mr. *Bannatyne*!" the receptionist said; she was a poised twenty-five, with flawless skin and a severe hairstyle that did little to blunt her good looks. "Of course, the actor! That's right, I saw you."

"Really?"

"No, I mean—*saw you*—just nearby, shooting a movie. I was there the day you fell on your behind." She giggled, then indicated his stick. "Sorry! Did it happen again?"

"Not quite!" It was interesting that someone who'd witnessed the accident that had begun this small saga was now playing a part at the conclusion. It had a bookend quality, a wry elegance of connectivity which he might once have thought of as fate. Now it just seemed ironic. "Is your boss in?" he said.

The girl smiled. "I'll check. You said you were friends?"

"Yeah—went to school together."

"Really? Cool! Just a minute . . ."

She picked up a phone and spoke to someone. After a brief conversation, she put it down again, looking surprised. "What?" Hal said.

"Mister Smithson's coming out. I never knew him do that before. Please, Mr Bannatyne, before you go in . . ."

"Yes?"

"Can I get your autograph?"

Presently, a nearby door opened and Vince appeared. His big grin froze when he took in Hal's appearance.

"Jesus, man! What happened? You look like something out of a James Bond movie."

Hal, who'd expected to feel anger at the sight of the one who'd caused so much pain, instead felt perplexed. Of course, Vince could have no idea of his personal involvement in the drama at Cowichan Bay. But seeing him standing there, mouth hanging comically, for all the world like a regular civilized person, was pretty surreal—like much that had been happening lately. Considering these matters earlier, he'd realized that not only was life often stranger than fiction, but his own life seemed lately to be becoming odder—and more dangerous—than the roles he played.

God, he hoped this wasn't going to become a pattern.

"What happened to me was no movie," he said quietly. "But it *is* why I'm here. I thought you might like to hear about it."

Vince frowned, then he gave an immaculately tailored shrug. "Come to provide your old bud with a little entertainment?"

"You could say that."

"Why?"

"It's something you need to hear."

"No kidding? Okay—shoot!"

"I think we should be alone."

"Alone!" Vince gave an amused glance at the receptionist. "Wow—always the performer, eh?"

"I'm not performing now, believe me."

"Really?" The man's geniality was an increasingly thin mask. "I've got a few minutes, I guess. Why don't you come inside?"

VINCE'S OFFICE WAS a glass-walled corner overlooking James Bay and the mountain-laced panorama of the Strait of Juan de Fuca. It had thick broadloom, a huge slab of red cedar for a desk, a computer, some comfortable chairs, a small bar, an Emily Carr painting on one wall, and little else.

Vince waved Hal to a chair and moved to the bar, where he fetched two bottles of mineral water. "Now I'm intrigued," he said, opening the bottles and handing one to Hal. "What *did* happen? You really look a mess."

Hal settled himself gingerly, his cracked collarbone and badly sprained foot making the process awkward. He accepted the water and drank. Only then did he realize how dry his mouth had become. "I was in a fire."

Rather than taking a chair, Vince perched atop his desk with his legs crossed, which gave him the appearance of an Old World tailor. The contrast of this eccentricity to the grim reality of the man was unnerving. "A fire?" Vince repeated. "Bummer! How did it happen?"

"I thought perhaps you could help me there."

Vince did a double take. "Come again?"

"Never mind. I'll explain later." Hal put down the water bottle and picked up his walking stick, passing it absently from hand to hand. "First I've got a question for you. It's about another fire, one that happened in Nanaimo a couple of years back. I wasn't here, but someone told me about it."

"Really! Go on."

"This blaze involved an eco-activist and his family. Seems they were burned alive one night in their home: a property that had stood in the way of a major development, which was then able to proceed. Sound familiar?"

Vince, in his tailor pose, was as still as an ornament. "Who told you this?"

"Not important. At first, I didn't realize that the outfit involved was yours: PacificCon. I only recently made the connection."

The small man nodded slowly. "Okay—yes—now you mention it, I do vaguely remember something like that. A tragic accident, which horrified everyone. That we were able to pick up the property was fortunate for the company. But, naturally, no one would wish to profit from such circumstances."

"Naturally." Hal agreed, continuing quietly, "So you're saying you had nothing to do with having that fire set?"

Vince broke his tailor pose and swung off the desk. "*What*? What the fuck kind of question is that?"

Hal changed hands with his stick. "Simple enough. I'm asking if you had the Nanaimo place torched, so you could—how did you put it the other night?—get your land parcel together. What do you say, old friend?"

The friend's face was very white. His nostrils flared as he took a small snorting breath. "You've got to be shittin' me, man. Either you're crazy or this is a sick joke."

He was good, Hal thought, no doubt about it. But pique at being rumbled could easily masquerade as the anger of someone unjustly accused, so the guy didn't need to be that much of an actor. "It's no joke, Vince. I remember from the old days that you weren't one to mess with. But the Nanaimo thing isn't really why I'm here. That's just background to the real story. That concerns *another* fire, the one I was in the other night—in Maple Bay."

Vince's expression drifted from anger to caution. "Maple Bay?"

"Yeah! Maybe you heard about it on the news: the fire on the Trail Property?"

His companion was very still. He'd been standing over Hal, not exactly threatening, but in a stance that bristled with ire. Slowly he backed off, a slim silhouette against the glass-walled sky. "What do you know about that?"

"I just told you, I was in it!"

"So you did."

"I also had a tussle with the guy who set the fire: the character I met at your party, actually. Penney, I think you called him. Except up in Cowichan Bay he was calling himself Iverson. That's how I connected all this together."

Vince didn't move a muscle. With the light behind him, it was hard to see his expression. But the silence fairly hummed with tension. After a long time, he said. "I don't know what you're talking about."

"Yeah, that's about right."

"What?"

"What I thought you'd say. It's okay. I didn't expect anything different. I'm sure you've got your ass thoroughly covered. And I'm not naïve enough to think you'd admit anything. I can't nail you, Vince. Probably no one can. Not yet, anyway. So I'm going to have to settle for something different."

Vince did a sidling movement away from the window. Significantly, he now seemed uninterested in any attempt at denial. He flicked a nervous glance at Hal's stick. "What's that supposed to mean?"

Hal chucked. "Oh—you think I might beat up on you? Sweet thought, but hardly practical. I did come here to fuck with you, man. You can bet on it. But not that way."

"So what did you have in mind?"

"To give you information."

"*What*?"

"Starting with the answer to a question that I'm sure's been bugging the heck out of you: why haven't you heard from your goon, Penney? Answer: he's dead. Burned to a crisp in the fire he set himself—in Fitz Trail's boathouse."

Vince inhaled a sharp breath.

"More important, the guy who was *supposed* to die in the fire—didn't. Thanks to the actions of a certain brave young man—though I'm happy to say I also had a hand in it—Fitz was saved. He's alive and well—and ornery as ever."

Vince moved in a pace. "Motherfucker! Why the crap are you doing this? What did I ever do to you?"

"Nothing, old buddy. It's what *you've* been doing that we're talking about. So let's stick to the point, eh? That means more information for you. Best for last."

"So get on with it."

"A pleasure. Today Fitz Trail signed over his property—the one you'd set your sick little heart on—into a trust. Upon his death—*whenever that happens*—the place will pass to the Cowichan Valley Regional Authority. For a park. To be named in honor of two friends."

There was a long silence. Vince breathed, "Why?"

"As a memorial. One was lost in the fire, the other at sea."

"No, asshole, why did he have to do that? We offered the idiot millions."

"He didn't *want* millions. All Fitz needed was to be left alone. The trust will make sure that happens."

"You think?"

"Buddy, I *know*! Vince, you may be a treacherous shit, but you're a realist. You know there's no point in messing with someone if it won't achieve anything. And now it won't. The old man's given over control. He couldn't change his mind if he wanted. And after he's gone, the family won't have anything to sell. I'm here to make sure you understand that completely. Do you?"

"Fuck you!"

"I'll take that as a 'yes.' So, that's about it—except for one thing . . ."

Hal heaved himself to his feet. Even hunched over, he towered over the other man. He lifted his stick, then extended his arm slowly so that the tip came to rest on Vince's chest.

Vince didn't move. His pale eyes dropped to the stick, which, though hardly making contact, seemed to hold him transfixed.

"If this was a movie script," Hal said quietly, "now would be the point I beat the crap out of you. But, that'd just be playing into your hands. And squishing bugs never did turn me on. Vince, I don't kid myself that you give a damn about what you've done, or even that I know you've done it. Just so long as no one can nail you, eh?

"But one thing you *do* care about, I know: that map you showed me with all the stuff you've developed says it all. You're obsessed. You've just got to be the best, have the lot, litter the world with shrines to your ego. But now there's one place on that map that will always stay yellow. Fucking forever! And you'll always know you lost, beaten by an old man you couldn't buy and couldn't scare, who showed you up for the bastard you are. He'll always have that property and know that when he goes it'll be safe. Guys like you will never get their greasy hands on it. That's his legacy. And what's yours? A pile of overpriced junk that's making this island look like a poor relation of California."

Hal surveyed Vince, still staring cold-eyed from the other end of the walking stick. Instead of performing the action that once would have given him huge satisfaction—cracking the prick's skull—he used the stick to propel the small man firmly backward, at last depositing him into one of the plush chairs.

"*This* isn't much of a script either," Hal said wryly. "It sure wouldn't make it at the box office. No big drama. No bloody retribution. But it's got to be a hell of a lot better than the one you had in mind."

Without another word he clumped out of the office, feeling relieved and frustrated and ridiculous and, ultimately, satisfied. There was no feeling of catharsis, let alone justice. But the meeting had done its job and would have to do.

Reaching his car, he performed the Houdini-like feat of inserting his battered frame into the driver's seat. Fortunately, the transmission was automatic and his right foot was uninjured. With that and one good arm he could reasonably navigate back to Maple Bay.

He'd just started the engine when his cell rang. It was in a pocket opposite his good arm, so it took time and a brace of curses to extract the thing.

"Hello?"

"Hal, laddie—where the hell have you been?"

The voice, deeply familiar yet seeming to belong to another life, was Hal's agent, Danny Feltmann. "Oh, hey—Danny." Hal said, actually needing to search momentarily for the name. "How's it going?"

"How's it *going*? Jesus Geronimo, what's happening out there? I've been trying to reach you for freaking *days*!"

"Guess my phone got switched off. Some—er—strange stuff came up."

"Yeah?" Danny laughed nastily. "You get into some of that West Coast weed?"

"Not exactly!" Hal said, thinking that if Danny knew what he *had* been into he'd really flip. "Anyway, sorry! You've got me now. What is it?"

Hal was one of Danny's best money-makers so, though he was thoroughly pissed, Danny couldn't afford to blow his cool too much. But Hal could almost hear teeth grinding as Danny said, "What it *is*, matey, is the voice-over gig. Remember that little number?"

"Oh, right . . . have they sorted out their legal problems?"

"Yeah—duh!!!—two fucking *days* ago! And they've been trying to rouse you ever since!"

The voice-over gig. Work. The real world. Such things still actually existed. Since the start of what had turned out to be the strangest of adventures, the rest of his life had been put on hold. Yet as he talked to Danny, that life seemed hardly real at all. And when he finally broke the connection, he felt as if he'd touched something irrelevant and not quite clean.

Nonetheless, the fact remained that he had to be at the studio to start work first thing in the morning. Considering his injuries, it was lucky the job required voice only. But if he was going to get to

Vancouver in time to check into his hotel, he'd need to start for the
ferry right away. No time even to return to Maple Bay to pick up his
things, let alone say goodbye. With a sigh of irritation—masking a
deeper regret—Hal dialed Mattie's number.

"Hello?"

That single word evoked such a powerful image of his friend he
could almost feel her presence beside him. "Hi, it's Hal. Mattie, I did
what I said I was going to do."

"With the man from PacificCon?"

"No way he'll ever admit to anything, of course. But I told him
about the land trust—and didn't give in to the temptation to bust his
ass—and he won't bother you guys again."

"That's wonderful. Thank you."

Her voice had an odd quality, but he ignored that as he continued. "Look, Mattie, I'm sorry, but my agent just called. The lawsuit's
settled and they need me back at work first thing tomorrow . . ." He
explained the situation and she seemed to understand. But as they
continued to talk, he making assurances that when the job was done
he'd be returning, it became impossible to ignore her strange under-
tone: something that finally registered as bemusement. "Mattie!" he
said at last. "What is it? Is Fitz okay?"

"Fitz? Oh—yes—he's fine."

"So . . . What's wrong?"

She didn't answer. The line was so silent that he thought he'd
lost the connection. As he was about to switch off, she said abruptly,
"Hal?"

"Yes. I'm here. What's going on?"

"I'm not completely sure yet," Mattie said, her voice low and flat.
"But it's possible we may have found my son."

FORTY

At the bottom of the cliff, where the boathouse had stood for nearly a century, nothing remained but dunes of gray-white ash, drifting through the charred hulks of the largest beams. Around the edge, the vestiges of pilings sprouted from the beach like rotted teeth. In the midst of the desolation was a cleared area sporting two flagged stakes. What had been in that place was long gone.

Surrounding all was a sagging line of police tape.

Hal descended the path, going only far enough to get a clear view. This evening was the first time he'd been there since the night of the fire. That was now long in the past, but returning still made him queasy. When fire trucks had finally arrived, the flames had at least been prevented from spreading beyond the immediate vegetation. But it still looked like a war zone down there, the effect enhanced by the sour ash smell that lingered.

Hal paused. His shoulder was on the mend and he no longer needed a stick, but the remaining stiffness in his ankle was a grim reminder—if any were needed—of the horror that had taken place below. Yet, he'd been the lucky one. Two others had perished, one tragically, the other by some blind twist of justice, while yet another had been rescued only just in time. An extraordinary accumulation of events had reached its climax on that fateful night. The result had been terrible, though not in the manner intended. Also the outcome had clear aspects of triumph, for those who'd set the dark wheels in motion had been thwarted.

Yet nothing that had happened had prepared anyone for the final surprise. Gazing at the ruins, Hal could see the focal point of that revelation clearly: higher up the beach, a short distance from where the two had died—was a third marker.

NEARLY THREE WEEKS had passed. The remains of the two known victims had been retrieved and enquiries set in motion. But since all proof of the cause of the fire—along with the culprit—had been destroyed, the facts known to the family were to the police mere speculation. There was no proof of any cause other than accident or negligence. That scenario, of course, didn't take into account the remains of Penney-cum-Iverson. Hal had volunteered his knowledge of the man's link to PacificCon, but with few illusions as to what it would achieve.

As to the fire's intended victim, Fitz Trail had recovered well enough from his ordeal. But the tragedy—especially the death of Con—had taken a heavy toll. When Hal had come up with the idea of putting his land into a trust, he'd agreed at once, desperate to protect his family from further threat. But the heart had gone out of him. The blaze that had taken his young friend, his carvings, and his beloved boathouse had sadly dimmed his own fire. Much more than lives and property had been lost on that dreadful night.

The funeral for Con had taken place after Hal's return to work. But he was told it had been well attended, the mourners including his brother and Stephanie. Con's mother—escorted by Mattie, who'd been largely responsible for the arrangements—was like a pale ghost. She'd been sober since the night of the fire and, incredibly, the loss of her son seemed to be the reason. But even Mattie, who'd lost a child of her own, could provide little comfort. The gaunt, hollow-eyed woman was as withdrawn as if she herself were already on the other side of the grave.

Though no insurance claim had been filed on the boathouse, an investigator arrived anyway and started to poke about in the ashes. He was the one who made the final discovery.

A third body.

The mummified remains had apparently been there for a long time. Though exposed by the fire, they'd been largely protected from its fury. Accompanying artifacts had provided identification: Brian Trail.

Not lost at sea, but concealed beneath the boathouse. Not drowned, but murdered.

HAL STOOD STILL on the cliff path, while evening slowly gathered the scene into merciful shadow. The charred remains had revealed at last the answer to the biggest puzzle of all: what had happened to Mattie's son? But with that had come new questions: *Why*? And, more important, *Who*?

Closing his eyes, Hal could picture the boathouse so vividly it was hard to believe that it wasn't still there. He recalled the strange feelings he'd had, almost as if the place had been trying to tell him something. But of course that was nonsense. He would not let fanciful thinking divert him from what was most important, the ordeal of Mattie. Being stuck in Vancouver during the mind-bending discovery had been torture. Talking to his friend on the phone had seemed to be of little help. He didn't even know if when he got back to the Island things would be any better. But he'd been determined to try.

Not surprisingly, Mattie had not wanted to view the scene of devastation again, but he'd felt compelled to look at it one last time. Now it was done, what had been accomplished? Apart from the revival of bad memories, not much.

Back at the house, he discovered Mattie at the window, gazing across the bay in her habitual position of waiting: for the son who'd never been out there anyway. "You saw it?" she said, as he entered.

"Didn't go too close, I'm afraid."

"I understand. Sometimes I feel I have to go down there, to remind myself where poor Brian was hidden away all these years. Other times I think I never want to go near it again. More often though, I just want to get away . . ." She turned back from staring at the ocean. "I'm sorry, Hal!"

"For what?"

"For being so . . . for not being able to talk when you were in Vancouver. I know you wanted to help."

"It's okay."

"I wouldn't have been surprised if you hadn't come back. But I'm very glad you did."

"So am I."

"Mattie . . . ?"

"I know. There's still one thing we still haven't talked about. You didn't ask on the phone and I couldn't bring it up. I still find it hard to even think about . . ."

"Who did it?"

Mattie nodded resignedly. "Yes! The police questioned everyone for ages. It was dreadful. I don't believe they thought anyone in the family was responsible. But who else was there? Well, there was one . . ."

"Con?"

"Yes. But when Brian disappeared, Con was in Vancouver . . ."

"Yes. Fitz told me."

Mattie shook her head, sinking down the kitchen table. "Oh, dear, poor Brian!"

Hal pulled a chair in beside her. "You don't need to talk now ."

"Actually, I do. Now you're here, I finally can. Is that all right?"

"Of course."

"Over the years, I never stopped wondering what deep, lonely place had taken him. Now that I at least know where he is, it's a strange sort of relief. And when all this is over, we can have a funeral. A proper burial. Brian can finally have some peace: or at least the rest of us can. We never held a memorial before, did I tell you?"

"No. I want to be there this time."

"I'm glad."

"But Mattie . . ."

"I know, there's still the other thing: I saw Brian sail away, so how did he end up under the boathouse? But if he was—killed—somewhere else, how did he get back here?"

"Could he have come back later?"

"Without his boat?"

"I see what you mean. Did the police have any ideas?"

Mattie shook her head. "They've been so busy trying to understand all the rest, I think that the discovery of Brian threw them for a complete loop. It's five years since he vanished, yet I get the feeling the police think *that* and the fire are somehow connected."

"Could they be?"

Mattie shook her head. "Five years ago, the idea of anyone wanting this property hadn't even come up. Nothing was going on back then that could account for whatever happened to Brian. When he disappeared, no one was here but me. The last I saw of him he was sailing away, and two days later his boat was found wrecked. But now we find he wasn't lost in the sea after all. You know, I sometimes felt— sort of *close* to him when I was in that old boathouse. Who could have known that he really *was* so near. Goodness, my poor darling."

Tears were finally flowing. Hal longed to put a comforting arm about her, but that felt too much like an intrusion. So he kept still and watched her and waited. After a while he said, "So where's Fitz?"

Mattie wiped her eyes. "I don't know exactly. Lately he's taken to going for long walks. Quite apart from Con, he's lost without his beloved boathouse. Though we know it was that terrible man who started the fire, Fitz still blames himself. He's given up smoking, as a sort of a penance, I think. Though I'm not sure for what. Like me, he's relieved that Brian's been found. But since it's murder—there, I've finally said the word—not knowing who's responsible is driving him a little crazy."

"You too, I'd think."

Mattie thought for a while. "Me not so much. Maybe it should. Perhaps after a while it will. But right now I'm just content to know where he is. Does that sound awful?"

"Hell, no! When something so extraordinary happens, I think everyone's got to deal with it their own way. Just so as you're coping. That's all that matters."

Mattie smiled wanly. "Coping! Yes, I guess that's what I'm doing—though sometimes it doesn't feel like it." She reached across and took his hand. "But you being here helps a lot. Thanks for coming back, Hal."

Hal nodded, trying not to show the pleasure that her touch gave him. "You're very welcome. Least I could do."

"How long can you stay?"

As long as you want, was the phrase that came to his mind. But he said, "Well, my work's finished out here. But I don't have anything lined up right away. So—when did you plan the . . ."

"Brian's funeral? As soon as Jennifer can get back from France."

"Well, at least until then."

"Good. Thank you." Mattie rose, pulling him to his feet. She moved in, placing her body squarely against his own without embarrassment, stretched up, and kissed him. The embrace was not sexy, nor yet something appropriate from a sister, rather the frank contact of two lovers who in some sense had never been apart. Finally, she disengaged and stood back with a smile. "You hungry?"

"Actually, no. I had something to eat on the boat."

"Okay, so let's have a glass of wine and sit a while. And then . . ."

"Then?"

"Then you can help me with one last thing."

FORTY-ONE

The house stood alone at the end of a wooded lane running off the Genoa Bay Rd. It had its own view of the water, but this was largely obscured by unkempt greenery that had grown up all around. The building was not as old as the Trail house, but large, built in the faux-cottage style favoured by well-off British émigrés after the Second World War. Time and neglect had turned it into a peeling ghost of its former glory, echoing the sad decline of its owner.

At the gate was a FOR SALE sign.

When Mattie rang the bell, there was a brief pause, followed by a rattling of the inside latch. Then the door was opened with surprising energy. Revealed was a small woman whom Hal had little difficulty recognizing as Con's mother; she had the same high forehead and dark, quizzical eyes. By all accounts, Claudia Ryan was younger than Mattie, but looked twenty years her senior. She was thin, her hair white, and she had the mottled, puffy features of the dedicated drinker. She was wearing a shirt and jeans, which hung like prison drab from her angular frame. In her mouth—at an incongruously jaunty angle—was a fat little cigarillo. Her glance darted swiftly between the newcomers: she was obviously cold sober.

"Mattie!" Claudia said, her voice cultivated and incongruously deep. "I'm so glad you could come."

"Well, of course!" Mattie replied. "You don't think I'd let you leave without saying goodbye."

Hal was introduced, and they entered, Con's mother ushering them in with a manner that—if not exactly cheery—was clearly welcoming. Hal recalled Mattie's account of Claudia's recent coldness and withdrawal, and they exchanged a glance of surprise.

The dark-paneled hall was cluttered chaos—furniture, ornaments, books, and packing cases competing for space, with hardly room to pass. They inched their way through a similarly dismembered living room to the kitchen, which as yet had been spared the rude winds of departure.

As with the Trail house, the windows looked out over the ocean, or would have done, but for the rampant outdoor foliage. The room was sparsely neat: table, four kitchen chairs, clear counters with appliances and dishes in a rack. On the stove was a simmering kettle, nearby a teapot, cups and saucers, and a plate of digestive biscuits. The table was bare except for two items: a wicked-looking kitchen knife and a full bottle of Johnny Walker Black Label whisky.

Claudia picked up the latter objects and with a grimace put them aside. "Reminders! If I open one, I may as well cut my throat with the other. Maybe it'll work. The jury's still out. Will you have tea?"

They both accepted and settled at the kitchen table. From what Hal had heard of past behavior, it seemed that a radical change had occurred in Claudia Ryan. A short time ago she'd lost her only son and apparently had exhibited all the expected reactions of shock and grief. But now that phase was definitely over. Though they'd just met, Hal felt that this was not just a persona donned for company. Physically ravaged she might be, but mentally Claudia seemed very clear, as if she'd turned some sort of corner.

After they'd chatted, a little awkwardly at first, Claudia said quietly, "Mattie, isn't it nice to think that at this very moment our boys may be together—in some place we can't begin to imagine—goofing off just like they used to?"

"It's certainly a . . . a pleasant thought."

Claudia smiled, and sipped her tea. "But it's just as likely that they're nowhere at all. That they're both gone into nothing and that's an end to it. But either way—at least for Con—it's for the best."

Mattie looked startled. "Claudia, what are you saying? Surely you don't mean that Con's better . . . ?"

"Dead?" The other woman sighed then deliberately relit her cigarillo. "I used to think that Con's life being so messed up was his parents' fault: his dad's for running off, mine for becoming a drunk. But none of that seemed to matter when he was young. Then he was happy as a boy could be. And clever! Good grades at school, as you well know. And all that lovely stuff he wrote; poems and stories. You said he could be a real writer. Remember?"

Mattie nodded palely, "Of course."

"But after Brian disappeared, everything changed. Con just wasn't—*right* anymore. I don't know if he blamed himself. For not being there. For not being able even to *find* his friend. But afterwards, something just went out of him . . .

"Me being a lush didn't help, of course. He was disgusted with me and I can't blame him. Thank God he at least had your family. After losing your own boy, I sometimes wondered how you could even bear to look at Con. But you did, and it was the only good thing in his life: hanging out at your place, fishing with Fitz, just being around where he and Brian used to play. I don't know what he'd have done without that."

The others watched silently as Claudia extinguished her cigarillo and poured more tea. Finally she looked directly at Mattie. "Dear, I don't know what happened with the boathouse fire, how it started, or who was to blame. If other people were involved, I certainly hope they're punished. But one thing I *do* know: helping to save your dad would have made Con very proud. I don't mean to sound sentimental, but I know he'd have considered the swap—his life for Fitz's—a fair bargain. And if he'd also known the fire would help find his friend . . . I don't think he'd have asked for more."

The room was very still. Mattie, with her cup half to her lips, had tears in her eyes. Hal felt a lump in his own throat.

"As for my drinking," Claudia continued, "who really knows. Maybe it's just shock that's keeping me sober right now. But, believe me, I'm going to try like hell to make it stick. Mattie, you lost a son *and* a husband, but you didn't give up. You just—what did we used to say?—kept on trucking. Taking care of the ones who were left and being a wonderful teacher. You rebuilt your life, while I pissed mine away. I've no excuse, I was just shallow and stupid." She shook her head sharply as Mattie made to interrupt. "No! It's true. If there's any hope for me, I must start by being totally honest.

"And now I know I have a simple choice: either to follow my son into the dark, or try—even though I'm a beat-up old wreck—to follow your example, Mattie: *do* something with what's left of my life. As you know, I've always had money. Too much for my own good, probably. If I'd had to get out and hustle my buns, maybe there'd have been less time for self-indulgence. Anyway, I'm going to try my best to make a new start, Not exciting but *better*. And AA full time, of course, to keep me on track. I've got a sister in Kelowna who had a stroke last year. I'm going to stay with her awhile. Give her some help, if I can. Then I'll try to figure how I can use this damn money of mine to do some good."

Claudia rose, poured more tea, sipped, then made a face. "Damn, I hate this stuff. But I'm going to grow to like it again if it kills me." She moved around the table to Mattie. "So that's it, dear. I wanted to say goodbye and thank you for all you've done. But mostly I wanted to make sure you understood what I know: Con's death was *his* choice: whatever the circumstances, he wouldn't have had it any other way."

After that there was little more to be said. Mattie told Claudia about the plans for Brian's funeral, but Claudia made her apologies and begged off. She was leaving for her sister's tomorrow and was unlikely to be back. On their way out, she asked them to wait and hurried upstairs. Presently, she returned, carrying a small bundle, which she handed to Mattie.

"Con's old notebooks. Came across them while I was packing. English compositions, mostly. I thought you might like them."

Mattie looked pleased. She took the books, extending the move into a hug, so strong that the thin woman gasped and laughed. Having planted a kiss on the white hair, she finally backed off.

They said goodbyes and left. As they swung the car around to head home, Claudia Ryan was still standing by the peeling front door, thin arm raised in mute farewell.

FORTY-TWO

They arrived back to find unexpected activity. Lights were burning in the dining room and busy sounds were coming from that direction. Entering quietly, they discovered Fitz hard at work. A tarp had been thrown across the table and upon this rested a thick chunk of log. The sounds they'd heard were of mallet on chisel. Already a considerable pile of shavings had been created, flowing from the table onto the floor. Sensing their presence, Fitz glanced up briefly.

"Doing Brian's boat again." he said, without pausing in his labors. "Dandy piece of cedar, eh?"

"Yes!" Mattie replied. "Where did you get it?"

"Hauled it out of the woods a while back. Hadn't got round to cutting it up, so I hadn't yet taken it down to the . . ." He trailed off. Since the fire, the boathouse was not easily mentioned. "Once I'd made up my mind, I couldn't wait to get started. Sorry about the mess."

"Who cares!" Mattie's eyes were shining. "I'm just glad to see you working again. I loved that boat. Of all your carvings, I think it was the best."

Hal found he could remember it vividly, the storm-swept sails and heroic figure alone at the wheel. That haunting creation, along with the rest of Fitz's work, was now ashes. Yet it still lived in the old man's mind, from which it was evidently about be reborn.

However, now there was a problem: the central premise, lone sailor bravely fighting the elements, was invalid, since Brian had not in fact been lost at sea. Unless after drowning, his body had washed up under his own boathouse—an unimaginable coincidence—the only possible conclusion was that he'd been murdered in an unknown location, his body then returned to be hidden in the one place no one would think to look.

But that was not being talked about now. Mattie must have gone over it with the police, but she'd not as yet mentioned it to Hal and he hadn't liked to bring it up. As for Fitz, since the fire he hadn't said much of anything. For now, recovery, or acceptance, or whatever was happening in his beleaguered spirit, seemed to require the re-creation of the boat carving. If that's what it took, more power to him. Life had to go on. But for Hal, who found it impossible to ignore the mystery of what had really happened to Brian, all this seemed extremely strange.

They left Fitz working and gravitated, as if by tidal pull, back to the kitchen. Outside the window, the broad sweep of the bay was fading to dark, the eastern sky laced with emerging pinpoints of stars. Mattie fetched the bottle of wine they'd started earlier and poured fresh glasses.

They sat, and some time later Mattie put on a lamp. It created a warm glow, a gentle haven in the enormous night, a place where the monsters of memory and misadventure were of diminished power. Later still, Mattie put down her glass and took Hal's hand. "Thank you," she said.

"For what?"

"Right now—tonight—just for being here."

"I wouldn't want to be anywhere else."

"I'm glad. Also for not talking about that *other*."

"You mean, what happened?"

"Yes."

"Don't you find it hard—not knowing?"

"It's been that way so long, I'm used to it. Anyway, I'm sort of swamped with relief just to have found him. Does that sound unfeeling?"

"Heavens, no! Anyway, what do I know? I can't imagine what it must be like to lose a child, so there's no way I could possibly judge. I'm just happy that both you and Fitz seem to be surviving."

She squeezed his hand and stared out into the dark. "Hal?"

"Yes."

"I want to ask you something. Probably I shouldn't, but if I don't now I'll probably never get up the nerve again. And I'll never stop wondering . . ."

"So ask!"

"I know we said that it's inevitable that our lives went the way they did. And I'm convinced that's true. But did you ever wonder what it would have been like if we . . ."

"Hadn't broken up?"

"Yes."

Hal thought for while. "To answer that," he said finally, "I have to go back to a certain day in Victoria, when I fell on my butt and looked up to see an old friend staring at me."

Mattie gave a little laugh. "I'm not sure I understand."

"Well, I recognized you instantly, you know that. My first thought was, *That's Mattie*! Then another one came right on top, though I tried to push it away, to sort of *unthink* it. And I guess I've been trying to avoid it ever since."

"What was it?"

"That letting go of you was the biggest mistake of my life."

Mattie's grip on his hand tightened, so much that it was almost painful. But on her face grew a smile of such depth and beauty that Hal would have endured any discomfort to witness it. Then she let go his hand and rose. "Dear Hal," she said quietly. "That's about the sweetest thing I ever heard. All the more so because I believe you really mean it. Now—if I don't go to bed, I think I may fall down. Goodnight."

Just like that she was gone. Hal sat in the window, sipping the last of his wine, the house silent save for the distant tap-tap of Fitz's chisel. The sound had a hypnotic quality: ancient, soothing to the spirit.

After a while he rose and headed upstairs also.

FORTY-THREE

He awoke with a start, thinking someone had called his name. The darkness of the room was split by a fuzzy bright haze, that came from the open door, which silhouetted a looming figure.

"*Hal?*"

This was not an echo from a dream, but a real voice, which emerging consciousness identified as Mattie's. Surprise, concern, and pleasure began a struggle for supremacy in the brisk run-up to his response. "Mattie—what is it?"

The figure drifted closer, and he realized that Mattie was dressed only in a nightgown. "Hal!" she whispered yet again. "Oh, God—Hal!"

The tone was so strange that any excitement he might have felt at this surprise nocturnal visit morphed into fear: *Fitz*, he thought. *Something's happened to Fitz.* Scrambling to sit up, he fumbled to turn on the bedside lamp.

"Mattie, what's the matter? Is it Fitz?"

Mattie shook her head. The light confirmed Hal's first impression of her attire—or lack of it—but she seemed unaware of this; even in a state of undress, and obviously distraught, she still retained an aura of dignity. This was enhanced by the fact that perched improbably on her shapely nose was a pair of reading glasses.

"What's the matter?" Hal said again.

Instead of replying, Mattie moved farther into the light and lifted her arm, revealing an exercise book. She held it out, her hand shaking.

The glow from the bed lamp cast her expression into sharp relief: wonder, and something more disturbing.

"*Jesus, Mattie—WHAT*?"

Mattie spoke at last, her voice a whisper. "This is Con's. One of the ones his mum gave me this afternoon. Full of old compositions. I started reading it when I went up to bed . . ."

"And?"

Mattie's eyes again locked on his own. "A lot of the exercises were graded by me. Some I even remember. But one is . . . different."

"How?"

"It was written later. A long time after Con left school, I think. It's more than just a composition. Like a real story—except . . ."

"Yes?"

"Hal, I don't think it's a *story* at all!"

"What do you mean?"

Mattie sat on the bed, forcing him to move over, and thrust the book in front of him. It was already open, folded back to the start of a section of writing. The letters were in blue ballpoint, small but legible, with a sharp, imperative quality that didn't look like the work of a young person.

Hal looked from the page to Mattie, then on impulse plucked the glasses from her face. The lenses were drug-store magnifiers and suited his own eyes just fine. Shifting the book into better light—which also necessitated putting his arm around her—he began to read . . .

FORTY-FOUR

Damn, Jack felt psyched. He'd finally found out where his dad lived and was off to Vancouver to root the old guy out.

His mum didn't know. Would have had a bird if she had. He'd fed her some bullshit about taking in a rock concert on the mainland. Not that she probably remembered. Lately she'd been bombed all the time. Totally out of it, when he went to her room to lift some green for the trip.

It was then he hit a snag. Except for chump-change, her cash supply was zilch. While tossing some juicy curses at the snoring bitch, he thought of Paul. His bud always went sailing early on Saturdays, but if he hustled he could catch him.

The quick route to Paul's pad—traveled a zillion times—was down some steps from his backyard, then a five-minute jog along the beach. Jack made it in less than that and found Paul's boat still moored at the dock. There were sounds coming from the boathouse.

"Yo, Man!" he called, heading in. "How's it hangin'?"

Paul was at the workbench, sanding something in a vise. Jack was glad to see that he was alone. He didn't need old Gramps on his ass when he was trying to mooch cash.

"Hey, freako," Paul grinned, pushing back the cruddy red baseball cap he always wore sailing. "You coming crewin' for a change?"

"Nah, dickhead!" Jack returned. "Gave that shit up for girls!"

"Yeah?" Paul sneered. "So how's that goin'? Still a hopeful virgin?"

"Like *you*, eh?"

"Whatever!" Paul took the object he'd been working on from the vise, a stout wooden handle with a narrow end to slot into the boat's rudder. He tossed it to Jack, who caught it easily. "What do you think?"

"What was the matter with it?"

"Kept working loose. Last time out I almost dunked. Should be cool now." He put the handle with some gear by the door. "Wouldn't have been such a bummer if I wasn't alone."

Jack laughed. "Yeah? Don't try that guilt shit on me, man. You fuckin' *love* sailing alone and you know it."

"Okay, maybe. But we used to have fun."

"We will again, fella—when you grow up." That was meant to be cool, but came out wrong. Jack saw the hurt in Paul's eyes and kicked himself: after all, he *had* come to beg a favor. "Sorry, guy. I just meant I don't get a kick out of it anymore."

"So why are you here, Loverboy? To tell me how you still haven't got laid?"

Jack decided to come clean. "Listen, Paulo, there's something important I've gotta do, so I come to see if I could mooch some moolah."

"Fixing to get yourself a ho?"

Jack ignored the dig. He'd wanted to tell Paul for a while about finding his father, but hadn't because he was embarrassed. Now there seemed to be no choice. "Okay!" he blurted, "if you must know, I'm going to see my dad."

That stopped Paul cold. "Your *dad*? The pisser who walked out when you were a kid?"

"That's right, yeah."

"Why would you want to see that loser?"

"I just *need* to, is all. But I'm short of cash. So I wondered—"

"Bullshit!" Paul cut in.

"*What*!"

"Why'd you want to hook up with *that* asshole. He doesn't give a fuck about you."

Jack's face grew hot. "You don't know that. And cut out that *asshole* shit. He could be a real neat old dude."

"Oh, yeah, *sure*!" Paul sneered, "And I could be fuckin' Elvis."

Jack felt furious, then it suddenly hit him: Paul didn't *have* a dad to find. He and Jack had always both been half-orphans, part of their cool bond. Now, just when they were growing apart anyway, he was doing something that Paul could never do.

His buddy was jealous.

But instead of helping, this understanding only made Jack madder. Shit, they were supposed to be friends. Paul should be happy for him. But all the prick could do was take cheap shots. Okay, two could play at that game. "Well, anyway, my dad's *alive*," he sneered. "At least *he* wasn't stupid enough to let himself get wiped out on the freakin' highway."

Right away he knew he'd blown it. What was meant as a cool retort had made him sound like an asshole. Seeing Paul's face go red with rage, he said hastily, "Hey, sorry, man! I didn't mean—"

Paul cut him off with a howl, punching Jack on the side of the head and sending him reeling. Then, before he could recover, Paul hit him again. The second blow connected with Jack's jaw and this time he hit the deck.

Stunned, Jack lay still. A violent kick brought him out of it. He turned his head to see Paul standing over him—and another kick coming. Quickly, Jack rolled away, then scrambled up. "Jesus!" he yelled. "For fuck's sake, man! Are you nuts?"

But Paul wasn't going to stop. His face was scarlet, clear to the roots of his hair. His eyes were like flames. His mouth spewed curses. His arms and legs were like robots as he came in again.

Jack backed off but was stopped by a wall. Paul was still coming, intent on murder. But by now Jack was getting it together and he knew he had to fight. As Paul rushed in, he raised his arms to block the punches, then banged a solid left to Paul's gut. It was a lucky blow, knocking out the guy's wind. Clutching his belly, Paul staggered away.

Jack knew what he had to do. He and Paul had sometimes fought, but never like this. Something really bad was going down and he had to vanish. Sidestepping Paul, he raced for the exit. He would have made it but for a wicked stroke of fate. The tiller handle, placed near the door, tripped him and he went down. He broke his fall with his arms, but before he could get up again, a body crashed onto his back, flattening him. In his ear was a deafening scream.

"*Bastard—bastard—bastard!*"

Savagely his hair was grabbed. Violently his head was jerked back then slammed down, so that his forehead crashed against the floor. It hurt like hell, but he was still conscious—and he now knew something else:

Paul really *was* trying to kill him.

This knowledge gave him new strength and allowed him to writhe out of his attacker's grip. Flexing every muscle, he threw Paul off, then punched and kicked to break free. Then he scrambled up and ran.

This time he made it outside, turning toward the beach, where he'd have a straight run for home. Gaining speed, Jack felt the first twinge of relief. He was a faster runner than Paul and once off the dock, he'd be in the clear. But leaping down meant he had to hesitate. Glancing back to make sure Paul wasn't close enough to jump him, his toe caught on something on the uneven dock. He stumbled, and for the second time went down.

But now he had a moment to think: Paul mustn't get another chance to pin him. So he twisted and rolled like a cat, all four limbs extended for protection.

Good thinking, because the crazy guy was almost on him. Paul yelled and leaped, hands clutching for the throat. But Jack was ready. As the body came down, he took the weight on the soles of his feet. He then used all the strength of his legs to throw Paul off, flipping him clear off the side of the dock.

For a moment Jack lay panting. Then he jumped up and backed off, expecting Paul to resume the attack. But nothing happened. Paul didn't appear.

Silence.

Paul must be hiding, Jack thought, waiting to nail him. Jack crept back then dropped off the other side of dock. He then worked his way to where he could see under the dock.

It was then that he realized that all his precautions had been unnecessary. His buddy was there, okay, but he wasn't going to jump anyone. Ever again.

JACK TRIED CPR, but that was a joke. You can't get someone to breathe again when their neck is busted.

When he'd approached he'd found his buddy lying on his back, eyes sightlessly staring, neck twisted like a pretzel. After falling off the dock, Paul must have landed on his head. There was neither breath nor pulse.

The guy was totally dead.

Jack felt sick. If he hadn't made that crack about Paul's dad, the fight never would have started. But how could he know that Paul would totally freak. And all *he'd* done was try to defend himself.

But who'd believe *that*? Everyone knew they used to fight, and it would look like they'd been at it again.

Oh, yeah—he was going to be charged with murder.

He had to do something. But what? Well, at least one thing was clear: he had to have time to think.

Meaning he had to hide the body,

Sickened, but made strong by fear, he forced himself to drag the thing that had once been his friend up into the dark under the boathouse, far beyond the reach of the highest tide.

Back on the dock, the first thing he saw was Paul's cap, which must have come off in the fight. He picked it up. It made him feel guilty again, but he couldn't put it down. What the fuck was he going to do now?

Then he noticed the boat.

Moments later he returned to the boathouse. He collected two things: the tiller handle that he'd tripped over, and a yellow slicker Paul often wore sailing. Then he made the boat ready. He wasn't a sailing genius like Paul, but he could manage. Casting off, and with a decent breeze to stern, he headed out into the bay.

By then he was wearing the slicker—and the red Cardinals cap.

FORTY-FIVE

Hal turned the page, but the next was blank, as was the rest of the book. Con had either been unwilling or unable to finish the account of that dreadful day: how, presumably, he'd wrecked the boat, how he'd returned and what he'd done to permanently conceal the body. All of this could only be imagined.

If one dared.

He closed the book and put it down carefully on the bed. His left arm, which had been around Mattie all the time he read, was numb. But he hardly noticed. Neither spoke for a long time.

A full moon had risen over the bay, its pale glow slanting through the window added a surreal quality to the tableau: two figures, transfixed in the wonder of awful revelation. Finally Mattie said quietly, "Poor boy!"

To whom was she referring? The survivor or the slain? Cain or Abel? For which, after all, was really which? Two young men had been lost on that long ago day: one physically, the other in just about every other way. Though not taken by the sea, at least Brian had gone quickly. Con had found no such mercy and had spent his life haunting the scene of the tragedy, till released at last by an act of fiery atonement.

Mattie was the first to move. She shifted her weight off Hal, picked up the exercise book, and drifted to the window. She gazed trancelike out at the water, which stretched away, dark and still under the moon.

How often had she stood thus, reliving the last passage of the boat she'd believed to have been manned by her son. Watching her, Hal couldn't even begin to imagine what her thoughts might be. The moon lit one side of her face, the lamp the other. The effect was ethereal. Her features looked ageless, showing no emotion.

Some time later she came back to the bed and lay down. The exercise book was still clutched in one hand. The other sought out Hal's. She lay back with eyes closed. Presently, the rhythm of her breathing changed. Hal lay still. After a while he followed her into sleep.

He awoke to discover dawn light in the window. As his eyes opened, it was as if Mattie had been waiting. She released his stiffened fingers, rolled over, and kissed him lightly. Then she left the room. Minutes later, he heard her steps pass his door and descend the stairs. Hal put on some clothes and followed.

A kettle was already simmering when he arrived in the kitchen. Two fresh mugs waited by the teapot. As she poured the tea, Mattie said, "Just before I woke I had this dream: Brian and Con walking down a long road. There wasn't much more to it than that. They were laughing at something and holding hands, but somehow their hands were *hurting*. Then I woke to find that the hurting was actually in my own hand. I was still clutching on to you, and my fingers were stiff as hell."

"Mine too. Sorry!"

Mattie smiled. "Don't be. It was a good hurt. Anyway, I think the dream was triggered by what Con's mum said: about the boys goofing off together some place. Remember?"

"Yes. Talking of her . . ." Hal indicated the exercise book, now on the kitchen table. "Do you think . . . she *knew*?"

Mattie shook her head strongly. "Absolutely not! And we never— *never* . . ."

Mattie put down her mug and grabbed the book. With decision, she flipped it open to the story they'd read, then ripped out the pages. Tossing aside the book, she looked about, her eyes finally coming to rest on the kitchen window. Beyond, sunrise streaked the sky yellow. She nodded to herself and headed for the kitchen door.

The air felt mild and sweet as Hal followed Mattie across the garden toward the ocean. Morning was growing out in the bay; fresh, new morning with the promise of a beautiful summer day.

Mattie walked to the cliff's edge. Beyond was the familiar panorama, islands and mountains and sky. The sea was calm, haunted no more by the image of the little sailboat that would never return. The beach below was silent, perhaps mourning the building that had stood sentinel for a century and the act of evil that had turned it to ashes.

Mattie still held the pages she'd torn from Con's book: the dark tale that had finally made its journey into the light. She tore them in half, then again and again, till the pieces were as small as her strength would allow. Finally she tossed the pile skyward, where it was caught by the wind and scattered like a flock of escaping birds. When the last one had vanished into the morning, she turned back to Hal, and together they returned to the big, old house.

EPILOGUE

Hal and Mattie were strolling along a beautiful beach. They were wearing period dress, which seemed odd until Hal remembered that they were in a play and—*oh, Christ!*—they should be onstage right now. In panic, he turned to Mattie—to discover that she was down in the surf, trying to snag a toy boat that was sailing by. When he called, she shook her head and kept vainly reaching for the boat, which Hal now saw had a tiny figure at the helm. "Nay, prithee, Milord, my heart is *here!*" Mattie cried . . . the words fading beneath a droning sound that, as he opened his eyes, Hal realized was the noise of jet engines.

He gazed out the window at the unbroken cloud-sea that seemed likely to stretch clear across the continent, and felt a moment of complete gloom. Then the emotional impact of the dream faded, and he gave a rueful chuckle, stretched, and sat up. *Jesus*, he thought, *if my subconscious was a writer, it'd be unemployed.* Then, ironically, *Or maybe making even more money than I do.*

Anyway, dreams aside, the fact was that he was back on the road—or in this case sky—on the way to the next gig; a response to a performer's powerful urge to keep following the work, in contrast to Mattie's equally strong need to stay put. Both knew this wouldn't change. So what was left? Clichéd Freudian dreams, apparently. After that? Regrets, certainly. But after *that*?

Getting on with it.

"Excuse me, you wouldn't, by any chance, be Hal Bannatyne?"

He turned to his seatmate, an earnest middle-aged lady who looked as if she might, hopefully, be recognizing him from something other than his ill-advised TV commercial.

"Guilty!" Hal said.

The woman was quiet-spoken, pleasant and not pushy. She had indeed seen some of his better work. And if *The Man from the West* had intruded on her intellectual radar, she had the grace not to mention it. They spent an hour in pleasantly un-fan-like conversation and were still chatting when the seat-belt sign came on, preparatory to their descent into Toronto.

He was home: or at least what would *be* home, if only he could manage to spend more than a few weeks out of a year there. But the day after tomorrow he was off again, down to the Caribbean to do a pretty decent role in another—this time, modern—flick.

Presumably, that enterprise would not produce the kind of unexpected excitement that had occurred on Vancouver Island.

But one never could tell.

Ron Chudley is the author of four other TouchWood mysteries: *Old Bones* (2005), *Dark Resurrection* (2006), *Stolen* (2007), and *Scammed* (2009). He has written extensively for television (including *The Beachcombers*) and for the National Film Board of Canada, and has contributed dramas to CBC Radio's *Mystery, The Bush and the Salon,* and CBC *Stage*. He lives with his wife, Karen, in Mill Bay, BC.

ISBN: 978-1-894898-33-1

ISBN: 978-1-894898-48-5

ISBN: 978-1-894898-59-1

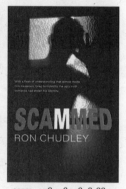

ISBN: 978-1-894898-88-1

"A moody psychological novel with a series of finely drawn characters." —*The Globe and Mail*

"His characters are skilfully realized and the redemption is startling and tempting. A satisfying read from cover to cover."
—*Hamilton Spectator*